AUTUMN BLUE

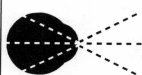

This Large Print Book carries the
Seal of Approval of N.A.V.H.

AUTUMN BLUE

KAREN HARTER

THORNDIKE PRESS

An imprint of Thomson Gale, a part of The Thomson Corporation

Detroit • New York • San Francisco • New Haven, Conn. • Waterville, Maine • London

LT
FIC
HARTER
11/07
Gale Grp.
28.95

LIBRARY OF CONGRESS CATALOGING-IN-PUBLICATION DATA

Harter, Karen, 1952–
    Autumn blue / by Karen Harter.
      p. cm. — (Thorndike Press large print clean reads)
    ISBN-13: 978-0-7862-9868-6 (hardcover : alk. paper)
    ISBN-10: 0-7862-9868-5 (hardcover : alk. paper)
    1. Single mothers — Fiction. 2. Domestic fiction. 3. Large type books.
    I. Title.
    PS3608.A78717A95 2007b
    813'.6—dc22
                                       2007026772

Published in 2007 by arrangement with Center Street,
a division of Hachette Book Group USA. Inc.

Printed in the United States of America on permanent paper
10 9 8 7 6 5 4 3 2 1

To Dan and Linda;
my happy haven in hard times.

ACKNOWLEDGMENTS

The production of this book was a family project. Since being diagnosed with the "C" word, they have rallied at my side, providing emotional, physical and practical support. Dad and Mom, Dan and Linda, Paula and Howie, Maria, Joe and Pam, thank you. I honestly could not have met my deadlines or even had a clear head without your help. I also appreciate the vacation therapy — cruising, dancing, zip lines and kayaks, swimming with sea turtles; I could go on. I am eternally grateful for your faith and that we can laugh so easily despite the circumstances of life.

To my huge bouquet of friends and extended family, thanks for the prayers and words of encouragement.

Ryan, Mike, and Jake, thanks for the love and for treating your mother like a queen. I hereby dub you knights in the kingdom in which love conquers all.

Christina Boys, my talented editor: By the time you get through with my manuscript I am confident that we've got a winner. Thanks also to Brynn Thomas and the entire team at Center Street who have helped to make this book a success.

1

If he came, it would be by the woods. It was always the woods. Even when it had been perfectly safe for him to lollygag along the street in broad daylight, Ty had always preferred a floor of decaying leaves and fir needles and a ceiling of sky or green boughs.

The woodlands behind their house edged a gully formed by Sparrow Creek which meandered all the way to the edge of Ham Bone, wrapping around the town's east side. Tucked between stands of trees were houses and pastures, churches and schools, all snuggled against the foothills of the Cascade Mountains. Surely by now Ty knew every square foot of his territory as well as the wild creatures that watched him come and go.

When her son was younger, he returned from his adventures with wildlife specimens: mud puppies, red-legged frogs, little tree frogs with emerald skin as smooth and damp as avocado flesh. Ponds and streams held more treasure for him than fleets of Spanish galleons. He spent countless hours combing his fingers through murky water and mud in search of baby catfish or wading through lily pads, jeweled dragon flies circling above as his keen eyes scanned for bullfrog nostrils breaking the surface of the water. Long ago, she had learned to let him go. Having the instincts of a wild creature, he was certainly safer in his beloved woods than on the county roads. Sidney always knew her son was on his way home when the dog, panting and covered with burrs, preceded him to the back door.

She stood at the kitchen sink, a cereal bowl in one yellow-gloved hand, the other submerged in gray soapy water with a scrub brush. Through the window, her eyes skimmed over the dog run where the grass was as worn as the knees of Tyson's old jeans, searching — as she had for days — the edge of the trees behind the house.

The landlord had not bothered much with landscaping. He simply cleared the lot and plopped a used mobile home in the middle of it with a For Rent sign in the front yard. Some grass just naturally filled in, seeded by overgrown pasture land on either side of them, but had not flourished due to a long, dry summer. The only shrubs were clumps of jagged Oregon grape and leathery salal spilling from the shade of cedar trees that formed the back boundary. The two dead azalea bushes in front didn't count.

Vaguely she heard her daughters' laughter from their bedroom. She felt the dog streak behind her and didn't notice until the girls ran past shrieking with delight that their brother's German shepherd looked like the Big Bad Wolf disguised as a grandmother. He came through again, shaking his head to rid it of a pink doll bonnet, limping every time he stepped on the shawl that had slipped around his neck. They would never get away with that if Ty were home. He had a thing about that dog.

"Come here, Duke." Sidney pulled the wool scarf over his head, snagging the bonnet along with it.

"Mom!" Sissy whined. "Why did you do that? He likes it. Don't you, Duke?"

"Look at his tail, Sis. See how droopy it is? That's how a dog says he'd rather be anywhere but here right now. Rebecca, put him outside, please."

"Should I put him on his dog run?"

Normally Sidney would have insisted on hooking the leash up to the long wire that ran between two posts out back. A dog should not be roaming the neighborhood free, even outside town. Some cars still sped through pretty fast. Besides, it wasn't fair to the neighbors. Old Mr. Bradbury across the street would not be pleased to find his peonies trampled or, worse yet, a pile of dog poop on his perfect lawn. "No. Just let him go."

Rebecca giggled as she opened the back door. "Now look at him! He's happy!" The dog's bushy tail swung like a reaper's scythe as he slipped through the opening and bounded into the yard. The girls went back to their play.

Sidney lingered at the window. If Ty was watching the house from the woods, con-templating coming home for a warm bed and a home-cooked meal, that dog would know it. They were normally as inseparable as twins. Duke bounded across the yard, sniffing and peeing here and there along the wire-fenced edges. Once he stopped, his nose lifted high into the wind. Her hopes rose. Then he turned and wandered off, not toward the woods, but on a haphazard trail with no apparent destination.

She had searched all morning, picking up where she left off the night before when darkness fell about a mile down the course of Sparrow Creek. She wondered as she trudged along trails made by animals and children, thrashing through thick tangles of huckleberry in less accessible spots, if she should have started upstream instead of down. Or if Ty had hidden himself far away from the creek in the deep, mysterious woods of the foothills or beyond.

A thin branch had whipped her face. The sting of it was all it took to bring on a good cry, one that needed to come. She had plopped herself down on a fallen cedar and let her sobs fill the woods. Birdsong fell silent as she rocked with her arms wrapped around her ribs to keep her heart from exploding. It was a lonely thing to raise a fifteen-year-old boy alone.

She rinsed a plate and set it in the draining rack while her eyes swept the terrain outside her kitchen window, across the rolling blue-green stands of evergreen trees to the east. Wherever Ty was, it was too far away. The tension she felt on that invisible cord that every mother knows is not really severed at birth was a constant, almost unbearable pain.

It was harder to cope on a Saturday. At the office, her worries had been interrupted by phone calls, working up insurance premium estimates, and the usual computer work. But today she just couldn't quell her imagination. He didn't even have his jacket.

Ty had been missing now for just over a week. On her lunch hours she had cruised the streets of town, checking the library, behind grocery stores, under bridges. The Winger County Sheriff's Department was searching for him too and promised to call her as soon as they had any information. She hoped to find him first. Her angry, rebellious boy. Was he safe? She had a need to touch him, to apply her love like a salve to invisible wounds, to make everything all right. This need overwhelmed her desire to bend him over her knee for a good old-fashioned spanking. It was too late for that; he had grown almost as tall as she was.

She finished the breakfast dishes and then, without planning to, found herself cleaning out the fridge. She dumped the last of the broccoli lasagna into the garbage disposal. Tyson's favorite. Well, it wouldn't keep for-ever.

"What's for lunch, Mom?" Seven-year-old Sissy crawled onto a tall stool, plopping her pudgy forearms on the breakfast bar. She peered through long brown hair, uncombed as usual. She was still wearing her T-shirt from yesterday with flannel pajama pants that exposed her belly. It was not a fashion statement.

"Didn't you just eat?" Sidney had left fruit and cereal out for the girls in case they woke up before she returned from her search, which she had started just after dawn.

"That was a long time ago." Rebecca joined her sister at the counter. Her lighter hair was pulled back in a neat ponytail, a style she wore often since getting her ears pierced. *All* the other girls in the fourth grade had their ears pierced, according to Rebecca, and Sidney had finally succumbed. She was learning to choose her battles wisely. Some things just didn't matter in the long run.

"Okay." Sidney began rummaging through the fridge. "How about egg sandwiches?"

"With tomato and avocado!" Sissy said.

"And onion," Rebecca added.

Sidney felt like a short-order cook, but didn't mind one bit. The only thing missing was the third face that should have been lined up at the breakfast bar. It was their gathering place — the center of her family's world, it seemed, where the day's stories and silly jokes were told, problems discussed, while Sidney sliced, chopped, sautéed, and stewed. Ty loved to taste-test her concoctions, especially muffins straight from the oven and too hot to hold.

"Mom, don't forget the fair tomorrow."

Sidney wiped her hands on a towel. "Oh, Sis . . ."

"We *have* to go. Tomorrow is the last day! And you promised!"

"I did?"

"A long time ago. Don't you remember?"

"But your brother might come home." If he wasn't home by then, she knew she had to be out combing his usual habitat, maybe above the bridge next time.

Rebecca shrugged. "If he comes home, he can just let himself in and we'll see him when we get home."

"He probably followed a wild animal way up to the mountain," Sissy suggested innocently. The girls didn't know the true circumstances of Ty's disappearance or their serious implications. Sidney didn't want to frighten them. "Don't worry, Mama. He's just having an adventure. He always comes home."

Sidney busied herself with frying eggs, slicing tomatoes, and toasting bread. She tried to banter with her daughters, but every sentence fell flat. Would he come home today? Or slip into his bedroom during the night where she'd find him safely curled beneath the covers of his own bed in the morning? She could only hope.

The girls chattered about the fair while

16

they ate their sandwiches. Sidney couldn't say yes, but then again she struggled with saying no. She'd been neglecting them lately. When they finished lunch and scooted off to their room she felt relieved.

With a deep sigh, she blew a strand of blond-streaked hair from her eyes, dropping her head back as if hoping to see the answers to all her questions through an open window to heaven. Instead she saw the dark crack that ran along the peak of the double-wide mobile home's ceiling. The house was coming apart at the seams — literally. And yet, she couldn't complain. It was better than their apartment in the old Victorian mansion in town on the corner of Elm and Prentice. At least here she had her own washer and dryer and the kids had a big yard to play in. They owed the move to the dog. The decision was actually made by their former landlord in response to complaints of a constant pounding — the sound of Duke's heavy tail beating against the wall in Tyson's room.

Sidney had been thrilled to find this house. Miraculously, it didn't cost that much more than the apartment and it was better for all of them, only a couple of miles from town and with a new stretch of woods for Ty to explore right from their backyard.

The house itself would never grace the pages of *Traditional Home* despite Sidney's talent for interior design. That was her intended major in college, before she got pregnant and dropped out to have Ty. No, about all she could afford to do with this place was keep it clean and try to have matching towels out for company when they came.

She should have married Jack Mellon when she had the chance. That might have changed everything. Surely it would have. Jack and Ty had really hit it off, right from the start. Had it been two years since she broke up with Jack? He used to take her son to baseball games and taught him to fly remote-control airplanes in the pasture across from the elementary school. There were other boys Ty's age there too, mostly with their dads, and they all met down at the Pizza Barn afterward. Jack was a nice guy, a butcher. Looking back, Sidney realized there had been a sparkle in her son's brown eyes that she couldn't remember seeing since.

The thought had been nagging at her for months now. So what if she hadn't felt any chemistry with Jack? Was that a valid reason for depriving her son of what he needed more desperately than protein or vitamin C or a good night's sleep? What was it about her that wouldn't allow the chemistry to happen? Was she waiting for another bad boy to come along? A man like Dodge? Someone who would keep her living on the edge? She shuddered. If she had it all to do over again, she'd marry Jack in a heartbeat.

She remembered Tyson as a small boy, the delightful sound of his giggles, the way he adored his baby sisters. He had been content to play alone for hours. Even while other children played tag nearby, Ty seemed to prefer the cavelike hollow beneath the big rhododendron outside their kitchen window, where she could hear the boy-sounds of rumbling truck engines while she peeled potatoes for dinner. Once she had waited for him at the edge of a stand of trees while he followed a brown rabbit into the underbrush. She heard him thrash through the dry leaves for some time and then a momentary silence before his tiny voice wafted through the low branches. "Mommy, where are me?"

But Tyson was really lost this time. It was as if he had been swept out to sea beneath her very nose. It all happened so gradually that she hadn't noticed how dangerous the undercurrent really was. By the time she realized how far her son had drifted, there seemed to be no lifeline long enough to reach him. He had slowly become a mere speck on the horizon — and then she couldn't see him at all.

2

Millard Bradbury's eyes opened at precisely 7:45 a.m., right on schedule and without the benefit — or the curse — of an alarm. He swung his feet to the hardwood floor, where his leather slippers awaited, parked side by side like a couple of polished brown sedans nosed to a curb.

At the bathroom sink he shaved the face of a stranger. Pouches had formed under the blue eyes, and lines arced away from the corners and down his cheeks like streams from a fan sprinkler. The mouth sagged downward as if it might soon slide right off his chin. He forced it up into a smile, searching the image in the mirror for any sign of the man he once knew. Gone. Not even a glimmer of recognition in the old man's eyes.

He dressed and made up the bed, fluffing the fat shammed pillows and leaning them against the headboard along with a smaller, decorative one just like Molly used to do. His floor exercises were next: the back stretches his doctor had prescribed, some leg lifts, and a few push-ups. After a cup of instant coffee (why brew a pot for just one person?) and a banana sliced onto a bowl of crunchy Grape-Nuts (at least his teeth were still good) he retrieved the *Winger County Herald* from the front porch.

There was a slight nip in the air but the sky was blue. He leaned against the porch rail and dropped the paper to his side. A red-winged blackbird emitted its liquid warble from the deep ditch at the edge of a vacant field on the west side of the house. From the woods beyond, other bird voices twittered and sang. Molly could have identified each of them by their voices alone. She would have made him stop to listen — if she were there. He scanned his lawn as he did every morning for any sign of an invading dandelion having successfully parachuted over the picket fence into his territory while he slept. His grass remained like carpet, the plush, expensive kind, with precision-cut edges curving along neatly landscaped borders where perennial shrubs shaded broad-leafed hostas.

The winesap apple tree strained under the weight of its dappled-red fruit. Hah! He had been right about pruning it back to only a small umbrella two seasons ago. Molly had wrung her hands and whined the whole time, warning that he was butchering the poor thing. Gave it a good military haircut, he did, and it was better off for it. What he would do with all those apples was a worry to him, though. His pantry shelves were still lined with jars of cinnamon applesauce and apple butter, his freezer stuffed with zip-closed bags labeled Pie-Fixings in Molly's flowing cursive hand.

A door slammed across the street. That lady from the trailer-house had emerged, arms full, bending at the knees while trying to lock the house up as her two girls headed down the steps and got into the car. He had met her at the mailbox not long after the family moved in and the For Rent sign was yanked out of the yard. She was a nice enough young lady, he guessed. No husband. Not much meat on her bones, but she dressed neatly and wore her dark blond hair like she put some effort into it. Not at all like her yard, which was a downright eyesore to the neighborhood with patches of grass and weeds growing down the middle of the gravel driveway, a couple of scraggly half-dead azalea bushes clinging to the cementlike dirt, and a bent downspout hanging off one corner of the double-wide house.

She had a boy, too, a boy old enough to be out there mowing those patches of grass and getting up on a ladder to secure that downspout. But on rare sightings the kid had clattered down the blacktop road on a skateboard, baggy pants at half-mast, his tufted hair, even from a distance, looking as mangy as their lawn. Millard blew out a disgusted sigh, remembering how he had hoped the kid's pants would slip down and hog-tie him. Why, when he was that age, every boy he knew had chores after school, and there was no fishing or pasture baseball games until the chicken coops were clean, eggs gathered, firewood cut, fences mended, and anything else that needed doing done. He shook his head, turning to go inside. Punk kids nowadays. Wouldn't know how to do an honest day's work if their life hinged on it.

He shook the paper open, pulled his reading glasses from his shirt pocket, and sank into the worn blue recliner by the picture window. First he perused the obituaries (seemed like the only contact he had with old peers anymore, their entire lives summed up in a few neat paragraphs). He then worked the crossword until his daughter's pale blue Chevy pulled into the drive. She pushed through the front door with a grocery sack in each arm. "Hi, Dad. How are you feeling?" She bent to kiss the top of his forehead. "You should be wearing a sweater. It's not summer anymore. Where's your gray cardigan?" She proceeded to the kitchen to begin her weekly ritual. He heard cupboards opening and closing. "Nicole has her first cheerleader gig Friday night — first football game of the season. I hope this weather holds. You know those girls are going to freeze their little tushies when it gets colder. And they just hate to bundle up and cover their cute little outfits."

"I need a six-letter word for 'jump.' Starts with a *p.*"

He heard the suction-release sound of the fridge opening. "Prance?"

"Pounce." That's right. Why hadn't he thought of it? He penned the letters into the appropriate boxes.

"You haven't even touched this squash, have you, Dad?" She sounded hurt that he had not appreciated her boiling and mashing the disgusting gourd's flesh into a stringy pulp. "You know you need the vitamin A, Dad. It's good for your eyesight. What are you going to do when you can't see anymore? No crossword puzzles, no

25

Wheel of Fortune. That won't be any fun, will it?"

Nine across had him stumped. He gazed out the window. Seven letters with a *d* in the middle, meaning "inner substance." "I just saw a starling drop a bomb on that shiny blue car out there," he said. The splat on Rita's windshield was purple. It was a good year for blackberries. They hung like grapes from tangled vines on the far side of the field next door. He might go out and pick another coffee can full if he felt like it that afternoon.

Rita came around the corner and peered out the front-room window as if she didn't believe him. She clicked her tongue and shook her head. "Nasty birds.

"Well, don't take anything for granted," she continued. "Not your eyesight or anything else. At your age every day of good health is a gift."

"Oh," he said, "and everyone else's is under specific warranty?"

"You need to take care of yourself, Dad. That's all I'm saying." Once Rita was on a certain track, she was not easily derailed. She headed back to the kitchen and he heard her loading this week's supply of frozen dinners — leftovers from her family's meals divided into sections in plastic containers — onto the freezer shelves. "Which reminds me, Dad. It's time to get your prostate checked again. What was your PSA count last time?"

He slapped his pen to the newspaper in his lap. So, his life had come to this. "I don't remember." Of course, he knew the moment the words escaped that they were grounds for suspicion of the onset of Alzheimer's. "I peed twice today so far. It was as yellow as lemonade and I flushed both times. My bowels are regular, blood pressure maintaining at 125 over 80. Is there anything else you'd like to know?"

Rita came out and stood over him, her arms crossed, her face pinched. His pretty little girl was beginning to look middle-aged. Her throat had become minutely wrinkled like the pink crepe paper hung for her birthdays back when she was a child and he was clearly an adult. Had it been so long since the feet she stomped wore little Mary Jane shoes? She tilted her head defiantly, clamping her hands on her full hips. "I'm sorry, Dad." She certainly was not. "But these things need to be discussed, whether you're comfortable with it or not. If Mom were here, she'd be the one asking, not me. But she's not here and I'm all you've got. This isn't easy for me either, you know. I lost my mother, but I'm not sitting around moping and giving up on life. And it's not like I don't have anything better to do. I'm in charge of the Girl Scouts craft projects this fall. I've got play costumes to make, soccer practices, piano lessons, you name it." She sighed, looking down at him like he was a hopeless cause. It was the resigned, dutiful sigh of a martyr bravely accepting her fate.

Giving up on life. What was there to give up? "Then don't worry about me," he scowled. "I told you before that you don't have to dote on me. I can make my own suppers, for Pete's sake."

"But you won't. You'd live on bologna sandwiches and corn dogs if I let you." She sat on the edge of the sofa, leaning toward him. "As long as you live here in this big old house all by yourself, I'm just going to worry about you, Dad. I wish you'd reconsider about going to Haywood House. It's a nice place. You get your own little apartment, so you'd have your treasured privacy, but there are other people just like you there. You can get to know them in the dining room at mealtimes, maybe meet some friends that like to play chess or put together jigsaw puzzles. And wouldn't it be nice to know that there are doctors and nurses right there on staff?"

It would take the self-imposed pressure off her, anyway. He wished she would go now. Leave him before the last hull of manhood was shucked away, exposing only a withered pea, a nothing, with no higher purpose than to put together cardboard jigsaw puzzles until he returned to the dust from which he came. He already knew this about himself, of course. But it was a truth better left untouched, unexplored. It was best to keep to the rhythm of his daily routine, biding away the hours with pleasant distractions and the self-imposed orders of the day. His battles were no longer fought against Soviet MiGs, but airborne dandelion seeds that dared invade the airspace inside the perimeter of his picket fence. Gone were the glory days of coaching the wrestling team at Silver Falls High School over in Dunbar — state champions six years out of ten. Not bad for a hick-town farm-boy team. But now his greatest mission was to solve the before-and-after puzzle on *Wheel of Fortune* before anyone bought the last vowel.

He glanced at his watch and pushed up from his chair. "The mail should be here now." He paused when he passed her to touch Rita's soft red hair. "I'll be good," he promised, "as long as you don't make me eat any more of that baby-puke squash."

3

Sidney and her friend Micki steered their children through the crowded fairgrounds toward the livestock exhibits. Attending the Winger County Harvest Fair was an annual tradition, one Sidney couldn't deny her daughters, though her heart was not in it, to say the least.

Today her girls wore matching pink denim jackets that their grandmother had sent from Desert Hot Springs last Christmas. Sissy's had a gray streak across the front from rubbing it against the corral fence where they had watched a friend from school run her pony through the barrel race. Andy, Micki's nine-year-old son, led the way down a row of wooden stalls to the Goliath of the hogs, a huge mottled gray blimp with legs. It tried to push itself up from the straw where it was sprawled, then seemed to think better of it, falling back with a breathy grunt. The children began to clap and chant as cheerily as Richard Simmons's disciples: "Get up! Come on; you can do it. Get up!"

The sow pushed up on her haunches, holding that immodest pose while she contemplated her next move.

Everyone laughed, including Sidney. "That's why I don't eat bacon," she said. "Fat, fat, fat."

"Oh, like you've ever had an adipose cell in your entire body." Micki held out her bag of popcorn but Sidney shook her head. Her perky blond friend looked great despite the garbage she continually consumed. The receptionist for Leon Schuman Insurance, she was known for keeping a stash of chocolate in her desk drawer at all times. They sat on hay bales in the middle of the barn, where they could see their children as they scrambled from stall to stall. "Now aren't you glad you came? I told you it would do you good."

Sidney pulled a bottle of water out of her straw bag and took a swig, her eyes roving the crowd on the slight chance that Ty might be among them. A handsome dad with one child straddling his neck and another held by the hand leaned over a gate and began making hog sounds. People around them laughed and joined in, though the pig seemed unimpressed. Sidney sighed. "That's what I want."

"What? A man who can grunt? They're everywhere; trust me."

"A man who spends Saturday with the kids. Look at that little boy looking up at him. His dad is his hero — and all it takes is a little snorting. He doesn't have to be in a rock band or send elaborate gifts to make up for all the visits that got postponed to some mysterious date in the future." Sidney saw a vision of Tyson watching expectantly for his father from the living room window, fidgeting, flopping from sofa to chair to floor, same scenario but different face as the boy grew from an excited six-year-old to a preteen whose eyes had grown dull from atrophied hope. At some point he had wised up, forsaking his post at the window and aloofly pretending he didn't care whether his father showed up or not. Sidney's soul tore open every time it happened, while Ty's heart had seemingly formed such thick scars from the repeated wounds that it had hardened into a clenched fist. The girls had never bonded with their father enough to care much.

Sidney's eyes began to flood again. She inhaled, filling her aching chest with the sweet scents of hay and cotton candy, forcing her eyes to focus on her daughters: Rebecca, a joyful and dramatic ten-year-old, thin and long-armed like her mother, and Sissy, still endowed with some cuddly baby fat, pushing eight.

"Dodge is going to be shocked someday to see that the girls aren't babies anymore," Sidney said. "He still sends them baby dolls for Christmas, if he remembers at all. Do you know what he sent Tyson when he was twelve? A truck. A big Tonka dump truck for a kid that was playing Internet chess with guys from France. I swear he must have sent one of his groupies to get Christmas presents for the kids."

Micki shook her head. "Time flies while he's having fun. How's he doing on child support?"

Sidney laughed. That was the least of her worries. "The band apparently has a new gig in a different town. Support Enforcement can't find him again. I wish he'd just get famous so he'd be easier to track down. Plus he'd be rich and that couldn't hurt."

They got up, brushing hay from the backs of their jeans, and followed their kids out of the barn toward game booths full of cheap toys and stuffed animals.

"Remember Jack Mellon?" Sidney asked.

"The butcher I dated a couple of years ago?"

"Sure. That was the Vegetarian-Meets-Beef-Every-Night-Guy chapter of your life," Micki said through a mouthful of popcorn. "You found him intellectually unstimulating, as I recall."

"Did I say that? Well, anyway, I've been thinking a lot about where I've gone wrong with Tyson. What I could have done differently, you know? I try to remember when he became so moody and dark — and you know what I keep coming up with? It was right after that time. The Beef-Every-Night-Guy chapter. Jack was good with Ty. He took him to do all kinds of guy things, played with the kids in the yard. Maybe I was just being too picky. I mean, what's more important than finding a man who loves your kids?"

"Well, mutual attraction is always nice."

Sidney sighed. "That would be good. What you and Dennis have. Your family is my unwritten standard, you know. You're still in love after all these years, and Dennis is the perfect dad. Oh, don't roll your eyes! You know what I mean. So he brings Andy home dirty and late and full of junk food. Stand back and look at it from my perspective. I've pumped every known vitamin and mineral into Ty since he was a little squirt, but it's not enough. It's not what he needs most. He needs a dad. One who actually loves him, I mean. So far my girls seem perfectly happy, but they never really knew Dodge so it didn't mess them up when he left. But Ty has been through it twice. He was six when his father left and it devastated him. Then he finally connects with a man again and I pull the plug."

"Jack still works at the Dunbar Traders Market," Micki offered. "At least last time I stopped in there. He was looking pretty good for a guy with bloodstains all over the front of him."

Sidney made a face. "What? You think I'm going to drive twenty miles away for groceries and show up at his department for a slab of corned beef? I'll bet you anything he's married by now anyway. He definitely had marriage on his mind. That's what sort of scared me."

"Did the girls like him?"

Sidney shrugged. "Sure. But they didn't connect with him like Ty did. It was a guy thing, you know?"

Sissy came running, stumbling at Sidney's feet. She stood, giggling, wiping her dusty hands on her pink sleeves. "Mom, can we have some money for the rides?" Her youngest, though a beautiful child, had been compared more than once to the *Peanuts* character Pigpen. Dirt was attracted to her like metal shavings to a magnet. If Sidney didn't insist on it, a comb would never slide its way through Sissy's long, dark hair, which today was braided into a thick rope, loose strands already hanging across her puppy-dog eyes.

Rebecca danced up to her mother, her jacket tied around her waist, and bowed. "Oh, queen mother, bestow upon us thy riches, we pray." Her long, slender arms were still tan (she had her father's skin coloring, but dark blond hair like her mother), and her hands were clenched pleadingly at her chest.

Sidney reached into her pocket and pulled out a $20 bill, enough to buy lunch supplies for a week the way she shopped. She hesitated only a moment before lifting her chin and smiling her most queenly smile. "Your wish," she said as she offered the bill with a flourish, "is granted."

"Oh, thank you! Thank you!"

Andrew had simultaneously made his own withdrawal from his mother. The three children ran toward an obnoxious-looking ride, grotesque arms raised spiderlike in the air while encapsulated victims screamed and spun in terror. Micki grabbed Sidney's arm. "Come on, Sid. Let's go on the rides!"

"Are you nuts?" Sidney pulled her arm away. "People like me don't go looking for panic. I've got enough stress in my life without buying tickets for it." Micki looked disappointed. "You go. Get rid of some adrenaline. You know what I want to do? I want to see the quilts and the art exhibits, all those things that bore you to tears. Why don't we meet up over there at the picnic tables by the taco stand after a while?"

Micki agreed and ran to catch up with their kids at the ticket booth.

Sidney wandered through a crowd of familiar faces. She nodded and smiled from time to time, feeling like a bottom-dwelling flounder in a school of happily darting perch. She didn't fit in there. Not today. She stopped and stared at the whitewashed building that housed quilts, rows of brightly colored canned pickles and peaches, paintings made by students and old women, photos of long shadows made by fences, and other attempts at black-and-white genius. It would be the same as last year and the year before and the year before that. She had won a blue ribbon at Harvest Fair once. It was for an old jam cupboard that she had painted with a toile fruit basket design on the front, and that was before she was even good at it. Of course, hers had been the only entry in the category of painted furniture, so it wasn't like she could take second place or anything.

Mary Hadley emerged from the exhibition building, making eye contact before Sidney had a chance to turn away. Mary had lived next door to Sidney back at the apartments, and her son had adoringly followed Ty from puddle to pond in the brushy lot behind the building, searching for creatures to put in washed-out mayonnaise jars. "Hey, Sid. How are you? Gosh, I haven't seen you since you moved!"

Sometimes it was the things that people didn't say that hurt the most. Mary asked about the girls. Was Rebecca playing soccer this year? What teacher did Sissy get? They chatted all around their overlapping lives, somehow never mentioning Tyson, the boy who had eaten macaroni and cheese at Mary's table as many times as her boy, Ricky, had dined at Sidney's. No, she didn't need to ask about Ty because Ty Walker was the kid everyone in Ham Bone, Washington, already knew about.

Sidney didn't go in to see the quilts. Instead she said good-bye to Mary, ducking between the horse barn and the back of the bleachers overlooking a dirt arena where a youngsters' rodeo was going on, so that she would avoid running into any more old friends. She wandered toward the old log cabin set back by the outer fence. It had been part of one of the original homesteads there in Ham Bone, sitting on the county fairgrounds now because the real estate it used to occupy had become a parking lot for the Cascade Savings and Loan. Members of the town's historical society had restored it, redecorating the inside to look the way it might have back in 1879 when William Dangle, the town founder, lived there while mining for gold. Since that didn't pan out so well for him, he began logging, making his fortune not so much from the timber as from the rich, mostly level farmland that was exposed.

It was quiet there on the back side of everything. Most of the locals were no longer interested in the old cabin with a rusty crosscut saw mounted on the wall of the covered porch.

Beside the cabin was a new acquisition: a miniature white chapel, the one that used to rest alongside the state highway leading to Mount Baker before the road was widened. The old sign had been moved, too: Weary Traveler, Stop and Pray. Sidney was curious. She had always wondered how many people could fit inside the tiny steepled structure. She stepped up on the creaky porch and pushed on the double doors.

Her girls would like this. It was like a playhouse, only it was a play church. There were four short pews, benches really, facing a small oak podium. If Rebecca were there, she would be behind that podium in two seconds flat, preaching flamboyantly to an imaginary congregation. Sidney smiled. She used to take her kids to the community church in town. It was not long after the girls witnessed their first baptismal service that she saw them baptizing other children down at the public pool. There had been a plethora of repentant sinners that day, waiting in line while Rebecca, a white towel draped over her shoulders like a robe, immersed them "in the name of the Father, Son, and Holy Ghost, 'til death do us part."

She stepped around the pews and looked up to the pine boards on the vaulted ceiling. In the distance she could still hear the voice of the rodeo MC and an occasional cheer from the small crowd.

The tears came unexpectedly, and she sank down onto the first pew, pulled a tissue from her pocket, and dabbed at the corners of her eyes as she stared at the pat-

41

terns in the worn hardwood floor. She had lost him. Despite all her attempts to protect, to guide, to prepare her son for this world. As a newborn she had wrapped him tightly in soft flannel because the maternity ward nurse told her it made the infant feel securely embraced in his mother's womb. Over the years she had buckled him into car seats, bundled him in warm jackets, held his hand so that he wouldn't wander into the street or get himself stolen at the mall. But it was all in vain. She had protected her son in body, but somehow failed to defend his vulnerable heart.

"Oh, God," she whispered. "I don't know what to do. Please bring someone to help me. Someone to help Ty. A father who will love him and the girls. I just can't do this on my own."

She sat still for some time, grateful for the solitude, a sense of peace settling over her. She felt calm, as if God really had heard her cry for help and the angelic Coast Guard had already been dispatched, hovering over Tyson, preparing to rescue him, wherever he was, his head bobbing among the dark waves.

4

Monday night there was still no sign of Tyson.

Sidney made a cup of licorice tea and plopped into the big green wing back her mother had given her, propping her feet on the coffee table with a sigh. Her first sip of tea scalded her lip. She jerked, lowered the mug to her lap, and dropped her head wearily to the back of the chair.

She had made it through another day of work at the insurance office, another evening of feeding the girls vegetable stew from the slow cooker and nutty whole-grain bread that she had thrown together in her bread machine that morning. She signed more papers from the school, barely reading them, and repaired a split in the seam of Sissy's backpack. It was getting harder with each passing hour to feign normalcy for the sake of her daughters. The girls were in their room now, reading and doing homework.

Sidney could no longer pretend that her son was just somewhere beyond the perimeter of trees at the edge of their yard camping out under the stars. It occurred to her that a boy on the run could get pretty far hitchhiking. Ty could be in Canada or California for all she knew, or in the dark alleys of Seattle where drug dealers and deviants preyed on kids like him — confused, angry children running like animals from forest fires that they hadn't kindled but that had burned them just the same.

It was after eight o'clock but not dark yet; they were still on daylight saving time. The September sky had deepened to soft violet. Across the street, Mr. Bradbury was spraying his garden with the hose. He reminded her of her dad a little. Not in looks so much; Mr. Bradbury was taller, with broader shoulders and long, gangly arms. But there he was, predictably doing what he did every night around this time — on the nights it didn't rain, anyway — wearing that same dove-gray cardigan sweater, faithfully spraying his black-eyed Susans and orange mums. Just like her dad used to do. Mr. Bradbury's entire life was packaged up as neatly, she was sure, as his immaculate yard. Checkbook always balanced, bills paid a week or two before they were due, that classic Lincoln lubed and oiled precisely on schedule. She missed her stable, dependable father, gone now for five years. She remembered how her mother had grieved for him, the man she had slept beside for forty years, and at the same instant Sidney had a twinge of revelation. Hadn't she heard that Mr. Bradbury's wife died just last year? He must be grieving, too. She should go over there, maybe bring him a pie or a loaf of orange oatmeal bread. Yes, he would love her bread; everyone did. And with the delay timer on her bread machine, she could deliver it to him after work tomorrow, still warm.

A car cruised up to her driveway and surprised her by turning in. Sidney's heart lurched. The sheriff. Hot tea splashed on her bare thigh and soaked into her khaki shorts.

She stood, gripping her tea mug, straining her eyes to see the shape of Tyson in the backseat of the patrol car. From the front door she waited for what seemed like a day and a half before the uniformed deputy opened his car door and stepped out. Mr. Bradbury had been headed inside for the night, but froze halfway up his front steps, staring curiously from across the road. The deputy walked toward Sidney without so much as a glance back toward his car. "Mrs.

Walker?"

"Did you find my son?"

He shook his head. Sidney's blood was charged, racing through her veins. She didn't know whether to be relieved or disappointed. If he had been in the car, Tyson would be on his way to jail. But if they hadn't found him, then he was still lost, still running, out there in that terrible unknown that haunted her with alarming visions every waking hour. The deputy stopped at the base of her steps, a tall, thick-shouldered man with some kind of Latin blood. Probably Mexican. His dark eyes were cold and she knew instantly that he had not come as a friend. "I need to ask you some questions."

Should she invite him in? No, she didn't want the girls to hear this. They knew their brother was on the run, but Sidney had tried to shelter them from the specific details. "Ask away," she said.

He stepped up to the porch. She read the name bar pinned to his starched khaki shirt just below the Winger County sheriff's badge. Deputy A. Estrada. Sidney drew back, leaning against the doorjamb, putting a comfortable distance between her and the ominous visitor. She hugged herself, running her hands over the goose bumps on her bare arms.

"When was the last time you saw your son, Tyson, Mrs. Walker?"

"The morning he ran off from school." He should know that. The school counselor had called the Sheriff's Department immediately that Friday afternoon to report that he had broken his probation, and Sidney had been in touch with them regularly since then. "It was the ninth."

He cocked his head, his piercing eyes narrowing. "You're telling me you haven't seen him since then? He hasn't come home at all?"

She nodded. "That's what I'm telling you."

He raised a dark eyebrow and inspected her face without speaking. He might as well have called her a liar. Sidney had a fleeting impulse, a vision of her leg shooting out karate-style, kicking the sour-faced deputy sheriff off her porch. Instead, she reminded herself that he was just doing his job. Mr. Bradbury had obviously changed his mind about retiring for the night. He was stooped over, popping dead heads from the mums growing outside his picket fence and casting furtive glances across the road.

"You wouldn't mind me taking a look in his room, then?"

She straightened, inflating herself to her largest stature, trying for the life of her to avoid being intimidated by the badge, the gun on his hip, his broad chest and shoulders, and those austere eyes. "Yes, I would mind. My girls are inside and I don't want them upset. What are you looking for, anyway? You know he turned himself in right after the incident at Graber's Market. The only thing he took was a bottle of wine and he didn't even make it out the door with that."

The store proprietor had been watching Ty via strategically placed mirrors, saw him tuck the Mad Dog 20/20 inside his jacket, and tackled the boy before he made it out the automatic sliding door. The bottle shattered. Sidney was shocked when she learned that her son had then rolled onto his back, pulled his pellet gun out of his pants, and pointed it directly beneath Mitch Graber's chin. Mitch backed off, thinking of course that it was a real gun, and Ty ran out the door. Sidney had heard the patrol car sirens from her bedroom that warm August night, never suspecting for one moment that her son was the cause of them, thinking that he was just in the woods out back cooling off after a heated argument in which she insisted that he would indeed be attending his freshman year of high school, whether all the teachers were idiots or not.

The deputy smirked. "I'd turn myself in too if I needed somebody to tweeze all those glass splinters out of my chest."

"Well, I'll bet you got a good laugh out of that down there at the Sheriff's Department," Sidney retorted. "He probably looked like he'd been shot, with all that Mad Dog bleeding into his jacket. You all must have been rolling on the floors."

The deputy's smirk disappeared. "Look, Mrs. Walker, I'm just trying to do my job here. I'm not the bad guy. Your son's crime got real serious the minute he pulled out a gun. He's charged with attempted armed robbery and that's a felony."

"But it wasn't a real gun."

"Yes, ma'am, it was. In the eyes of the law, anyway."

"The thing shoots little plastic BBs. The boys around here shoot one another with them all the time."

"Even threatening someone with a squirt gun is a crime nowadays. Anyway, the judge released Tyson to your custody with strict stipulations, including that he was to go nowhere but school and home until his sentencing hearing. Now he's on the run and I have reason to believe he's committed another crime."

Sidney's heart sank in her chest. "What kind of crime?"

"A burglary in town."

She shook her head. "Ty wouldn't do that. He's not a bad boy, Deputy." But she immediately wondered. Who was the angry young man who had taken over sweet, compassionate Tyson's body?

"That's why I'd like to take a look inside. To see if he might have stowed any of the stolen items in there."

"He hasn't been here," she stated firmly, sliding her body directly in front of her door. "Believe me, if he had, I would know it. I'm not going to let you come into my home with that gun on your hip and scare my daughters."

His full lips pulled into a straight line and he gazed at her as if pondering his next move.

The front door suddenly opened behind her, and before Sidney could stop her, Sissy was on the porch, eye-to-eye with the deputy's Glock, or whatever he packed in his black leather holster. Her youngest daughter peered up at him with a sweet smile. "Hi."

"Sissy, you go on back inside," Sidney said.

She began to back up. "Are you the sheriff that came to my class?"

His face softened slightly. "I might be. Who's your teacher?"

"Mrs. Gilbreath."

Sidney gently pushed Sissy behind her. Rebecca peered curiously around the door-jamb. "Will you girls please go back in and let the deputy and me talk in *private?*" She emphasized the last word, hoping old Mr. Bradbury's hearing was good enough to take the hint. It was dark enough now that he was probably plucking off perfectly good blooms just for an excuse to stand out there within earshot.

Sissy called out a friendly " 'Bye" as the door closed.

Deputy Estrada ran one hand across his jaw. He would have been a strikingly hand-some man without the pinched forehead and squinty eyes. "Something tells me they're not afraid of me."

"Just the same, I'd rather you not come in."

"You know, Mrs. Walker, if you're knowingly possessing stolen goods . . ."

"I am not doing any such thing!" Now she was indignant, outraged. How dare he insult her like that? She felt branded, as if someone had burned the letter *L* for *loser* on her bare arm. Like she was one of those pathetic, dysfunctional women on *COPS,* only she still happened to have good teeth. It was as if he knew all about the past, all those sordid situations that Dodge had dragged her through. But her ex-husband was gone now. Cut off. She was making a new life for herself and the kids.

Maybe it was the shards of truth that sliced into her from his comment that enraged her so. Like the shattered bottle hidden inside Ty's jacket. She was guilty. Guilty of being an idiot. Believing that Dodge had really won that big-screen TV in a poker game. That all the nice things he brought home had been gifts from friends or incredible deals that he just couldn't pass up. The first time a pair of officers from the Bellingham Police Department had shown up at their door, she had been shocked. Ty was a baby on her hip then. And now, it was like déjà vu, standing out there on her porch and staring into a badge, only this time Ty was the suspect. The phrase "Like father, like son" popped into her mind uninvited.

"Look, Deputy . . ." She sighed, rubbing one temple that was beginning to throb. "If you had a search warrant, you would have pulled it out by now. Whether you believe me or not, I'm not hiding anything. I'm just tired. Please, go away now. I have to get my kids to bed."

He nodded curtly, glaring. "Have it your way, Mrs. Walker."

She watched him turn and walk to his car, head high and shoulders back like a marine. He glanced up at her again before ducking his head, sliding in, and slamming the door. The official green sedan accelerated quickly once on the road, and Sidney stood there massaging her hammering chest until the car's red taillights disappeared around the bend.

"Good night, Mr. Bradbury!" she called, adding "You nosy old coot" under her breath.

He looked up as if startled to see her there. "Oh, good night now," he stammered almost inaudibly, then turned and headed down the path to his front door.

5

It was a terrible shock, catching Millard Bradbury so off guard that he stumbled backward several steps and caught the front doorjamb for support. The *Winger County Herald* lay forgotten at his feet.

A mole. Dad-blasted blind-as-a-doorknob mole! It had pushed up a string of mounds from the picket fence that bordered the grassy field on the west halfway to the center of his immaculate lawn, where the tunnel was punctuated by a pile of rich brown earth.

His breath became short as he strode down the concrete steps. Stopping abruptly at the bottom, he detoured to his left toward the garage, which was set back at the end of the driveway, and emerged from it with shovel in hand. As he approached the scene of the crime, he tiptoed, holding the rough, wooden handle like the shaft of a spear, ready to send the mud-sucking rodent to its maker the moment it showed its snout.

He waited. The mound of dirt was still. Birds trilled and swooped through the sky, oblivious to the weighty drama playing out beneath them. A squash-colored school bus screeched to a stop across the unlined county road, rumbling and smoking as the little girls from the house across the street boarded. A row of curious faces peered out its windows at the seemingly frozen man, knees slightly bent and arm raised like a statue of an old warrior, but Millard did not see them as the bus roared past.

Still no sign of movement. He slowly lowered himself to one knee, using the shovel for support. Then, down on all fours, he listened. Perhaps if he put his ear right down to the earth like the Indians used to do to tell if the buffalo were coming . . . He lay flat out, his face on the cool, damp lawn. At first there was no sound other than the current of his own breath. Of course, his hearing wasn't all it used to be. He waited patiently, closing his eyes to enhance con- centration. This invasion was an act of war and he could be as stealthy as, if not more than, the enemy. After all, he was the one with superior intelligence. His mouth spread into a sinister grin as his fingers fondled the handle of the shovel. He was the master of the guillotine.

Finally he heard something. Yes. The ground was definitely vibrating. He forced himself to remain still, as still as a cat hunting in the tall grass.

"Mr. Bradbury!"

His heart leapt to his throat. He sprung to his elbows, his head jerking toward the alarmed female voice.

"Please, don't move. It's me, Sidney Walker, from across the street. Let me get help."

"No!" he stammered, awkwardly pushing himself to his hands and knees. She dropped to her knees, her hand on his back. "I'm fine." He tried to stand but the blood rushed from his head and he abruptly sat back onto the shovel blade, causing the handle to spring upward, wobbling in the air.

"Are you sure? Did you fall?" She reached out to brush something from his cheek.

"No." Confound it. Couldn't a man lie down on his lawn without some female assuming it was because he couldn't stand on his own two feet? He pushed the shovel out from under him. "I've got a mole," he stated, as if that explained everything.

His neighbor seemed confused at first; then her eyes fell on the pile of dirt near

Millard's head. She sighed in relief. "Too bad. Your yard usually looks like a picture right out of *Sunset* magazine. Makes me feel so embarrassed about mine. I keep meaning to do something about it, but it seems my days get all used up, what with work and the kids and all."

He suddenly remembered the sheriff standing on her porch a couple of evenings ago. He was not one to pry, but he might just lift up a loose board and take a peek under it. "What about that boy of yours? What is he, fourteen? Fifteen?"

She averted her eyes to a pile of white clouds beyond his roof. "Fifteen."

"Well, why don't you get him out there on that yard? A boy that age ought to be helping his mother. A woman was never meant to do all those outdoor chores. She's got enough to do cleaning house, sewing, cooking, and the like."

She smiled a little, as if he had said something amusing. "Well, I can't say that I do much sewing." She toyed with the zipper-tassel on her blue cardigan. "Anyway, we don't own a lawn mower."

Well, that complicated things. Millard glanced across the street, but from his vantage point there on the lawn, the view of her scraggly yard was blocked by the peonies along his fence. He still saw the hanging downspout, though. He *could* offer his lawn mower. But he had just sharpened the blades a couple of weeks ago. If the kid hit any hidden rocks or debris, which surely lurked behind every tuft of grass, it would definitely ruin them. On the other hand, it would be nice to look out his window without the annoyance of that tainted scene. He still couldn't get over the fact that somebody knocked out all the alder and vine maples (which would be going red by now) to stick a boxy old trailer-house there. "You tell him to come on over here and borrow my mower. I'll show him how to use it, but make sure all the sticks and rocks are picked out of the yard first."

Sidney dropped her head and let out a slow, steady breath. "Well, that's very nice of you to offer, Mr. Bradbury. But the truth is, I'm having a little trouble with Tyson right now."

Aha. It figured. Even from a distance a guy could see the kid had rebellion written all over him. "You just send him over here. I'll tell him where the hogs eat corn."

She sighed again, her angular but pretty face losing what he now realized had been a pleasant, almost cheery facade. "My son isn't home right now. He, uh, ran away recently."

"So, that's why the sheriff was there the other night?"

She clamped her lips between her teeth momentarily as she seemed to study his face. "Mr. Bradbury, I'm going to be honest with you. You're a nice neighbor, and living right across the street from us the way you do, it's just a matter of time anyway until you know the truth. You know that so-called attempted robbery at Graber's this summer?" He nodded. "Well, that was my Ty." Her stunning green eyes fell away for a moment before returning to his.

He tried not to seem shocked, though he was. First the mole and now this. He had been living across the street from an armed criminal — and to think that he rarely remembered to lock up his house when he went to bed at night. It had never seemed necessary before. According to Red, the barber, the kid had almost shot the proprietor — would have killed a guy with a wife and two kids over a bottle of booze if he hadn't tripped and smashed the bottle tucked into his jacket. "But I've seen him around since then, haven't I?"

"The judge let him out to await his trial. Being a juvenile and the fact that it was his first offense, plus that he turned himself in, he let Ty come home until his hearing. But he had a curfew and was supposed to be in school every day and no place but home after that." She looked away. "Now he's messed that all up. Got in a fight at school and ran away. I guess he thought they'd slap him right in jail for getting suspended." Her eyes watered up. "He's really not such a bad boy, Mr. Bradbury. It's just that something's got him by the heart and it's squeezing the life out of him. I see this dull pain in his eyes but I don't know what it is. I don't know how to fix his hurts anymore."

A mole, a criminal for a neighbor, and now a crying woman. If this wasn't a day to beat all. It was half-past nine and he hadn't even touched the newspaper yet. His whole neat world, it seemed, was being cracked open like a walnut. He should do something but he didn't know what. His hand reached out to pat her knee, but he thought better of it and grabbed the shovel, using it as a crutch to stand to his feet, leaning heavily on it as he stretched his stiff knees.

Sidney stood also, dabbing her face with the underside of her sleeve. That was the way Molly did when she cried over old movies or sad telephone conversations so as not to smear her makeup. Molly wore rouge and a little mascara right up until she took sick and even then sometimes pinked up her cheeks when someone came to call. "Sorry to lay my troubles on you, Mr. Bradbury." She chuckled through her tears. "I don't know why I did that." She glanced at her watch. "Well, it looks like I'll be working past five tonight to make up for it." She offered a brave smile. "Anyway, I'm glad you were just hunting down a mole and not having an aneurysm or something."

"You lay your troubles on me anytime you need an ear," he heard himself say, immediately wondering where that came from. If he could have sucked the words back, he would have. But the thing about words: once spoken, they're poker chips on a table, there for the taking. Odds are somebody's going to cash them in.

She tipped her head, smiling softly. "Thank you, Mr. Bradbury." She reached out and hugged him, just like that, letting her cheek brush against his, then turned and strode quickly back down his driveway and across the road. He stood there while she tried to start her banged-up little Ford, which finally kicked in with a rattle-roar on the third try. Feebly returning her wave, he watched as the car chugged away.

6

Sidney's boss leaned over her shoulder, perusing one of her files for some information he needed before returning a client's phone call. Leon Schuman was an intensely serious man, no good at small talk, with a deeply lined face that was hard to read. She prayed he wouldn't notice the stack of insurance quote requests piled to the left of her computer as she casually covered it with a notebook, breathing a sigh of relief when he closed the file and returned to his glassed-in office. Pushing the notebook aside, she covered a yawn and began to enter data into her computer. Her eyes watered from the yawn. It had been a long and sleepless night.

As far as she knew, Micki was the only other employee at the Leon Schuman Insurance office that knew Sidney's son was on the run. Sure, the others knew about Ty's initial arrest, even though the paper had not stated his name because he was a juvenile. Word, distorted as it was, got around in Ham Bone, long before the weekly paper hit the porch steps. But her coworkers seemed to assume that Ty was either still at home or at school per the judge's mandate, awaiting his fact-finding hearing. Most of them politely avoided the topic, sensing that Sidney was a little sensitive about it, though surely her private family business was being discussed in whispers between donuts and sips of coffee in the break room when she wasn't there.

She remembered ruefully how Ty's court-appointed attorney, a pale, pregnant woman in her early thirties, had warned him of the absolute urgency of adhering to every rule set by the judge who had mercifully released him into his mother's custody after the incident — without bail. She warned him that the consequences of breaking the court orders would be severe. Ty had nodded gravely without taking his eyes off her face.

Sidney contemplated the framed photo on her desk, one that Jack Mellon had taken of a twelve-year-old Ty holding a remote control and gazing with wonder into the sky. The red model biplane, which Jack had painstakingly built and painted, was out of the picture. The very fact that the man had focused the camera on Tyson rather than on his masterpiece should have been a sign to her. Where had her head been back then? Where would Ty be today if she had married Jack? Certainly not on the streets or in the tangled woods living on blackberries and tree roots. She pictured Ty the way he could have been if he had a strong man to guide him — safe and content, flourishing in school, proudly displaying his own model airplane at the science fair. She forced her eyes back to the computer screen.

Micki finally saved her from the pandemonium in her mind. "Hey." Her friend's blond head appeared at the top of her cubicle. "Let's do lunch."

Sidney blinked. She hadn't accomplished a complete task all morning that she could remember. She saved the work on her computer with a click. "Okay. Good idea."

It had been a beautiful September so far, but today autumn hovered in a chilly fog. The usual view of evergreen-covered foothills and the Cascade Mountains was shrouded with gray. They grabbed their jackets and walked to the little Mexican restaurant next door to their office — like many of the businesses in town, a home remodeled into retail space when commercial zoning was extended to the end of

Center Street, the main drag through town. They sat by the window and looked out at the sidewalk and the Hair Place salon across the street. Micki ordered chicken enchiladas; Sidney, as usual, a veggie burrito.

"I miss you," Micki said.

"What are you talking about? You see me every day, like it or not."

"But it's not the real you. I miss your famous laugh."

Sidney's mouth spread into a heartless smile. "Got any good jokes?"

Micki took a sip of iced tea and lowered her glass to the table. "Knock, knock."

"Who's there?"

"Interrupting cow."

"Inter—"

"MOO!"

They both giggled. "Okay, I've got another one," Micki said. "Knock, knock."

"Who's there?"

"Interrupting starfish."

"Interrup—"

Micki's open hand shot across the table, spreading across Sidney's face, her palm firmly plastered against Sidney's mouth. She couldn't speak. Micki pulled her arm back, laughing at her own joke. "Get it?"

Sidney rubbed her nose. "That hurt! For Pete's sake! Starfish move like glaciers —

65

not torpedoes."

"Sorry." Micki reached for Sidney's glass. "Water?"

She nodded. "And an ice pack."

"I was just trying to get your mind off Tyson."

"Well, it worked until just now. Now I'm thinking about him all over again. Here I am devouring mounds of good food and he's out there somewhere eating . . . I don't know, maybe tree bark or something." A horrible thought occurred to her. "Do we have anything poisonous growing around here?"

Micki shook her head, causing her silver dangling earrings to swing. Her hair was cropped in the latest style, her tangerine blouse a little trendy — something a teenager might wear, but she could pull it off. Micki had the body of an athlete. Sidney reminded herself to work out more, put a little muscle on her slender arms. "About the worst he could do around here is cascara bark. They make laxatives out of it."

"Oh, great. Runs on the run."

Micki sighed. "You've got to stop worrying about him. He's Nature Boy; you know that. He's spent more hours roaming the forests around here than a lone wolf. And he's smart. If anyone can survive out there,

Ty can."

"Did I mention that he didn't have a jacket when he took off?"

"A few times." Micki raised her eyebrows. "I'll bet you anything he has one now."

Sidney didn't want to go there. She couldn't bear to think that her son made stealing a habit. That Deputy Estrada might be on to something by suspecting Ty as the culprit of that burglary in town. The attempted robbery at Graber's Market may not have been just a crazy, stupid, spontaneous, onetime event. She had found empty beer bottles in the back of his closet after he ran away, plus a full six-pack under the bed, and there was no way that her baby-faced son could pass for twenty-one even if he had fake ID.

"I finally called my mother last night."

Micki's eyebrows rose. "And?"

"I woke her up. I tried to sleep until 2:00 a.m., lying there worrying about whether that deputy was going to come back with a search warrant, imagining Ty in every possible scenario under the moon. Finally I just reached over and punched in her number. Good old Mom. She wasn't even mad.

"I told her everything this time. Right down to the gory details. All about the arrest, the charges, and that Ty ran away."

Sidney pursed her lips and sighed. "I guess I should have told her what was going on sooner, starting with those black moods he falls into. At least then it wouldn't have been such a shock to her. She still sees him as the sweet-faced little boy that used to bring her jars of centipedes and potato bugs. She, of course, always oohed and aahed like he had just bestowed jewels from Tiffany on her."

"She didn't freak out on you when you told her, did she?"

"No. That's not her style. She was annoyingly calm and rational. She said Ty is going to come through this just fine. That someday we'll look back and thank God for the wonderful man he's become."

"Wow. At least she's positive. Why didn't you tell her before? I go crying to my mom about things like the toilet backing up."

Sidney stared at the chunk of burrito on her fork and shrugged. "I don't know. Mom has this family-portrait image of my world in her head — everything's fine; the kids are always squeaky-clean and smiling. I used to clean for days before her visits, trying to make my house look as perfect and organized as hers. We weren't rich growing up, but you wouldn't know it by the way she kept the house. She served tea in bone china cups and saucers, poured it out of a silver teapot on a silver tray. She dressed my sister and me in matching dresses — the kind you have to iron! I'm lucky if I can get two matching socks on Sissy before I push the girls out the door in the morning, let alone iron anything. And of course, she always had her hair done and lipstick on when Dad came home at night. She managed to stay happily married too, by the way."

"How many years?"

"Dad died just before their fortieth anniversary. The funeral was on the actual day. August 12."

"Oh, how sad."

Sidney tipped her head and smiled. "Yes, it was. But for once Dad was there with flowers — enough to make up for all the anniversaries he forgot. He never was very good with dates."

Micki leaned back and crossed her arms, looking at Sidney like her fifth-grade teacher used to when she couldn't diagram a simple sentence. "So you're comparing yourself to your perfect mother, who — correct me if I'm wrong — had a husband to pay the bills and help raise the kids, and she never worked an outside job a day of your childhood."

"Not comparing, exactly," Sidney said.

69

"Just trying to live up to. Please pass the salsa."

"Too bad she lives so far away. I think you could use some mothering right now."

Sidney stared at a papier mâché parrot that seemed to be eavesdropping from its perch above Micki's shoulder. Her mother lived in a suburb of Cleveland with Sidney's aunts, Clair and Aggie. The three now-single middle-aged women were crazy best friends. Sometimes Sidney couldn't carry on an intelligent phone conversation with her mother for all the laughter and commotion going on in the background. She wouldn't do anything to break up that happy trio, no matter how bad things got for her there in Ham Bone.

"My sister needs her worse than I do." Sidney shook her head, still disbelieving that her younger sister, the one who once claimed she didn't have a maternal bone in her body, had somehow ended up with five kids under the age of ten. She and her husband were in a standoff, both refusing to have their bodies permanently altered to prevent any future surprises. "Mom watches the little ones in the mornings while Alana works."

She glanced at her watch. The school bus would drop Rebecca and Sissy off at their driveway at about 3:45. With Ty gone, the girls would be home alone until she got home after 5:00. But maybe it was actually better that way for now. Lately, she had worried more about them being *with* their brother than without him.

A green sheriff's car sped past the restaurant window, lights flashing. Sidney was surprised when it jerked to a stop abruptly in front of the insurance office next door.

"What's going on?" Micki stood, dropping her napkin to the floor. Another patrol car appeared from the other direction and braked, and an officer stormed from the car. Both women bolted for the door of the restaurant, leaving their half-eaten lunches behind.

"We'll be right back," Sidney called over her shoulder to the waitress.

The officers ran, shouting, toward the gravel alley behind the Leon Schuman Insurance building where another deputy was wrestling someone facedown to the ground. A guy in a big brown jacket. He wasn't going down easy. Adrenaline shot through Sidney's bloodstream. "It's Tyson!"

Micki reached out and held her arm. "No, Sidney. I don't think so." They stopped a safe distance away in the middle of the small parking lot between the two buildings. Leon

71

Schuman and several coworkers spilled out of their office to observe the incident from the side porch. A dark-haired officer with a broad back and shoulders — unmistakably Deputy Estrada — jerked the captive's arms behind his back to be cuffed, causing his face to drag on the gravel. The body on the ground let out a plaintive cry.

Tyson! It *was* her son lying there, pressed to the ground. She ran toward him on legs like ribbon, but just before she reached him another deputy caught her, firmly holding her back. Estrada yanked the boy roughly to his feet. Tyson's eyes were wild and fevered, his hair a shaggy mess. "Ty!" He looked directly at her, blinked, and dropped his head. His cheek was bleeding. Estrada thrust him past, pushing and dragging him across the parking lot. She had never seen that brown canvas jacket. The sleeves were too long; thick rolls of fabric were bunched at Ty's wrists. Just before they reached the awaiting patrol car, Ty defiantly jerked his arm away. Estrada grabbed it again, roughly shoving him forward and then pushing her son's head down into the backseat.

Micki was at her side, supporting Sidney's elbow when the car door slammed.

"Please, let me talk to him." The deputy hesitated before reaching inside the driver's door and lowering the window partway. There were a thousand questions to ask. Why did he run? Where had he been? How had he been eating and sleeping, surviving the cold autumn nights? She lowered her head, resting it on the upper rim of the window opening. "Ty," she said softly.

The cuffs made him lean forward awkwardly. He didn't look up. "I just wanted to tell you I'm okay," he muttered.

Her tears threatened to choke her, but she wouldn't let them come. Not yet. "Tyson, we're going to work this out. You cooperate in every way. Do you hear me?"

"I won't stay in jail. I can't. I'd rather die."

A chill ran through her body. This was something he had obviously given a lot of thought. "Nobody said you're going to jail, Ty. A lot depends on you." She really didn't know how true that was. After all, he had committed a felony by pulling that pellet gun. "Now you be good. I'll do whatever I can to help, but you have to quit making stupid mistakes. You got yourself here; now you'd better decide if you're going to do the right things to get yourself out." He finally looked up at her. He had the dark eyes and long lashes of his father. The eyes of her perdition. "I love you, Tyson."

He tried to speak, but all that came from

his quivering lips was a stifled "Ma . . ." She saw his face screw up like it did when he was small, like the times his little heart was broken by a father who found a better life and simply lost interest in the family he had started. Ty whipped his head away from her. A blade of dry grass stuck in the back of his dirty, tousled hair.

Sidney's tears came then. Micki held her, kept her knees from hitting the ground as the bulletproof window slid up and the patrol car rolled away.

7

Sidney waited for almost three hours in the austere Winger County Juvenile Detention building before being allowed to see her son. How long did it take to *book* someone anyway? The place was eerie, with no daylight in the wide, echoing corridor except for the slice that ventured through a tiny oblong window at the far end. She sat against the wall in the middle of a row of vacant green plastic chairs that must have been there since before she was born. When a uniformed deputy finally escorted her to a visiting room, she passed him Sybil Tanner's card. "Can you please call our attorney and let her know we can see him now?" Sybil's office was just across the street in the courthouse, a much friendlier building with lots of windows, surrounded by neat gardens and stately trees.

Sidney waited alone in a room with a chicken-wire window in its door. Sybil arrived, her pregnant belly swollen dramatically since Sidney last saw her, barely having time to drop her neatly organized briefcase to the table and remove Ty's file before the door opened again.

"Try to keep it to a half hour," the deputy said, guiding Ty into the room with a firm hand on his upper arm. After the door latched behind the deputy, his uniformed shoulder remained visible through the small window.

Sidney's breath caught. Tyson's wrists were cuffed, chained to a belt locked around his waist. He wore a blue, short-sleeved jumpsuit and an expression of shame or hopelessness, maybe both. She inhaled deeply. *I will not cry. I will not cry.* Her chair scraped the floor as she rose to hug him. His body was slightly rigid, but he let her rub his back as she held her cheek to his. She savored the moment, the sensation of finally holding her son's slim but developing body next to hers. There was a new firmness in his back, small but sinewy biceps now palpable on his arms. He smelled clean; he must have showered before donning the garb that marked him as a detainee.

"Sorry, Mom," she heard him whisper through her hair.

"Hello, Tyson," Sybil said. "Why don't you join us here at the table? We don't have much time."

He dropped into a chair across the table from her.

"Okay." She sighed deeply. "We have a real challenge in front of us. Why did you run? Didn't you believe me when I warned you about breaking court orders?"

His eyes narrowed. "I got in a fight at school."

Her intense blue eyes looked directly into his. "Tell me about it."

He shrugged. "This jock kept riding me about what happened at Graber's. He and his friends were on me since the first day of school. And lying about what really happened. They said I meant to kill that guy." He scoffed bitterly. "With a pellet gun?"

"Who threw the first punch?"

He stared down at her pale, freckled arm as she scribbled notes. "I guess I did, but actually he hit me first. He's a big dude. Has longer arms."

"I'll bet you were glad when the teachers broke it up."

"Yeah. Until the counselor called the sheriff. That's why I ran." His voice cracked. "I knew they'd throw me in jail because of what you said. That I couldn't get in any more trouble before my hearing." His eyes searched her face. "What's going to happen now?"

She hesitated, tapping her pen on the table with clamped lips. "I think you would have been better off facing the situation head-on." She flipped through his file. "You were charged with a felony, in which case you may be tried as an adult. The judge was surprisingly lenient when he released you to your mother's custody after the robbery." She looked at him squarely with a slight shake of her head. "I'm not going to lie to you, Tyson. Judge Renkin is not one to mess with. He's tough. Especially when he feels he hasn't been taken seriously. I'm going to do the best I can." She glanced over at Sidney. "If you've got family, gather them up and get them in that courtroom. Showing that Ty has support may have some influence on the outcome." She turned back to Ty. "Prepare yourself. I'm sorry to say that you're going to do some time. If you're tried as an adult, the worst-case scenario is five years."

Ty's face went pale. He wheeled his head toward the wall with an audible whine. "No!" His chained hands struck the table's edge and the terrible sounds resonated in the stark room. Sidney watched his shoulders rise and fall convulsively and heard the resolve in his breaking voice as he uttered, "I'd rather die."

Sidney parked her car in front of the Dunbar Traders Market and took a good, hard look at herself in the visor mirror. Her eyes were slightly red from crying, but no longer swollen. She swept a coat of mascara on her lashes. What did she think she was doing? Jack Mellon was probably married or at least engaged by now. He had wanted to settle down, to have a family. He was that kind of guy. A man who held a steady job, loved kids and sports — and, at one time, her.

But as long as she was already in Dunbar and Micki had the girls, it occurred to her that this might be the perfect time to connect with him again. She knew she was fooling herself, yet the image of Jack sitting beside her in court next Tuesday kept popping into her mind. Her mother was in Ohio. Micki and Dennis were the closest thing to family that she had locally, but they would be in Arizona for Dennis's business convention on the day of the hearing. She ran a comb through her hair. It was longer now than when she and Jack had dated, falling on her shoulders, dark blond with lighter streaks that were no longer the result of spending hours in the sun like the highlights in Rebecca's sleek tresses. Sidney's rays of sunshine came from a box and were painted on. She applied tinted lip gloss and glared at herself one last time. "Okay, if you're going to do this thing, do it," she murmured aloud.

Inside the store, she grabbed a cart and began throwing a few items into it on her way to the meat department. Nothing frozen; it was a half-hour drive back to Ham Bone. How she would explain the out-of-town shopping trip to Jack, she still didn't know. She was not one to lie. The seafood case came into view. Behind it, a young man wearing an apron and plastic gloves stooped to arrange salmon fillets on a bed of crushed ice. Sidney took a sharp right, not even daring a glance to the left where the red meats were displayed. After all, she never touched beef or pork. Jack knew that better than anyone. It had been a standing joke with them while they dated. A red meat–loving butcher and a fanatic vegetarian. Jack had insisted that opposites attract, while Sidney was repelled by the hormone- and chemical-infused slabs of flesh that he consumed. He had corrupted Tyson on their outings, sneakily buying him hot dogs and pepperoni pizzas, barbecuing hamburgers on a portable hibachi that Jack kept in the back of his canopied truck. Long after their breakup, her son had begged her to stop at the Burger Barn every time she drove past.

In the safety of the organic produce section, Sidney collected her thoughts while weighing bunches of romaine lettuce in her hands. At $1.99 each, she was determined to get the heaviest one.

The red-meat thing was not the reason she gave Jack the "Let's just be friends" line two years ago. It had been more than that. When Jack fell in love with her, she just panicked. Suddenly the fun and comfort of having a relationship with someone of the opposite sex had drained away. He wanted a commitment. 'Til death do us part. It shouldn't have terrified her; she could see that clearly now. Jack was a good man. He was nothing like Dodge.

Besides, hadn't she known from the start that Dodge Walker was a dangerous man?

She had met Dodge the winter of her freshman year. Sidney had grown up in Ohio, but came out west to attend Western Washington University. It seemed like a good idea at the time. A grand adventure. If she had known back then what she knew now, that a stranger named Dodge Walker would pop out from between a couple of those famous Washington State evergreens to reroute her life forever, she would have stayed close to home and gone to OSU like most of her friends.

Sidney and her cousin Tara were stomping through a tree farm searching for the perfect Christmas tree for the lobby in their dorm. It was dusk when a young man suddenly emerged between two firs, wielding a crosscut saw.

"Ladies, I couldn't help overhearing your discussion. You need something big. Something all you college women can gather around in your shorty pajamas while you paint your toenails." He grinned mischievously and winked. "I've got the tree of your dreams." He walked away without looking back. They followed the dark and dashing stranger down a path of slushy snow between rows of fragrant evergreens, both girls more intrigued by the salesman at that point than the prospect of a perfect tree. He eventually stopped short of a nine-foot-tall alpine, surveying it from top to bottom, and whistled. "Trust me. They don't make 'em any better than this." His eyebrows shot up and he flashed another cocky grin. Black curls fringed the edges of his wool knit cap. His eyes were brown like coffee with the sun shining through it, and when they stayed fixed on Sidney too long, she felt herself blush.

"I wouldn't sell this to just anybody," he said. "This baby took a lot of coddling, years of precision pruning. Look at the symmetry. These branches are so level you could serve dinner on them."

"The alpines are, like, $60, aren't they?" Tara asked.

"What's the matter? You don't like it?"

She nodded. "Sure, but —"

"It's yours then." He gave Sidney a long and suggestive look, raising his saw. "It happens that I'm in a very good mood today."

"Wow. Thanks. But it's too big," Tara lamented. "There's no way we can tie that on the top of my Honda."

Dodge had answered her without taking his eyes off Sidney. "I deliver." He reached out to brush a snow crystal from her lip.

It made her angry whenever she thought back on it. Not that he, a perfect stranger, had the gall to touch her like that. Not even when she found out after the tree had already been erected and decorated that Dodge didn't work for the tree farm. He had tossed the artfully sculpted evergreen into the back of his pickup truck, which was parked in a roped-off field-turned-parking-lot, as if he owned the place, without so much as a glance over his shoulder toward the pay station in the barn. What irked her was that she had fallen for his blatant seduction like the naive schoolgirl that she was. Blinded by infatuation.

Sidney gazed at the produce. She needed some things, but she couldn't think of them now. Instead, her mind reasoned. She had imagined flaws in Jack. She had let certain mannerisms bother her as a means of self-protection. How stupid was that? He had been the very salve to heal her wounds and those of her children, but she had sent him away.

For all Sidney knew, Jack wasn't even working today. If he wasn't there, she would know this encounter, this reconnection, was not meant to be. That would be that. From then on she would do her shopping in Ham Bone, where she knew her way around the store and she could get the frozen blueberries home before they became a sloppy mess. She tossed a bag of fresh broccoli into the cart and pushed it around the corner again, this time heading straight for the meat department.

Jack was nowhere in sight. The disappointment caught her by surprise. She stopped and stared into a cooler case of bacon and sausages, not really seeing them. She was suddenly weary. It had been an emotionally wrenching day. Hadn't it been enough seeing her son thrown to the ground and hauled away by the sheriff? Driving frantically to the detention center only to be kept waiting for hours? The attorney's frankly pessimistic forecast of what was to come at the hearing? This whole idea had been idiotic. She should be home now helping the girls get ready for bed.

She sighed, hugging herself against the chill of the refrigerated display case, too consumed by hopelessness to move on. She was all alone with nobody to help. Nobody but God. She wished she knew Him like her mother.

Her mom had the kind of faith that expected miracles and got them. Like the time she emptied out her wallet for a homeless woman while shopping in downtown Cleveland and then realized she didn't have bus fare to get back home. She had just shrugged and smiled. "The Lord will provide." Sidney and her sister were hungry. Their mother led them back to the bus stop and they waited. Then out of the blue, there was their neighbor, Mrs. Sanford, coming out of the florist shop. A neighbor, from way out in the suburbs! They all piled into her big Cadillac, and Mrs. Sanford, delighted with their company, had insisted on springing for dinner on the way home.

When things like that happened, Mom was not surprised. She just cast a glance and a wave to the sky. "Thank you, Jesus!"

"Excuse me. Have you decided yet?"

The woman startled her. "Oh, I'm so sorry." Sidney pushed her cart out of the way. "How long was I standing there?"

The middle-aged lady laughed. "Well, long enough to plan a few menus, I suppose."

Now Sidney laughed. "I was off in la-la land. It's a good thing you said something. I might have kept you waiting until they turned the lights off on us."

"Sidney?"

She whipped her head around. "Jack."

"I'd know that laugh anywhere," he said. He was pushing a tiered cart laden with beef. The other shopper placed some sausage links in her cart and moved on. The first thing Sidney noticed was his tan. Her eyes flitted to his hand. His ring finger, along with the others, was concealed inside yellow disposable gloves.

"How are you? You look great, Jack." He really did. He was pretty buff for a guy who ate beef and potato chips and greasy fried chicken. He wasn't terribly short, but Sidney remembered feeling a little uncomfortable around him when she wore high heels.

He smiled, a little cautiously. "Thanks. You're as pretty as ever yourself. What are you doing in Dunbar? Did you move?"

"I moved, but not out of Ham Bone. We've got a house now — well, a double-wide mobile home anyway. It's got a big yard and backs up to a wood full of cedar and firs. I can't see moving out of town as long as the kids are in school. We have good schools."

"Yeah. That's what I've heard. How are the kids?"

"Good. Growing like they're standing in fertilizer." This was not the time to tell him that Ty was locked up. "So what have you been up to? Do you still fly model planes?"

He swiped at his nose with his rolled-up sleeve. One of the things that had annoyed her back when she was looking for reasons not to fall in love. "Not much. I started building one about a year ago, but there it sits, unfinished. I played baseball on the Traders Market team all summer; we took second in the tournament. Now I coach peewee football."

"Good for you. You were always great with kids."

There was an awkward silence. She thought she should fill it before the "What are you doing in Dunbar?" question came up again. "I'm really glad to run into you, Jack. I've missed you."

"You have?"

She looked him square in his blue eyes. "Yes. I've actually been thinking of you a lot lately."

He stared at her blankly. Oh, crap. He *was* married.

"I mean, we had some good times, didn't we? My kids sure liked you. Do you have any kids of your own yet?"

He wheeled his cart across the aisle and began stocking beef roasts in the cooler case. "Nope." He glanced back at her as if reading her face, then went back to work.

Had she been dismissed? It seemed, if she had any dignity at all, like a good time to wrap this conversation up and head for the dog food aisle. "Well, I can see you're busy —"

"Why did you break it off with me?"

His question shocked her. She had expected only small talk. Her eyes were riveted on the back of his head while his arms swiftly packed roasts as if they were sandbags and the river was about to flood. "I don't know. I can't even remember anymore."

He straightened and looked at her like she had just broken out with a highly contagious rash. "You can't remember? I think at the time you said something about incompatible goals and a bunch of other ethereal reasons that never made a lick of sense. Not to me, anyway."

"Jack, I —"

"Sorry," he said, giving his head a quick shake. "Never mind all that. It doesn't matter anymore."

A man with a child on his hip walked up to Jack. "How can I help you, sir?" Jack asked.

"Those steaks over there look a little flimsy. Got any man-size cuts in there?"

Jack rummaged through the packages on the lowest shelf of his cart, producing two thick steaks with white fat borders. "Look at the marbling in these babies."

"Ah, beautiful. Thanks," the man said as he tossed them onto his frozen vegetables and walked away.

Jack returned to his work.

"Are you married now, Jack?" There. She said it.

He lined up stew meat in a neat single-file

row. "Nope."

Well, he certainly wasn't making this easy for her. "Jack, it's possible that I might have been an idiot back then," she said to his back. "That's not a definite, you understand, so don't quote me on it, but the thought has entered my mind."

He turned and a smile twitched at the corner of his lip. "Funny," he said as he cocked his head. "I had the very same thought."

8

It took only a few seconds when Millard awoke the next morning to remember that this was no ordinary day. Throwing off his blanket, he slid into his slippers, hastily wrapped a blue plaid bathrobe over his cotton undershirt and briefs, and, after a stop in the bathroom, headed straight down the hallway toward the front door.

He was surprised when the door did not fly open with a twist of the knob. The dead bolt. In his anticipation he had almost forgotten about the armed hoodlum who lived across the street. Millard had even double-checked the window latches the night before to assure himself that everything was secure. Sure, the kid was supposed to be in jail, but that didn't mean some wishy-washy judge hadn't merely slapped the kid's hand and let him out again. Millard twisted the bolt free, a flutter of excitement overshadowing any trepidation. In his mind he already saw his furry little marauder lying belly-up on the lawn, tongue hanging out and cheeks bulging.

A tip from Red, the barber, yesterday while Millard had his hair trimmed had saved him the $39.95 that Art Umquist down at the Hardware and Sporting Goods would have charged to special order a mole trap. Highway robbery! And the contraption might not get there for three to six weeks! A mole could drag the thing by its hind leg all the way from Milwaukee faster than that. But for less than a buck, Millard had bought the one thing moles couldn't resist, despite the fact that it choked them to death: Juicy Fruit gum.

What he saw brought instant tears of fury to his eyes. A word escaped his lips that he had not used since taking a bullet in the wing of his F-86 Sabre over North Korea. Millard bolted down the concrete steps, tripped on the *Winger County Herald,* and suddenly began a running dive that landed him face-first on the spongy lawn.

For a moment he just lay there. His heart was pounding too fast, his world spinning out of control. It occurred to him that this was the second time in two days that he had been this intimate with his land, lying prone like a subject before his lord. Worse yet, like an old man who could no longer stand on his own two feet. The thought of the latter, and especially a fear of the neighbor lady catching him in this position again, propelled him upward to his bare knees, and then with a labored grunt to his feet. He pulled his bathrobe together and retied it, took a deep breath, and turned to survey his formerly perfect lawn.

The mole's new tunnel branched off from the first, meandering toward the apple tree, where it stopped abruptly beneath the overhanging limbs. Must have bumped his noggin on a root, Millard thought. He stepped gingerly forward, peering at the fresh pile of earth. He stooped, brushing the dirt aside until he could see the new hole. Nobody home as far as he could see. Yesterday's tunnel seemed undisturbed, the dirt piles having dried out a bit under the sun. He reached down and felt through the soil, pulling out two perfect rectangles of Juicy Fruit gum.

That afternoon the crossword puzzle might as well have been in Swahili. Millard just couldn't get it. Every time he stared out the window, which was how he normally concentrated on a word clue, his eyes went to the jagged scars on his lawn. He tried looking beyond them, but that landed his gaze on the eyesore across the street. That downspout hanging there was an ominous sign. Once one house in the neighborhood went to pot, it wouldn't be long before others followed. The inversion of keeping up with the Joneses.

Rita stopped by. She cheerily congratulated him for eating most of his frozen dinners during the past week but compensated for the positive note by complaining that he should have called if he had planned to be gone all yesterday afternoon. "I didn't know where you were, Dad. For all I knew, you were lying in a ditch somewhere or flat on the kitchen floor, dead!"

He didn't mention the two episodes of lying flat on the lawn though very much alive. He did tell her in detail about his mole infestation, which seemed to concern her about as much as if he had said the sky was blue. She only looked over her shoulder at the damage through the picture window. "Well, yes. Look at that," she said. "It's a regular mole Disneyland." And then she proceeded to tell him that Audrey Milhall was in town and how they hadn't seen each other since their ten-year reunion but planned to get together on Friday night. Nicole's football game was going to be out of town that night so Rita probably wouldn't have gone to watch her lead cheers anyway, and Petie would be staying overnight with a friend. Dan could just fend for himself at home.

"I haven't seen the kids since Fourth of July," he said.

"Oh, Dad." She patted his knee sympathetically. "You know, they're teenagers now. Their lives are just so busy, what with all their practices and school events and friends. Dan says he's thinking of installing a revolving door, the way they come and go so quickly. But you know Nicole has her driver's license now. I'll tell her to come on over here and see you sometime soon."

He put the paper on the lamp table and stood, stretching out his legs. "You tell her to bring her brother. I'll take them out for root beer floats like we used to."

Rita's lips flattened out. "Well, if you do that, let Nicole drive." She sighed and paused long enough that he knew this was going to be something he didn't want to hear. "About your car, Dad. About you driving it, I mean. I'm wondering if, at your age, you shouldn't just park that thing for good."

"Confound it, Rita!"

"Hear me out, Dad. It's just that there

was this story about older drivers on a news show, and the statistics are absolutely scary. You'd be amazed at how many of your peers are driving in imaginary lanes and running into telephone poles!"

"So you think I've gone senile? Or blind?"

"No! I just think your reflexes may not be all that they used to be, that's all."

He began pacing the floor in front of her. "What are you really afraid of? That I might die? Well, so what if I do? So what if you come over here someday and find me in a heap on the kitchen floor because I ate corn dogs instead of shepherd's pie and creamed peas? What difference would it make, as long as I don't leave you with a mess to clean up? Who on God's green earth really gives a hoot?"

"Dad, you're blowing this way out of proportion. I just want you to take care of yourself, that's all."

"Maybe taking care of myself is not in my best interest! Did you ever think of that?" He strode to the front door and slammed it behind him. The first thing his eyes fell on was the cockeyed downspout on the trailer-house across the road. Rita came out and followed him all the way to the garage. He yanked his keys from his pocket.

"What are you doing? Where do you think

you're going? Dad, do *not* get in that car just to spite me!"

He ignored her, unlocking the garage door and walking past the Lincoln, then pulled the metal ladder off its hooks on the back wall of the garage. The drawer of his red tool chest stuck at first, but gave way with a violent jerk that almost pulled it off its track. Millard gathered nails, hammer, and screwdrivers, anything he thought he might need, stuffing them into the leather tool belt that Molly gave him one Christmas and strapping it around him. His daughter watched silently from the open door, hands planted on hips. When he proceeded forward, the ladder in front of him like a battering ram, she backed away.

"I've got some work to do," he said.

He felt her watching as he strode across the street. Though the ladder was somewhat heavy, he deliberately held it high, back straight, chin up. He might be pushing his mid-seventies, but he was *not* pushing up daisies. Give up his car! He'd sooner give up Sundays. Move to Haywood House! Pull a wheelchair up to the window and watch for Jesus to come again on the clouds. Wouldn't that just sew everything up neatly for Rita and Dan? Dan, her real estate agent husband who kept getting market appraisals

97

on Millard's house, practically salivating as he told Millard that the value would go up now that the new supermarket and strip mall were going in down on Highway 12. Rita, no longer looking up to him, not so much as a glint of admiration in her eyes. He remembered how she used to beg him to twirl her in his arms, how proud she was of her daddy when he came to her school on career day. At her wedding she hugged him so tightly that he knew she had a hard time letting go. At what point had he become nothing but a worry and a burden to her?

Millard lowered the ladder to the weedy flower bed at the far corner of Sidney Walker's house and leaned it up against dirty, gray siding. He could see that it was a simple fix. All he had to do was reattach an aluminum strap meant to hold the downspout in place. With each step up the metal rungs, he relished the knowledge that Rita was still standing over there, holding herself back, biting her tongue. He would show her. He was still useful for something.

It was not until he found himself staring through a bedroom window that he began to feel like a Peeping Tom. Was anyone home? His being there was really as much a surprise to him as it would be to anyone. It had not even occurred to him prior to that moment of frustration to fix the neighbor's downspout, but here he was, peering into the window of a pink bedroom with two unmade twin beds. It was too early for the little girls to come home from school, and their mother was usually at work during the day. He glanced across the yard, dismayed to see that for once her oxidized red car was actually parked at the end of the gravel drive. Perhaps he should have knocked first.

He would just get the job done and be gone. He knew Rita was still watching, whether from his driveway or in the house he didn't know, but as sure as fleas on a stray dog she was fretting and fuming right now because he wasn't sitting safely in his recliner, where he belonged. He placed a couple of nails between his lips and grasped the metal tube, hoisting it up toward the gutter. It was heavier than he'd thought. This was a bit difficult with only his left hand. He leaned to the left, his knees braced against the ladder. Stretching his right arm across his body, he pushed upward with both hands, his head tipped back awkwardly. At first the aluminum spout refused to match up with the mouth of the gutter. He grunted and adjusted his aim, blood draining from his head. There. Got it! He held it firmly with his left hand, fumbling for his hammer with the right, wishing for a third hand to pull a nail from his clamped lips.

A shrill scream sliced the air. Millard jerked backward as if stabbed in the chest. The downspout fell from his grip, clattering against the side of the house. He grabbed for the ladder, fighting an immediate case of vertigo.

The bedroom window slid open. "Oh, Mr. Bradbury! It's you. What are you doing? You nearly scared me to death!"

Sidney Walker had no idea who was nearly scared to death. His fingers clenched the ladder as if rigor mortis had already set in. Millard forced one hand loose and held his palpitating chest. "I didn't mean to . . . I mean I wasn't . . . your downspout. I was fixing your downspout."

"Oh." She cocked her head. "Well, God bless you. I've been wanting to fix that, but I didn't have a ladder. Just a minute." The window slammed shut, and seconds later she came out the front door and down the steps. "Let me help you with that."

There were some advantages to being old, he guessed. If he were a younger man hovering outside her daughters' window, Sidney would surely have called the sheriff. The sirens would be howling their way up Boulder Road from town right now. She helped him push the downspout onto the funnel of the gutter and held it in place while he nailed the strap to the siding.

"I thought you would be at work," he said. "Didn't notice your car there until I was already up on the ladder." He backed down the rungs and lowered the ladder to the ground.

"Well," she said with a sigh, "something came up today. I had to make a bunch of phone calls. Would you like to come in for some iced tea, Mr. Bradbury?"

He should be tending to his mole problem. He had a new plan of attack and was sure it would get better results than the Juicy Fruit gum. He glanced over his shoulder toward his neat, white ranch-style house. Rita's car was still in the drive. She didn't normally stay this long. What was she waiting for? To give him a good scolding, that's what. "I think I'd like some tea," he said.

Millard followed Sidney into her house. The place looked surprisingly cheery and a lot cleaner than one would suspect, judging by the outside. Quite tidy, really, with matching curtains tied back with fancy rope braids, an elegant cloth on the dining room table, and a huge bouquet of dahlias and daisies (which she certainly didn't cut from her own yard). A painted coffee table held stacks of neatly folded clothes. He wandered to a wall of framed photos while Sidney commented from the kitchen on the nice Indian summer they were having and how she hoped it would last. The pictures were of her children from newborn to missing teeth to the awkward school photos where their front teeth looked too big for their faces. There was a mustached man in the family shots up until the boy looked to be maybe six or seven and the girls were still babies. Sidney cradled an infant or toddler in each of the poses, her thick, dark blond hair and big eyes almost too intense for her slight frame. The next portrait in line showed the father conspicuously missing, a blank spot where he belonged, almost as if they were expecting him to show up any second and breathlessly take his spot next to their mother, his hand resting as it had before on the shoulder of the dark-haired boy. A normal-looking boy he was — actually quite handsome, with wide brown eyes and long, dark lashes.

"That's Tyson," she said, noting the photo that held his gaze. She passed Millard a tall, cold glass. "My precious jailbird." She went to one of the chairs, motioning him to do the same. "Please sit."

"He's still doing his time, eh?" Sidney had given him a brief update on her son's situation when they had met at the mailbox on Saturday. He lowered himself into a chair.

She nodded grimly. "His sentencing hearing is tomorrow. That's why I didn't go to work today. I've been talking to his attorney. She says the judge could try him as an adult, because the charge is a felony, and he could get up to five years." At that she teared up. "Tyson is like a wild creature. He just can't stand to be indoors for any length of time. He likes to take his sleeping bag and sleep out in the woods sometimes, all by himself." She sighed. "I can't bear the thought of him in that cage one more day."

"Have they let you talk to him?"

"Yes. He's terrified of jail. That's why Ty bolted from the school counselor's office the minute he reached for the phone to call the sheriff. He'd been camping out down by Sparrow Creek the whole time he was runaway. The day he was arrested, he had sneaked up to the window of my office through the back alley just to let me know he was all right. He said he missed me," she said with a half smile. "But someone thought he looked suspicious and called the sheriff. A deputy apparently got there in about two seconds flat."

She hadn't touched her glass to her lips, but twirled the liquid gently, watching the ice cubes go around and around. Neither of them spoke for what seemed like a long time. Millard thought he should say something but couldn't come up with anything appropriate.

"He's so angry," she said. "It's like he's got a fire smoldering inside him, and it doesn't take much to fan it to flame." She shook her head slowly. "I don't know what I've done wrong. Well, I do know I'm at work a lot. I wish I could be home when my kids get out of school." She glanced up at her son's childhood photo, the one where he held a caramel-colored puppy on his lap, boy gazing at dog and dog at boy in mutual admiration. She shivered, pulling her sweater around her, though it was a mild September day. "I don't know what's going to happen." She sighed. "I'll find out tomorrow morning at his hearing, I guess."

Millard glanced nervously out the window just in time to see Rita's car pull out of his driveway across the street. The blue Chevy cruised slowly past, his daughter no doubt straining her eyes to see what he was up to, wrinkling her forehead the way she did whenever she disapproved. The coast was clear now. He gulped down the last of his tea and set his glass on the coffee table next to a folded pile of washcloths. "Well, it probably won't be as bad as all that," he said, searching his mind for a *Perry Mason* episode to justify his statement but coming up blank. "You just get a good night's sleep tonight. Things have a way of looking better in the morning."

He stood slowly, thanking her for the iced tea.

"Here I've gone and spilled my guts to you again." She smiled through teary eyes. "I guess you remind me a little of my dad. I used to confide in him about everything, but I don't have him anymore. He passed on a few years ago. Anyway, I haven't even asked. Did you solve your mole problem?"

"I'm about to. I'm going to flood that sucker out. Mole soup, that's what I have in mind."

She laughed and walked him toward the door. "Sounds delicious!" She placed her hand on his arm. "It was so kind of you to fix my downspout, Mr. Bradbury. I'm sure you have more important things to do. You let me know if there's anything I can do for you." She leaned forward, kissing him on the cheek. "I mean it."

He nodded a smile and stepped gingerly down the wooden steps, remembering his morning dive.

More important things to do. Did she really believe that? Her words echoed tauntingly in his mind as he crossed the street toward home.

9

If his yard was a regular mole Disneyland, as Rita had put it, Millard's furry friend had just had the ride of his life. Millard chuckled as he wound up the hose and hung it on a bracket against the house. *Pirates of the Caribbean* gone wild. He had shoved the nozzle into the main tunnel and let it run full blast all night — to hell with the water bill. Lo and behold, this morning there were no new tunnels, no piles of freshly dug earth, but surely somewhere in the underground labyrinth was the bloated corpse of one dearly departed rodent who had dug his own grave.

"Sayonara," the old man said with a quick two-fingered salute. He stooped to pluck the paper from the porch, grasping a handrail for support. His back was talking to him this morning, telling him the weather was about to change — as if he couldn't figure that out just by looking at the sky. Clouds

as dense as chocolate mousse spread across the western horizon. Maybe he could have saved some money on his water bill after all. Looked like a pent-up flood looking for a place to happen. He shivered. Good day to hole up indoors.

Once settled into his easy chair, he snapped the *Herald* open, still gloating about the mole. He heard his little neighbor across the street trying to start her car. It was a familiar whine — every morning the same, usually sparking ignition on the third or fourth try.

He scanned the obituaries, shocked to see a familiar face grinning at him from the black-and-white page. Millard gasped and adjusted his glasses. Art Umquist! He stared in confusion. It was a flattering photo, one taken before the jowls hung from his face like icing melting from a cake. Not Art! Why, Millard just saw him down at the hardware store a few days ago. What happened? He skimmed the article. Died in his sleep? What does that mean? That's not a cause of death! He read on. Graduated from Ham Bone High School in 1948 (he was two years behind Millard and dated his sister, Glory, a couple of times, God rest her soul), worked as a carpenter until he opened Art's Hardware and Sporting Goods in 1961. Millard remembered when the building was brand-new; Art built it himself with the help of his brothers. Millard used to hunt and fish with the Umquist brothers before the wives and kids came along.

He closed his eyes, dropping his head to the back of the chair. Art Umquist — gone. Just like that. One day he's jawing with customers about the silvers heading upriver, telling them they're biting on corkies or whatever other jigs he had overstocked, then tells Millard he's fresh out of mole traps but he can order him one for $39.95, and a couple of days later he's reduced to a column of newsprint — the story of his life — soon to be wrapping fish or kindling fires.

Died in his sleep. What if it had been him? No one would know for a few days — not until Rita came by with a week's supply of frozen leftovers. She would find the hose still running, his yard as swamped as the Everglades. She would be shocked when she found him, then sad, then relieved. The grandkids might cry. He hoped they would, but wasn't sure. At least the funeral would get them out of a day of school. Peter would be grateful to him for that. Dan, of course, would have his real estate sign up in the yard before all the cheese puffs and Swedish meatballs were gone.

Art Umquist had been younger than Millard. Molly had been, too. Al Bender, Joe Seaton, Annabelle Watts . . . he could go on; they had all left him here — alone. For what? All he was good for anymore was to weigh down this faded blue armchair, as if without him it too might waft up into the great unknown. Not that it mattered. Nothing really mattered anymore.

He kept his eyes closed, imagining his own obituary. Graduated from Ham Bone High School in '46, bachelor's degree from the University of Washington, a stint in the Korean War, married Molly Elliot from Seattle, two kids (one deceased), taught at Silver Falls High in Dunbar until his retirement in 1989. His entire life wrapped up in a neat little package, sounding about as exciting as a pair of argyle socks.

The annoying whine from the car across the street grew weaker with each try until it faded out altogether.

Molly's eulogy had actually been quite beautiful. Her sister, Lena, came over from Idaho to give it, Millard being too beside himself with grief to speak at the service. There had been a slide show set to music, showing his wife as a girl at camp, a young woman in a svelte camel suit and heels, topped with a pheasant-feather hat, and then as his lovely bride. Photos of them with each of the babies, Molly walking Rita through her first steps, Molly pinning a Superman cape to little Jefferson's shoulders. Millard had been behind the camera much of the time, so he was invisible in most of the shots.

If he were to write his own epitaph for his tombstone today, it would be this: he tunneled blindly through life and left this molehill to remember him by.

The knock on the door startled him. He dropped the newspaper to the floor and pushed himself out of his muse and the chair. It was Sidney Walker, standing on his porch with a worried look that made her features appear sharper, her smooth cheeks a little hollow.

"Mr. Bradbury, I'm so sorry to bother you. I just don't know what else to do." She glanced back at the red pile of junk in her driveway. "This is just the worst day for my car to go kaput on me. I'm supposed to be at the courthouse for Tyson's hearing. I *have* to be there."

"Oh." Millard's mind had not yet joined him in the present tense. "Uh, well, I guess you need a jump, then," he stammered, looking over his shoulder as if he might see a pair of jumper cables draped over the back of his easy chair.

She shook her head and her brows rose imploringly. "There isn't time for that."

He stared blankly for a moment. What was she asking? To borrow his car?

"Is there any way — I mean, if you're not too busy, I was wondering if you could drive me to Dunbar?"

Millard drew back. Dunbar was twenty miles from there. He hadn't been that way for so long that they'd probably changed all the streets by now. But of course, that was the county seat. The courthouse, the jail, and the big library were all on the same block. He could tell by the way Sidney was clenching her hands together and trembling that he didn't have all morning to decide. "Well, I guess I could," he said, about as enthusiastically as if she'd asked him to help her shop for women's under-things. At least she didn't think he was too old and useless to drive his own car.

"Oh, thank you!" Sidney grasped his hands in hers. "Mr. Bradbury, you are a wonderful man!"

10

The sentencing hearing was held at the Juvenile Justice Center, a newer building located adjacent to the Juvenile Detention facility, better known as juvey jail. Mr. Bradbury sat next to Sidney in an open waiting area. She had insisted that he not sit out in the car for who knew how long in that miserable rain. The lobby was infested with teenagers, many in strange outfits and hairdos that made Mr. Bradbury gawk openly, along with their weary-looking parent or parents also waiting on black vinyl-covered chairs. Others sported fresh haircuts and even crisp shirts with ties, any brow and lip rings removed probably at the advice of their attorneys. A bailiff came through the double doors to call out a name and another party rose, gathering paperwork, the mother inevitably smoothing out a wrinkle or pushing back a wayward strand of her delinquent child's hair in hopes of making him or her look innocent before being swallowed up by the heavy doors.

"Mr. Bradbury, I appreciate this so much," Sidney said. "Not just the ride, but having you here for moral support."

He nodded. "I'm happy to oblige." He didn't look very happy, though. He was still gazing around as if he had somehow fallen through the pages of a book into a sci-fi world. "You might as well call me Millard," he added.

"Oh, sure."

Sidney had rolled up a pamphlet about the Job Corps and was tapping it rapidly against her other hand, her legs crossing and uncrossing every few seconds. "I wish I could see Tyson," she said. "I just want to talk to him. I don't even understand what's going on. Where is that attorney?"

Millard patted her arm. He probably thought she was going to cry again. Surely he was learning to see the signs. He seemed so uncomfortable there, but relaxed a little once he found the newspaper on one of the end tables and the crossword puzzle inside. He pulled a pen and reading glasses from his pocket. "Why don't you go up and ask at the desk?" he said. "I'll listen for your name to be called."

Sidney approached the dark-skinned

woman at the check-in desk and waited as she flipped a page on a clipboard. "Oh, it looks like your son's attorney went into labor last night. Just a minute." Sidney's heart fell. The receptionist punched in a phone number and waited, smiling at Sidney reassuringly. "Leonard, this is the front desk," she said. "According to my records, you've taken over the Tyson Walker case." Sidney heard the loud expletive that came out of the phone. The receptionist smiled. "He'll be right down."

Ty's new attorney still had traces of acne and could barely call the dark fuzz on his upper lip a mustache. He approached their row of chairs as if it were a train leaving the station, briefcase with protruding papers shoved under his arm, his shirt collar sticking out from a suit that had surely been handed down by a burlier big brother. "Mrs. Walker? Sorry, I'm running a little late this morning." He shook her hand and then reached for Millard's. "I'm Tyson's new attorney, Leonard Eggebraten."

"Millard Bradbury," he offered. He made a move to get up. "I'll let you two discuss this alone."

Sidney reached out for him. "Please stay." He sat back down.

"I'm taking over for Sybil," the new attorney said. "She went into labor early. Did you get a call?" Sidney shook her head, frowning.

Leonard Eggebraten pulled a chair in front of them, opening his briefcase on his lap. The black leather was brand-new. Probably a graduation gift from his mother. He pulled out a clipped-together pile of papers, smoothing out the creased corners and flipping through, skimming as if reading them for the first time. "Just refreshing my memory," he said.

"Okay," Leonard continued. "I see that Tyson has been incarcerated since last Tuesday. He's been charged with attempted armed robbery." He shook his head. "Oh, not good. Released on personal recognizance, and then he violated court orders."

"He ran away only because he got in trouble at school," Sidney said, leaning forward. "He thought they'd automatically throw him in jail. He has a terrible fear of jail, Mr. Eggebraten. Ty can't be cooped up. He'll go crazy. Please — we've got to get him out of there."

"Your son has been advised to plead guilty. Are you aware of that?"

"Yes, but Sybil told me that the fact that he turned himself in after the incident would work in his favor. He confessed. He also wrote letters of apology to the court and to the victim at the grocery store."

Leonard began flipping pages again. "Oh, yes, I see. That's good. Yes, I'll remind the judge of that. Also the fact that he has no priors and the judge can see that he has family support with both you and his grandpa here." He nodded toward Millard. "You'd be surprised how many kids don't have even one parent show up."

Millard opened his mouth, but Sidney opened her eyes wide and gave her head a quick shake. Millard's lips clamped tight and he nodded as if he understood. If his being perceived as family was going to help, he seemed willing to cooperate. He cleared his throat. "What exactly is your plan, young man?"

"Well, Mr. . . ."

"Bradbury."

"Yes, sorry. Mr. Bradbury. This is a very serious charge. I know that the deputy prosecuting attorney will ask for your grandson to be detained for at least part of his sentence."

"What does that mean?" Sidney asked.

"Juvenile jail. Tyson's probation counselor will also make a recommendation, based on his experience with him and his case so far. It's a long shot, but here's what I'm going to propose. We ask for a deferred disposition based on the positives here. That means he does *no* jail time. Zero, zip. He's placed on maybe six to twelve months' probation, probably has to do about forty hours of community service and keep his nose clean. I mean, he asks, 'Mother, may I?' and doesn't step over the line one time."

"Oh," Sidney breathed, "that would be perfect. What are the chances of the judge agreeing to that?"

He shrugged. "Slim."

The door to the courtroom opened again. The bailiff stood aside as a tearful mother emerged with a grim attorney, a fat folder stuffed under his arm. The boy who had gone in with them did not come out. "Walker!" the bailiff called.

Leonard gathered up his papers. "Showtime."

Sidney stood, clutching her purse close to her chest like a teddy bear. She gazed back at Millard, waiting. He dutifully pushed himself out of his chair, tucking the paper with its partially worked crossword puzzle under his arm. She felt his hand on the small of her back as they followed the green attorney through the oak doors.

Though it was juvenile court, the small hearing room looked as official as the courtrooms on *Matlock,* complete with a robed judge sitting behind a desk on a lofty platform. Millard and Sidney sidestepped to one of the hard wooden benches. Tyson's disheveled attorney plopped his briefcase onto a long, bow-shaped table up front while a woman in a gray suit and the more casually dressed probation officer took their seats adjacent to him. Sidney's hand inadvertently clutched Millard's arm as a door at the back opened and a uniformed officer led Tyson into the room. She caught her breath once again at the sight of her son dressed in that blue jumpsuit, his hands cuffed and locked to a chain around his waist. His shadowed eyes searched until he found her. She smiled reassuringly as if this were just his first piano recital, unaware that her fingernails were digging into Millard's arm until she felt the old man reach over and place his gnarled hand over hers, patting it like her own father would have done if he were there. Tyson's gaze dropped to the floor, his head down, as the officer guided him to the seat next to his newly appointed and still apparently floundering attorney.

Leonard leaned over and spoke to Ty in whispers while the judge perused the file placed in front of him. Other people came and went for several minutes, passing paper-work back and forth and speaking in hushed tones.

"Young man, please state your whole name for the court."

Ty leaned into the microphone on the table in front of him. "Tyson Holyfield Walker."

The fifty-something judge peered over his glasses. "I'm not even going to ask."

Sidney still resented Dodge for insisting on that name for their son. She knew Holy-field was her ex's favorite boxer, having become world heavyweight champ not long before Tyson was born. It wasn't until Evander Holyfield, a born-again Christian, had to have his ear sewn back together after convicted criminal Mike Tyson bit off a chunk in their famous 1997 rematch that Sidney realized why Dodge had insisted on Tyson for a first name. It seemed Ty was doomed to a life of conflict between good and evil from the start.

The prosecutor, Mrs. Rayburn, a prim-looking woman in her forties, stood to read the charges against him. "Your Honor, the defendant is charged with count one attempted first-degree robbery. On August 10, with intent to commit a robbery, Mr. Walker entered Graber's Market in Ham

Bone, stashed merchandise inside his clothing, including a bottle of alcohol, and attempted to leave the premises. He was apprehended by the store owner, at which time Mr. Walker threatened the victim with a previously concealed weapon. The victim managed to knock the gun from the defendant's hand and the defendant fled the scene." She dropped her papers to the desk in front of her.

It was a pellet gun, Sidney's mind screamed. Tell the court that! That it shot little hot-pink plastic balls. Oh, please, God, don't make him go to jail. Ty was too vulnerable right now. It seemed to her that sticking him in with a bunch of other angry, messed-up kids could only make things worse.

"Mr. Walker," the judge said, "do you understand the charges against you?"

Ty nodded. "Yes, sir."

"This is a very serious crime, punishable by up to five years in adult prison. Has your attorney informed you of your rights in this matter?"

"Yes, sir."

"And how do you plead?"

"Guilty, Your Honor." His voice cracked.

The prosecuting attorney spoke again. "Your Honor, the State is advising that Mr.

Walker be held in confinement at the county Juvenile Detention facility for the maximum standard period of thirty-six weeks."

The numbers whirled like dry leaves in Sidney's head as she tried to do the math.

Tyson's probation counselor stood next. Sidney and Ty had met with him only once before Ty ran away. He had seemed like a decent man, but tough. "Your Honor, the defendant was duly advised of the possible repercussions of breaking court orders when I met with him after his arraignment. He returned to school when it started in September, but within four days picked a fight with another student and took a swing at the teacher who tried to break it up. He then ran away from the school and was missing for eleven days until his arrest on September 20. I concur with Mrs. Rayburn except, considering the fact that this is the defendant's first offense, I think his detainment could be cut down to the minimum standard of fifteen weeks."

A minimum of three and a half months in jail or eight-plus max. Sidney's limbs went limp. Oh, God, could he survive it? Could she?

When the counselor finished, Leonard stood, still flipping through his papers as if something might jump out at him that he hadn't previously considered. It wasn't fair that their case had been handed over to this rookie at the last minute. At least Sybil had sounded somewhat competent.

"Your Honor," Leonard finally said, "what we have here is a young man who made a stupid mistake, and he knows it. If you read the letters that he wrote to the victim and the court in this case, you'll see that he is truly remorseful. Mr. Walker had no intention of threatening anyone with the pellet gun, which, by the way, he had not considered a real weapon due to the fact that it shoots only plastic beads. He realizes now, of course, that ignorance is no excuse for breaking the law. According to his statement, the gun had been in his pocket simply because he and his friends had been playing war in the woods earlier that day. He can provide witnesses to attest to that. I apologize for not having affidavits, Your Honor; this case was just passed to me this morning."

Sidney and Millard exchanged hopeful glances. The kid was doing all right.

Leonard ran his hand through his mop of dark hair. "Tyson has been in confinement for eight days, Your Honor. He tells me he's learned his lesson and that he will do anything to keep from going back to jail.

Based on his repentant attitude and the fact that this is his first offense — after which he did turn himself in to the sheriff without force — I propose the following: not fifteen weeks but the entire thirty-six, deferred dependent on his adherence to all court stipulations during that thirty-six-week period, along with forty hours of community service. The defendant has strong family support." Leonard glanced over his shoulder. "His mother and his grandfather are here in the courtroom. I suggest that my client be allowed to walk out of here in their custody today."

Tyson turned around to get a good look at the grandfather he didn't know he had. Sidney caught his eye, shrugging ever so slightly.

The judge raised one eyebrow, peering over his glasses at Leonard. "A slap on the knuckles considering the crime, don't you think, Mr. Eggebraten?"

Sidney could see only the back of Leonard's head, but he held it high. "Yes, Your Honor, but I feel strongly that locking the boy up will do more harm than good in this case."

At that moment Sidney wanted to run up there and hug their scraggly young attorney. The judge perused Tyson's file, making notes. He finally lifted his head.

"Let's make it a one-year sentence. Since the minimum recommended detainment for count one attempted first-degree robbery is fifteen weeks, I'm going to require the defendant to do that much time, but at school and at home. You are not to be anywhere but those two places for the next fifteen weeks; do you understand, Mr. Walker?"

Tyson nodded. Leonard elbowed him. "Yes, Your Honor."

"Mr. Walker, that means if you fail to abide by every stipulation of this court within the next year, you will be arrested and put behind bars to complete your sentence. You will be accountable to an assigned probation officer, who will give you a call within the next couple of days. In addition to his recommendations, this court mandates forty hours of community service and a fine of $100 to be paid to the crime victims' fund." The judge adjusted his glasses and flipped through the file for a moment. "That is, assuming there is adequate adult supervision at home. Otherwise, those fifteen weeks will have to be done in confinement."

Sidney's mind began to spin. She couldn't be there! She had her job.

Tyson whispered something to his attorney. Leonard leaned over and Sidney watched his profile. His brows drew together and he ran his hand over his mouth. "Your Honor, may I have a moment to confer with my client and his mother?"

"Certainly."

At his beckoning, Sidney stepped forward and sat in a vacant chair to Leonard's left.

"Mrs. Walker," he whispered, "we have two issues here. The first one is that you work full-time. The judge is not going to agree to leaving Tyson unsupervised. Second, Ty tells me he's been expelled from school for this entire semester. That's going to be major. The court is adamant about kids getting their education."

Sidney's heart sank. "What can we do?"

"How about Grandpa? Is there any reason he can't take responsibility for Tyson while you're at work?"

She sighed, her eyes meeting Ty's questioning stare. "Mr. Bradbury is not actually related. He's just a close neighbor."

Leonard winced and blew out a stream of air. "Okay, great. I just lied to the judge." He glanced back at Millard. "Do you think he'd agree to watch out for him?"

Sidney shook her head. "Oh, I don't know."

Leonard motioned for Mr. Bradbury to join them. Millard stared at him blankly for a moment, and then turned to look over his shoulder for someone else the attorney might be summoning. The poor man. Sidney had not only inconvenienced him, but now it seemed she had lured him from his comfort zone to the dangerous edge of a cliff. She pleaded with apologetic eyes. The grooves in his face seemed to deepen as he stood, slowly making his way to the front of the courtroom. He leaned forward, resting his long arms on the table.

"Mr. Bradbury, we have a situation here," Leonard said in a hushed voice. "Ty can't stay home unsupervised while his mom is at work. Are you home during the day?"

Millard recoiled. "Well, yes, but —"

"Here's the deal. You heard what the judge said. He's going to send him out of here today in shackles and lock him up for three and a half months unless we can come up with a plan."

Millard's mouth hung open. He began to stammer, his gaze falling on Tyson, whose face was expressionless. He didn't even know the kid. "There must be someone else . . ."

Sidney shook her head. "I'm sorry, Mr. Bradbury. Millard. I'm so sorry to even put you in this position."

His eyes said it all. He looked at her like a cornered wild thing, his unruly brows clenched in worry. Clearly he wanted no part in this and she didn't blame him one bit. His lips parted several times as if he wanted to say something, but no words came out. Ty was sizing the old man up, looking a little worried himself. Finally, Millard just shook his head.

"All right," Leonard said. "Does anybody have a plan B?"

Sidney's mind raced through her options in two seconds flat. Her mother lived in Ohio. Besides, even if she was willing to fly out to Washington, her mom was already obligated to watch her sister Alana's kids while Alana was at work. There was no one else she could possibly ask. She lifted her eyes to her son's desperate face. "Ty, I'm sorry."

"Mr. Eggebraten," the judge said, "can we move on here?"

Millard trudged back to his seat, his shoulders sagging. Sidney remained where she was seated.

Leonard sighed, shooting Tyson an apologetic glance as he stood. "Yes, Your Honor."

"Is there a problem here?"

"Your Honor, Mrs. Walker works full-time; however, her job is only minutes away from home. She could check in with Tyson throughout the day and could get there quickly if she needed to for any reason."

The judge shook his head at Leonard like he was a naughty child. "You know better, Mr. Eggebraten, but nice try. You didn't mention school. Why is that?"

"Tyson was expelled, sir, just for this semester."

"Well, that wraps it up." The judge looked directly at Tyson. "Young man, due to the circumstances, I have no choice but to return you to confinement in Juvenile Detention until you have completed your fifteen-week sentence. You can also get your schooling there. I will, however, withdraw the deferred sentence of one year, which was added in deference to allowing you to do this fifteen-week period on house arrest."

Tyson had been stoic through the whole thing, but suddenly his head dropped and his chin began to quiver. Tears immediately flooded her own eyes as Sidney reached behind Leonard to touch her son's arm. She wanted Ty to shrink back to a practical size so that she could bundle him in her arms and carry him away from that awful place. The uniformed corrections officer stepped toward the wild boy whose native floor was moss and leaves, his ceiling as high and wide as heaven. There were no walls in the world Ty loved — just the trees that welcomed his coming like brothers and stood aside whenever he chose to come home for a while. But he was about to be locked up like an animal in a concrete cage. Ty looked over at her as if to say good-bye, tears beginning to form on his lower eyelids, his lips clamped into a quivering frown. He raised his hands in an angry attempt to swipe them away, but the chain attaching the handcuffs to his chain belt stopped them short. Sidney fought for control, but lost. Silent sobs overtook her and her shoulders began to shake.

"Your Honor." Sidney whipped her head around. Mr. Bradbury was pushing himself up using the back of the oak bench in front of him for support. He cleared his throat. "May I address the court?"

The judge nodded.

"My name is Millard Bradbury. I live across the street from the Walkers."

The judge glanced down at his paperwork. "Are you not Tyson's grandfather?"

Leonard Eggebraten stood abruptly, his chair almost crashing to the floor. He caught it in the nick of time. "Your Honor, I was mistaken about that. I apologize. I had no intention of misleading the court. It turns out Mr. Bradbury is just a close friend of the family."

The judge glared at the attorney, then switched his gaze to Millard. "Go on, Mr. Bradbury."

"I could watch the boy." His eyes darted to Sidney, then Tyson. "I'm home most of the time anyway. I guess he could stay over at my place during the day. I could teach him something, too. That's what I did before I retired. Taught history and coached wrestling here in Dunbar, over at the high school."

That wonderful man. Sidney wanted to jump up and smother him with kisses.

The judge's pen tapped a slow, silent rhythm on his desk. His eagle-eyed stare burned a path to Leonard Eggebraten, whose face had grown noticeably flushed.

Sidney held her breath.

"Mr. Walker, are you willing to submit to Mr. Bradbury's authority while your mother is away?"

Tyson nodded. "Yes, sir."

"Mr. Bradbury, this is a big commitment. Tyson is not to be left unsupervised for any length of time. Are you sure about this?"

Millard hesitated slightly before nodding.

"All right, then. Mr. Walker, you may walk

out of here today under your mother's and Mr. Bradbury's custody. Your probation counselor will meet with you to go over the details of the court's requirements, which will include satisfactory completion of all assigned schoolwork. Failure to comply will put you back in confinement, and your sentence will automatically increase from fifteen weeks to one full year." His gavel smacked the desk and he stood. "Court is recessed."

11

Outside the courthouse everything looked brighter to Sidney. The sky was still gray and the streets wet enough to spray rooster tails behind passing cars, but the torrential rain seemed to have drained the saturated clouds.

Millard hardly spoke. He unlocked the doors of his red Lincoln and Tyson crawled into the backseat. Sidney sat up front, pouring out her gratitude to Millard for saving the day. He looked a bit dazed, probably still in shock from the overwhelming commitment he had just made. Tyson too was quiet. Sidney found herself chattering like a goldfinch just to fill the awkward silence.

It was all she could do to refrain from jumping into the backseat with her son where she could see him and touch him. He'd been gone so long, and she had feared that she might have lost him for good. Now here he was, safe. But of course, at fifteen, he was too cool for his mother's coddling and she respected that. She could no longer play with his cowlick or smooth the worry from his forehead. Those things were taboo now. Ty was trying to be a man. If only he knew how. If only he knew what a real man — a man of character — looked like, talked like, lived like.

Once again her mind drifted back to her encounter with Jack Mellon at the Traders Market. It had been a week and he hadn't called. She had watched him tuck her phone number into the pocket of his stained white apron before she wheeled her scantily loaded shopping cart down the pickle aisle toward checkout. Even if he had forgotten about the little scrap of paper and ran it through the wash, he could easily find her number through directory assistance. If he wanted to.

"Oh, look at those maples," she said. "They're as bright as pure gold. I just love this time of year, don't you?" Millard only nodded. "I can't believe it's almost October already. It seems like we were just out baking in the sun a few days ago. Tyson, we'll have to go get some pumpkins soon for our front porch." She wished she could retract the "we." Ty couldn't go anywhere for fifteen weeks, not even the woods behind the house. He could make a straight line from his front door to Millard's every weekday morning, and back again at night when she got home. The probation officer had warned against any detours en route. Ty was to be monitored by a telephone voice recognition system. A computer would call him at random throughout the day — weekdays at Millard's, nights and weekends at home. He had all of two minutes to get to the phone — or else back to jail to do his time.

"What was it like in there, Ty?" she asked.

He grunted from the backseat. "Stupid."

"Can you elaborate on that?"

"There are no stinkin' windows."

"Oh. What else?"

"The food sucks, it's noisy, and there's nothing to do."

Millard clucked his tongue. "That's why they call it jail instead of the Holiday Inn." Sidney heard the theme song from the TV series *Baretta* in her head: *don't do the crime if you can't do the time.* She hadn't seen or thought of that show since she was a kid. Her father had loved cop shows. She wondered if Millard was transmitting it somehow from his mind to hers when he added, "Don't do the crime if you can't do the time."

Sidney flipped down her visor mirror in time to see the scowl cross Ty's face. He sat back against the seat, his arms locked tightly across his chest. Oh, boy. Perhaps Ty had just hopped from the frying pan into the fire, as her dear old dad used to say. Spending his days with old Mr. Bradbury might prove to be worse than a damp dungeon and a steady diet of bread and water.

After a while she gave up on making pleasant conversation. As the miles passed, she turned her thoughts toward seeing the girls, who would be home from school by now. With Ty back at their dinner table for the first time in weeks, they should have a celebratory meal. What would Ty like? Spaghetti with lots of fresh mushrooms, some crusty garlic bread. That would be easy and he loved it.

She breathed a relieved sigh as Millard drove up the hill toward their houses. The clouds parted and a beam of afternoon light shone through the trees on either side of the curvy road, lighting up the leaves like red and orange neon. Almost home. Everything was going to be all right now. Ty could sleep in his own bed tonight, and she relished the thought of tucking him in. He might talk to her more then. That had become his way, to open up to her in the dark where there were only words and no faces. But it had been a long time since even that dwarfed communication had taken place between them.

Her eyes followed the weathered posts and wire fence along the right side of the road to her mailbox — and the car in her driveway. Winger County Sheriff's Department, it said on the door. Deputy Estrada sat inside and he was not alone. Adrenaline shot through her system. What was he doing here?

Tyson swore.

"What on earth do they want?" Millard asked. He stopped at the end of her driveway.

"I don't know, but I guess I'm about to find out." Sidney opened the car door. "Mr. . . . Millard. Thanks again." She glanced over her shoulder and saw the two deputies getting out of the car. "I guess Ty and I will be over at your place about eight o'clock in the morning. I hope that's okay."

He winced.

"Eight-thirty?"

He nodded grimly. "That will be fine."

"All right, then," she said and closed the door. Ty got out and Millard turned into his own driveway across the street. She walked straight up to Estrada, who was leaning against the hood of the official sedan. Dry leaves scurried across the gravel near his boots like a herd of red land crabs.

"Hello, Mrs. Walker."

"How can I help you?" She held her head high and her voice was terse. She felt Ty lingering just behind her.

The deputy looked right past her to her son and nodded. "Tyson. I'm surprised to see you here."

"Why?" Ty asked.

"Thought you'd be locked up for a while, that's all. Who did you get for a judge?"

Ty shrugged. "I don't know. Some old guy."

"Deputy," Sidney asserted, "what are you doing here?"

He pulled a folded paper from his shirt pocket. "I have the search warrant you suggested. I noticed your daughters were home, so I thought we'd wait for you." He tipped his head toward his partner. "This is Deputy Shingle." His sidekick looked a little frail and timid, younger than Estrada, with wide blue eyes peering through wire-rimmed glasses.

Ty stepped forward, his eyes narrowing into angry slits. "What are you looking for?"

"I think you know the answer to that question." Deputy Estrada's glare reflected the hostility in Ty's face. Estrada turned toward Sidney and gestured toward her front door. "Shall we, Mrs. Walker?"

She had no choice this time. They all walked to the porch in silence, where Sidney paused. "Let me take care of the girls before you start anything." He didn't argue, so she went inside. Estrada leaned against the doorjamb, while the other deputy lingered just outside.

"Girls, we're home!"

They came running from the kitchen, followed by Duke. The dog barked once before hurling his huge body forward. Deputy Estrada's right hand jerked toward the gun on his hip. Duke leapt onto Ty, paws on his master's shoulders, and began licking him as if he were an ice cream cone melting in the sun.

"Hey, buddy." Ty ruffled the hair on Duke's neck.

Sidney frowned at the deputy and shook her head. Oh, that would have been just great. Their beloved Duke blown to smithereens right before her children's eyes. Estrada sheepishly dropped his hand to his side.

"Ty!" Sissy hugged her brother, and his free arm rested on her shoulder though he stood as stiff as a signpost. "Hi, Ty," Rebecca said, staring at her brother almost shyly. Sissy's attention shifted to Deputy Estrada. "Why were you sitting out in our driveway so long?"

"We'll answer all your questions in just a little while," Sidney said. "But right now I need you girls to take the dog outside for a while. Put him on his leash, and Rebecca, hold on tight." Duke seemed torn. The German shepherd loved to go for walks but he kept throwing his heavy body back toward Ty, pouncing playfully at Ty's feet and then watching over his shoulder for Ty to follow each time Rebecca tried to drag him to the backdoor.

As soon as the door slammed behind them, the deputies began poking around the living room — halfheartedly, it seemed. Perhaps they didn't think Ty would be careless or brazen enough to hide something in such a public area. Estrada perused her bookcase where *Moby-Dick, Treasure Island,* and other classics stood shoulder to shoulder with vegetarian cookbooks and a collection of Oprah's picks. He pulled a few books out, running his fingers behind them, finding nothing but dust. At least the house looked clean and tidy — not that she needed to impress them. It was just that she had her pride and did not care to be perceived as trailer trash, even — or especially — to these contemptuous deputies.

Deputy Estrada headed for the hallway. Pushing open the first door, he entered the bathroom. She heard him remove the heavy porcelain lid to the toilet tank, vanity drawers and doors opening and closing. He moved on to Ty's room, the first door on the left. Sidney and Ty followed him, watching from the open doorway as the swarthy deputy began poking around, running his hands behind things on the shelf, even lifting the golf balls out of Ty's bird nest to peer beneath them. Whatever he was looking for must be pretty small. Deputy Shingle joined him, lifting the mattress from the bed, running his hand beneath it, feeling the corners of the contour sheet and the freshly washed pillowcases. Sidney glanced at Ty's expressionless face as the deputy headed for his closet. If Ty had snuck in and hidden something in there, he was Cool Hand Luke. The sooner that awful man finished invading their privacy and got out of there, the better. She just wanted to spend some time alone with her son.

"Mrs. Walker," Deputy Estrada said after running his hands through and beneath the dresser drawers, "I'd like to take a look in your bedroom."

Sidney's face grew instantly hot. "Why on earth —"

"It's not that I suspect you of anything. It's just a hunch I want to check out, that's all. I'm sure you don't want me coming back."

She laughed out loud. He turned to look at her. "Nothing personal," she added, though somehow it did feel personal, especially now that he was invading her bedroom. Would he go so far as to ransack her lingerie drawer? For the first time, her eyes went to his left hand. No ring. She might have felt a little more comfortable about this if he had a wife — not that that meant anything anymore. She studied his stony face as he surveyed the room. He had dark eyes set like shallow caves beneath a ledge of high forehead, a square granite jaw, and a straight nose. He was handsome, strikingly so, but that hard face and rigid body might have been chiseled out of granite. What woman would want to snuggle up to that on a cold night?

He walked straight to her highboy, opening the Italian inlaid wood jewelry box she had received as a wedding gift, while his partner stepped into the master bath. The music box began playing a cheery version of "Some Enchanted Evening." Estrada pushed aside the gold bracelet her father had given her on her sixteenth birthday, her silver locket, Great-Aunt Louise's sapphire and diamond ring, and a tangle of costume jewelry, picking up her wedding ring from the red velvet lining. She didn't know why she kept it. Dodge had probably stolen it; there was no way he could have afforded a rock like that back then. Of course that hadn't occurred to her at the time. She had been blinded — not just by love, but by the brilliance of the three-carat diamond set between two smaller stones. The rest of the jewelry her ex had given her over the years had gradually and quietly disappeared. He would have pawned the ring, too, no doubt, if it had not been snugly attached to her finger.

"Nice," the deputy said, fondling the gold ring.

"Put it back," Ty ordered from the doorway. "That's my mom's wedding ring."

The deputy's eyes darted to each of their faces as if to detect any sign of guilt. "Is that right, Mrs. Walker?"

"That's right, Deputy." She caught her reflection in the dresser mirror and tucked a wayward strand of hair behind her ear. "So, it's a ring you're looking for."

He nodded grimly. "If you don't mind,

I'd like to take this temporarily just to confirm that it's not part of the stolen property. It's just procedure, you understand, and I'll give you a receipt."

Tyson spat out a word that shocked Sidney. "I didn't steal any ring! There's nothing here for you to find, so why don't you just leave my mom alone!"

"I'm not the one that got her involved in this." He stared hard at Ty for a moment. "I don't know what kind of a sweet deal you got in court today, but I'll be talking to your probation officer, and believe me, you better not slip — not once, because I'm going to be your shadow. I'll be watching. And next time you screw up, you're not going to get off so easy! Not if I have anything to do with it."

12

Millard sat uneasily in his faded blue easy chair, trying to work the morning crossword puzzle, suspecting that hell was not a hot place after all but his own living room in the presence of a sulking teenager. Was he supposed to entertain the kid all day? Pull rabbits out of a hat, maybe do a little tap dance on the old coffee table? He tried to ignore the glares radiating from the sofa where Tyson Walker slouched with his arms locked across his chest. It was like in that article Millard read in the paper about dangerous radioactive waves escaping from faulty microwave ovens. You couldn't see them, but they were deadly just the same.

Fifteen weeks. He hadn't done the crime but here he was doing the time right along with this skinny little delinquent. Millard didn't get out much anymore, but he suddenly felt trapped. What if he decided to go on down to Clara's Café to see the old gang one of these Wednesdays? He hadn't joined them for the weekly ritual since Molly passed on, but the temptation had been lingering at the back of his mind. What on earth had he been thinking when he stood up in court and volunteered himself? It was the boy's mother, Sidney. She had looked so pale, those wide green eyes of hers so plaintive, so desperate. And then when the officer came forward to haul the kid away, her shoulders had deflated like a parachute hitting ground. He wanted to save her somehow, like she was his own daughter. The next thing he knew, he was on his feet and those fateful words had fallen out of his mouth. Damn.

Millard finally sighed, dropping the paper to his lap. Hopefully the kid's mother would bring his schoolwork tomorrow. She said she would try anyway. "Do you have any plans, young man, other than sitting there like a bump on a log all day?"

Tyson stared out the window. Rain spilled over a blocked gutter on the west side of the house like slender silver prison bars. He shrugged. "I thought you'd have a computer." The toes of his stocking foot poked at a stack of thin discs on the coffee table. He had pulled them from his backpack that morning while his mother left last-minute instructions and wrote her work number on a pad by Millard's phone. "*Everybody* has a computer."

"Everybody but me," Millard said, "and about two-thirds of the world, many of whom don't even have a bed to call their own. What do I need a computer for? I'm not suffering just because I have to crack a book open for an answer every now and then instead of searching all over cyber-space." Millard congratulated himself for knowing some of the terminology. He had picked up bits and pieces of computer jargon through his reading, but the whole concept of information scattering itself all over space and then coming together in some organized fashion at the click of a mouse still boggled his mind. Sometimes he felt as out of place in this modern world as Huck Finn suddenly catapulted into the flight control center at NASA. He clucked his tongue. "I've got the Yellow Pages, a telephone, and a library just down at the bottom of the hill. If I need to add up my bills or figure how many square yards of bark it takes to cover my gardens, I do it the old-fashioned way: pen and paper. Works every time. Don't even have to plug anything in."

"How about games?"

Millard glanced down at his crossword puzzle, then peered at the boy over his reading glasses. "You want games? Go take a look in that cupboard over there. Under the bookcase. I've got Scrabble, checkers, Monopoly. . . ."

The kid scoffed.

"Oh, not enough action for you, eh?"

"Nope."

"What kind of games do you like? Those race cars?" His grandson, Pete, had nearly driven him nuts with the loud Indianapolis raceway video game he played last Christmas.

"They're okay. But war games are better."

Millard nodded grimly. "Shoot-'em-ups."

"Huh?"

"If you ever get yourself into a real gunfight — and I don't mean with pellet guns — you might start thinking a quiet game of Scrabble looks pretty good."

For the first time all morning, the boy turned to look at him head-on. "What do you mean? Were you ever in a gunfight?"

"Sure was. In the air over North Korea." The forgotten war, some called it. But Millard would never forget. "Did they teach you about that war in school?"

Tyson shrugged. "I don't think so."

Millard frowned. It seemed schools nowadays were shooting out ignorant kids like spit wads from a Browning automatic. Back when he taught history at Silver Falls High over in Dunbar, he made sure they knew their stuff or they were back in his class the next year to try again. "Back in the early fifties. I flew an F-86 Sabre. It was a single-seat, single-engine fighter-bomber."

The boy turned his body to face him, leaning forward slightly. "Did you shoot down any MiGs?"

Well, look at that, Millard thought. Maybe there was somebody home behind those dark, sullen eyes after all. He nodded. "Harry S Truman was our president back then. You know all the presidents?"

Tyson flopped back against the sofa with a scowl. Millard took that as a no.

Just then the front door flew open. Rita, with a full sack in her arms, froze in the doorway and stared at Tyson as if there were a brown bear with muddy paws sitting there on her father's white sofa.

It was the moment Millard had simultaneously dreaded and anticipated with rebellious delight. "Well, shut the door before the rain gets in." He pushed up from his chair and took the bag from her. "Rita, this is Tyson Walker. The boy from across the street." He gestured toward Rita with a tip of his head. "My daughter, Rita."

"Hello," she said.

Tyson didn't budge. "Hi," he murmured. The kid didn't know enough to stand when greeting a lady, but Millard decided now was not the time for an etiquette lesson.

Rita followed him to the kitchen, where he began emptying plastic containers from the paper sack. "What's he doing here?" she whispered.

"Hmm? Oh, the kid? He'll be staying here for a while. The next fifteen weeks, actually, while his mother is at work."

"You're babysitting a teenager? How old is he?"

"Fifteen."

"Why isn't he in school?"

Millard peered under the lid of a covered bowl labeled Stew. As usual, someone had picked out most of the beef, leaving only mushy potatoes and carrots in a mud of gravy. "He got kicked out."

"Dad, what is going on here?"

He turned to face his daughter. "The kid tried to rob Mitch Graber down there at the market. He was sentenced to house arrest, except he has to be supervised and his mother works full-time." He was doing his best to sound nonchalant. "So he comes here during the days until she gets home."

150

"Oh, my gosh!" She rolled her eyes, shaking her head. "You don't know what you've gotten yourself into! He almost shot Mitch! I heard all about it down at the Hair Affair. What are you thinking?" She peered around the doorjamb as if to catch the would-be killer and thief in the act of pillaging. Apparently he was not in the middle of a heist. She pulled her head back and closed the kitchen door. "What makes you think he's not going to rob *you?*" she hissed. "Or, worse yet, murder you?"

Millard snickered.

"This isn't funny, Dad. You hardly know these people. You're being taking advantage of just because you're a widowed old man with a good heart."

He felt his blood pressure elevate. "There you go again," he growled. "You just insist on pegging me as an old man with nothing left to offer this world. You want to take away my car keys and check me into Haywood House, nothing but an old horse waiting for the glue factory. Well, maybe — just maybe, Rita Lynn — your old man still has another race or two in him."

She turned away and then turned back, taking a deep breath and stepping closer to him. "Dad, you're not thinking straight. I'm not saying you're senile, believe me. But you're more vulnerable now than you used to be. I know you don't recognize that, but sometimes the people around us can see things we just can't see. Why do you think so many scams are directed at the elderly? They're from an era where they learned to trust everybody, and without a spouse there to discuss things with, well, sometimes people get sucked into things. Like signing over their entire net worth to perfect strangers. It happens all the time."

"Is that what this is about? You're afraid I'm gambling with your inheritance?"

She looked shocked and hurt, and he immediately regretted his words. His son, Jefferson, was gone now. Rita and the grandkids would get it all. This encounter was turning out all wrong, though honestly it was what he had expected. It was just that he had hoped, for a fleeting second anyway, that his daughter might be proud of him.

She lifted her chin defiantly. "I just think you're in over your head, that's all."

He touched her elbow. "He's just a boy. I still know a thing or two about boys."

"This isn't sweet, benign Jefferson, Dad. I got the willies the moment I saw this kid." She ran a hand through her short red hair. "He can't be trusted. I know you think I'm wrong — and I hope I am. But I saw something in his eyes, something that tells me you'll regret this." She shuddered. "Maybe we all will."

13

Sidney packed the girls' lunches as well as a bag with oranges, a fresh loaf of nutty bread, and cheese for Ty and Millard to share. She reminded Ty to feed the dog, signed Rebecca's field-trip permission slip, braided Sissy's hair. "All right, girls, make sure you lock the door behind you when the bus comes. We'll be just across the street." She grabbed her coat. "Come on, Ty! Let's not keep the man waiting!"

She rushed across Boulder Road, Ty lagging behind her. It was 8:15. She had forty minutes max before she would have to leave for work. Jobs didn't spring up like fir saplings in Ham Bone and she certainly didn't need any more stress in her life.

Yesterday, day one of Tyson's sentence, had not gone well. Millard had practically pushed Ty out the door when she came for him after work. She felt the tension snapping between man and boy like a fuzzy sock being pulled from the dryer. That evening Ty had taken his aggression out on Duke, wrestling wildly on the living room floor. The dog, of course, sprang up and barked between pinnings, swinging his scythelike tail at full speed as if to make up for all the evenings his boy had been gone.

Millard was just presenting Ty's probation officer with a cup of coffee when they arrived. The man set it on the coffee table and stood holding out his hand. "Mrs. Walker, Mark Dane."

He was tall with receding brown hair and a neatly trimmed beard. There was confidence in the way he stood, the way he gripped her hand and looked her directly in the eye. "Mr. Dane, thanks so much for meeting us here. This is certainly above the call of duty."

"Oh, I like getting out of the office every once in a while. We can do things here in the county that just can't be done in the big city justice system." He turned to Ty, offering his hand. "Tyson, I presume."

Ty's head was lowered. He raised his eyes warily, extending his hand as if using his arm for the first time after having a cast removed. After the obligatory handshake, he slumped into an upholstered chair by the window. Millard shot him a disapproving look. Surely a young man from *his* generation would have shown more respect.

They all sat. Mr. Dane took a sip of coffee, his head drawing back almost imperceptibly as he stared into the mug and then put it down. Apparently he wasn't used to instant coffee, which was what Sidney had seen Millard prepare for himself when she brought in lunch yesterday morning. "All right, Tyson," he said, "let's get started. I'm going to go over the court requirements with all of you to make sure that everyone understands. My job is to monitor your adherence and to report to the court immediately any failure to comply. Your life is not your own right now. Consider yourself in jail" — he glanced around — "but with the benefit of windows and home-cooked meals." He leaned forward. "Look at me, young man."

Ty dragged his gaze from the wall to the officer's face.

"I have no problem with sending you back to juvey." Mr. Dane's voice was firm and steady. "Where you do your time is up to you. So make sure you're getting all this, because I've spoken with Judge Renkin and you've been shown all the mercy you're going to get."

Ty glared at him without speaking.

"Normally you would be confined to your own home, but I understand in this case special arrangements were approved. As of today you're going to start receiving calls at random to confirm your whereabouts. The voice recognition system is set up to call you at this phone number on weekdays and at your home on evenings and weekends." Millard leaned forward intently as Mark Dane explained the system while Ty feigned disinterest. The probation officer then pulled out some court documents stapled in one corner. He went over community service and the $100 fine that Ty would be expected to pay into the crime victims' fund, and stressed that Ty must complete and receive passing grades on all his schoolwork. The latter rule pleased Sidney but caused Ty to sink a little lower in his chair, his frown deepening. At least she would have a reprieve from being the bad guy.

"And as I'm sure you've read, because your crime was a felony, you've lost the right to possess firearms of any kind."

Ty had not read his court paperwork. His head whipped toward Mr. Dane. "For how long?"

"The rest of your life."

Sidney was surprised by the way her son's eyes narrowed, the way this news seemed to affect him.

He shook his head defiantly, huffing an angry breath. "That sucks!"

Peanut butter, whole wheat flour, toilet paper. Sidney's shopping-list entries popped out of her head and onto the paper on her desk in random order. If she could pick up some groceries on her lunch hour instead of after work, she would be home that much sooner to relieve Millard of Tyson and vice versa.

She was just reaching for her purse when she heard Micki greet someone who had entered the office. "Does Sidney Walker still work here?"

Sidney's heart leapt. She rolled her chair clear of her cubicle and waved. "Hi, Jack! Just a minute." She met him up at the reception counter, where he stood looking a little awkward, his hands thrust into the back pockets of his jeans.

"Hey," he said, "have you been to lunch yet?"

She smiled and shook her head, wishing Micki would do something about the silly grin on her face. "No. Your timing is perfect."

She grabbed her coat and purse and followed Jack outside. White clouds stampeded

across the sky toward the westerly mountains, and a chilly wind thrashed her hair across her face. She pulled a strand from her mouth so that she could speak. "I'm glad you found me."

"Yeah, me too. I forgot to ask if you were still working here when I saw you at the market. I had to come to Ham Bone today for a meeting, so I thought I'd look you up."

Sidney felt a twinge of disappointment. So he didn't drive twenty miles just to see her. It had been an afterthought. He certainly would have called her if it had been a planned thing; he had her number. Jack's pale green cotton shirt undulated across his stocky body, but the wind didn't budge a wiry hair on his blond, short-cropped head. He looked pretty good; it was definitely a better look than the stained butcher's apron.

"You wanna go to Clara's?"

Sidney's mind raced through the vegetarian options on the menu at Clara's Café. Slim pickings. She'd probably have to settle for a salad. "Sure."

After driving three blocks to the west end of town in his polished black SUV, they seated themselves at a table against the wall. Jack did not pull out her chair. He immediately sat and flipped his menu open, scouring the entrees. Sidney couldn't compete with the colorful pictures of patty melts and French dips. She stared at the blue floral wallpaper until he pushed the menu aside. "Okay." He looked for a waitress. "You know what you want?"

"Yes." She leaned back casually. "So what is the meeting that brought you all the way to Ham Bone?"

"Peewee football. I'm coaching again this year. The Ham Bone coach lives up on Sparrow Hill. That's where you moved, isn't it? Dave Petrie. Do you know him?"

"Petrie. I think his son is in Sissy's class, and he rides the girls' bus. Well, sure. David Petrie, obviously named after his dad."

"Yeah, David's on the team. He's a good little kicker. We're doing tackle this year — no more flag."

"Really? How old are these kids?"

"Seven or eight years. Eighty pounds or so." He chuckled in response to her expression. "Don't worry. They're fully suited up, shoulder pads, helmets, and all."

"You're a good man, Jack."

His blue eyes sparkled. "Why do you say that?"

"Because you volunteer your time for the sake of those kids. You don't even have one of your own."

His friendly smile straightened into a thin line and he shrugged. The waitress came to take their order, returning quickly with a Pepsi for Jack and a cup of steaming chamomile tea. Sidney felt Jack's eyes on her as she dunked her tea bag, but when she raised her eyes, he glanced away.

She followed his gaze out the window. The foothills rose like dinosaur backs behind the false-fronted shops lining Center Street. Blotches of amber and burnt red marbled through the predominantly evergreen hills. The hot tea was comforting, warm in her hands. "I've always loved autumn," she said. "Especially here in Ham Bone. You can smell the snow in the mountains long before it falls this low."

"Yeah, but once it covers the ball fields, it's all over. Nothing to do but order a stack of pizzas and watch sports on TV."

She scoffed. "You and your sports. Are you still a junkie?"

"Don't start in with me. What do you want me to do, paint little birdies on junk furniture like you? You still do that stuff?"

She lifted her chin, smirking. "Oh, if you only knew. When I run out of old furniture, I paint cigar boxes, apple crates, you name it." She lowered her fork and leaned across the table. "People buy my things, Jack! Hannie Mays put one of my chests in the entry of her gift shop and set a lamp on it. She has to tell people all the time it's not for sale. Hannie says I should get a card made up and go into business."

"Well, why don't you?"

"Capital. More specifically, lack thereof. I pick up cheap used furniture at yard sales in the summer, but once school starts, it's pretty hard to find." She poured hot water from a tiny teapot into her mug. If she could just save up some money — or if Dodge would ever get around to paying child support — she would start her own business as quick as she could slam the door at Leon Schuman Insurance.

"Don't you miss good old Ham Bone?" she asked.

"Hah! Not really. Dunbar isn't exactly a metropolis, but at least we have a semipro baseball team and stadium, a bowling alley with ten lanes, and multiple places to get a steak after 9 p.m."

She smiled softly. "The important things in life."

"And my job is there, you may remember. I make almost double what I did at Graber's. I could commute, but why? No, I made that decision after you and I broke up." He glanced away again. "Getting out of Ham Bone is one of the smartest things I ever did."

"I guess it's different for someone who's lived here their whole life. After Dodge left, I thought about going back home to Cleveland, but it was too late for me. I'd already fallen in love with this three-lane-bowling-alley-everything-shuts-down-around-dinnertime town. I don't find it boring, not for one minute. I like the fact that I can go out on my porch and breathe air that's been filtered by the thousands of Christmas trees on those hills. My children wander the woods instead of city sidewalks and noisy, smoggy streets. I feel safe here."

Jack grew quiet, chewing, gazing at her face. "What's new with Ty?" he finally asked. "Is he doing well in school?"

She took a deep breath and blew it out, dropping her head momentarily. *Oh, God. It's time.* "He's in trouble, Jack."

His eyebrows pinched. "What kind of trouble?"

"To summarize, he shoplifted at Graber's Market, and when Mitch tackled him on his way out the door, Ty pointed a pellet gun at him. It counts as a felony because of that. He's on modified house arrest for fifteen weeks."

Jack let out a low whistle. "I can't imagine

Ty doing a thing like that."

"He's changed, Jack." She was saying too much too soon. She stopped herself, relieved when the waitress appeared with their lunches. Jack's burger was as thick as a cow pie, filling the air with greasy fumes. She squeezed lemon onto her salad, dropping the rind into her water glass.

Jack's mouth was full when he resumed their conversation. "Changed how?"

She shook her head. "Maybe it's normal teenage boy stuff. He just seems chronically unhappy, that's all." She avoided stronger adjectives like *dark, angry, rebellious* — anything that might scare Jack off. She guessed that the first thing to assess was whether there was any chance of reviving what she and Jack once had together.

"I'd be unhappy too if I had to stay indoors for fifteen weeks," he said. "What is that? Almost four months." He shook his head, the light from the window giving his eyes the look of blue glass. "As I remember Ty, he came out of the woods and ponds only when he was hungry or to show off his animal friends. That kid stalked bullfrogs like a heron. I've never seen anybody catch those wise old frogs, the big ones that have been around awhile — not by hand, anyway. Normal people can't even see them. I watched him wade into a lake at the edge of a ball field once," he laughed, "back when I was trying to get him interested in playing baseball. He moved about as fast as the hour hand on a clock and came out of the lily pads dangling a big old boy by its armpits, legs like that male ballerina, Baryshnikov. Or is it ballerino?"

That struck her funny and she laughed long and hard. "A bullfrog ballerino. I can just see Sissy dressing him up in a tutu and dancing him around." She noticed a couple from a nearby table looking over at them, smiling.

Jack grinned. "Anyway, it was all Ty could do to hang on to the thing with both hands. Pretty soon the dugouts were empty and the pond was full of boys in muddy knickers. Ty coached them on the fine skills of frog hunting." He chuckled. "We had to call off practice for the day."

She smiled. "He liked going places with you, even though he was never very good at sports. His dad never threw him a ball as far as I can remember. By the time you started taking him to games, all the other boys had been competing for years. Ty didn't even know the rules. That embarrassed him. He cried in my arms about it one night and it nearly broke my heart. Flying your model airplanes, though, he liked that."

"Yeah. I should get back to that sometime. I have to finish building this little biplane I'm working on." He popped a thick french fry into his mouth. "How does this house-arrest thing work? Is he home alone right now?"

She told him the whole story about how poor, kind Mr. Bradbury had been squeezed into this predicament and was now doing time for fifteen weeks behind his own picket fence.

"So, Ty didn't even know the old man before this?"

"Nope."

"How does he feel about the arrange-ment?"

"Oh, he hates it. But that's tough. He deserves worse for what he did. I just feel bad for Millard. It's no fun being around Ty right now. He seems set on making everyone around him just as miserable as he is. We met with the probation officer this morn-ing." She smirked and shook her head. "He's mean and very blunt. I liked that about him. One of my problems is I'm not mean enough. I don't know how. So this guy is going to monitor Ty's community service and his schoolwork. I've never been able to get that boy to finish his homework — ever." Her eyes widened dramatically. "But now if he doesn't do it, he goes straight to jail."

Jack grew thoughtful. "Do you still think he has ADD?"

She frowned. "That's what some people call it."

"Do you medicate him?"

"No. And I never will. He's not sick; he's unique. He's also extremely intelligent." She sighed. "Jack, you know I've been battling this for years. Since way before you and I were together. He has never fit in at school, and because he doesn't sit still and learn like other kids, he's been pegged as a bad kid. He's been *treated* like a bad kid, and maybe that's the one thing he *has* learned at school. He's bad."

"But maybe if you put him on Ritalin or something —"

"No drugs. I don't know what the answer is, but I know in my heart it is *not* pumping harmful chemicals into him."

She glanced at her watch. "Oh, my gosh! My lunch hour was over ten minutes ago."

Jack paid the bill while she applied fresh lipstick and put on her coat. Ten or fifteen minutes late might be overlooked on occasion. But she had showed up late for work several times in the past few weeks and had taken two unscheduled days off — all on behalf of her rogue son. On the day of Tyson's arrest just outside their office, Mr. Schuman had allowed her to leave early. Sidney had been no good for anything, as upset as she was. Her employer of three-plus years had exhibited neither anger nor sympathy. Whether he was about to fire someone or give them a raise could never be told by looking at his deadpan face.

Jack drove her right up to the front entrance of the insurance office. "Nice to see you again, green-eyed lady."

She flashed a smile. "Ditto, dude. Hey, thanks for lunch. That was a nice surprise."

He clicked his tongue and winked as she opened her own door and stepped out to the curb, then he shoved his Suburban into drive and pulled away. She stood on the sidewalk in shock. That was it? No "When can I see you again?" No "I'll be calling you." Nothing. She had done it. She had gone and done exactly what she had warned herself not to do. Spilling her guts about Tyson that way. What perfectly happy single man would willingly subject himself to that environment?

Sidney looked down at herself. She had worn sensible shoes today, her brown loafers with the chunky heels, simply because they were near the front door when she dashed across the street with Tyson to meet the probation officer. She looked like a mom. Her eyes misted up. Like a mediocre agent in a dwarfish insurance office in a hick town called Ham Bone. Maybe that was all she was. There wasn't time or energy for anything else. She dabbed the corners of her eyes. She didn't even know how to seduce a man.

She turned to go into the office. Leon Schuman stood at the window, staring at her blankly with his arms folded across his chest.

14

Yellow leaves were losing their grip on Molly's apple tree, but the red winter fruit hung like ornaments from its spindly branches. Millard snapped off the last bite of a cold apple, letting the tangy juice run down his chin. He stomped down the fresh dirt on the newest molehill, remembering with chagrin when the mole invasion was the biggest worry in his life, then tossed the apple core into his pile of leaves and continued raking. It was a good day to be outdoors. Even a rain squall would be more comfortable than the environment indoors. That kid was sucking all the oxygen out of the house. There was this silent sensation like just before a twister descends, vacuuming you up along with everything you hold dear and dumping you someplace like Oz. Maybe Rita was right. Maybe something was on the horizon that would cause him to regret his involvement with this troubled boy even more than he already did.

But he was a man of his word. Millard Bradbury did not go back on a promise.

A gust of wind stirred his pile of leaves, scattering some across the grass like flitting birds. And then he heard it again — Jefferson's innocent laughter. It was a sound that rang out in his head when he least expected it, and then he would look around him and remember. It was a day like this, sometime in October, the mountains like purple slate against a hazy blue sky. He leaned against his rake and sighed, blinking at the sting the memory brought to his eyes. Millard had spent all afternoon raking a yard full of leaves into a single pile that day and then had gone into the garage for some matches. He heard his son's jubilant shouts, ignoring them at first. Jefferson was always celebrating something. It could have been the discovery of an inchworm or a pot of gold — equal causes for rejoicing in Jefferson's world. But it had been the pile of leaves. Millard came out of the garage to see flurries of red and gold dancing against the cold sky and Jeff flinging another armload into the air with a loud cheer. His beaming face was upturned, arms spread like a statue in the park inviting autumn birds to land.

Millard squinted up at the weeping birch

by the corner of the picket fence, the tree's branches dripping with leaves that shimmered like gold medallions against a backdrop of pure blue. A breeze sent a flurry of them into the sky and they drifted down to the lawn. Jefferson had turned fourteen that autumn. Millard remembered it with a chill as he watched the leaves stir at his feet. Fourteen and still a child. He swatted in frustration at the pile of leaves with his rake, watching them scatter. He had ranted and raved about the mess Jefferson made of his neatly piled leaves. Oh, what terrible things he had shouted, driving his son back into the house in tears. If he could only get that day back — all of them — he would do better next time. But it was too late. Next time would never come. Millard bent down, scooped an armload of dead leaves against the prongs of his rake, and tossed them violently to the wind.

He suddenly remembered the kid in the house and felt foolish. Raking leaves into neat piles just to spread them over the lawn again could be construed as insanity, and proving to people that he was not losing his marbles had become a preoccupation recently. Millard glanced furtively toward the front window. Tyson was no longer at the dining room table cheating at solitaire. What was the kid doing? With a twinge of uneasiness, he stepped toward the garden for a better view. Not slouched on the sofa. Oh, there he was, standing at the side window. Millard followed the boy's gaze westward, out to the untamed five-acre field beyond his picket fence. And then he saw what the boy must have seen: a buck emerging from the woods with a rack big enough to display every forgotten hat in Red's Barber Shop. The deer raised its snout to the wind before dropping its powerful neck to graze. He was majestic, Millard thought, suppressing the urge to grab his rifle and pump some lead into the hide covering the buck's heart. His days of hanging deer by their hindquarters from the maple tree behind the garage were over. Too much work and too much venison. But if that old boy dared to even look over the fence at his apples, well, that would be a different story.

Millard headed for the garage, shuffling through his scattered leaves. He hung the rake in its appointed place on the pegboard along the back wall with a sigh of defeat. God commanded man to take dominion over all the earth, and then he sent things beyond his control to try him. Moles, gales of wind, rampant boys. He tossed his gardening gloves onto the work bench. His once ordered life was a flurry of dry leaves, spiraling out of control.

As he approached the front steps, he paused. The eave of the house sheltered the window from glare and he could see Tyson clearly, still across the dining room at the west window, his back to Millard. The boy's shoulders drooped; his arms hung at his sides. He looked for all the world like a juvenile gorilla Millard had once seen at the zoo, staring at the glass that enclosed him. Like the ape, Tyson looked as lifeless as if a plug had been pulled from his soul, draining all hope of living in his native habitat again. Millard cleared his throat loudly, stomping a warning of his approach on the porch steps, and removed his dirty shoes.

He found Tyson back at the table again, his back to Millard, flipping cards from the deck in his hand.

"There's a big old buck out there," Millard said. "Don't think I've ever seen that one before."

"I have."

"You sure? He's not the only four-point in the forest."

"I know him." Tyson slapped a series of cards down in rapid succession. "He knows me, too."

Wild deer weren't exactly sociable in Millard's experience, but something made him ask, "Would he let you walk right up to him?"

"Not anymore. He wanders off if I get too close. Somebody got to him. There's a nick out of his ear. I think he got shot at."

Not even an eagle could see a nicked ear from that distance. Millard pulled his high-power bird-watching binoculars from a drawer next to his easy chair just as the phone on his lamp table rang. "You might as well get that," Millard said. "It's always for you." Tyson got up and took the phone from its cradle. Sure enough, it was the court's computer monitoring system calling again to confirm that Tyson was where he was supposed to be. The calls were random, anywhere from two to five a day. A robotic voice would ask to speak to Tyson and he had two minutes to get to the phone. Millard heard the boy repeat a series of numbers back to the voice recognition software (the numbers were different every time) and hang up the receiver.

The buck raised its head, sniffing the air. "Well, I'll be darned." Millard dropped the field glasses to his side. "That's a bullet hole all right."

"He beds down at the bottom of the hill. Not far from Sparrow Creek."

Millard turned to look at Tyson. "Do you know the whereabouts of other animals?"

Tyson nodded.

Millard dropped into a chair at the table. "Like what, for instance?"

The boy shrugged. "Like skunks and coyotes and mice. There's a big old cedar stump on the other side of a pond." He gestured in the direction of the woods behind his house across the road. "Some skunks live in there. I usually see them come out only at night. I watch coyotes in the daylight sometimes, though. There's a whole family of them in this little cave behind a fallen tree over there beyond this pasture."

That was the longest paragraph Tyson had ever spoken to him. Millard glanced out the window. The buck was gone. "I hear those coyotes at night. Sounds like a boys' choir tuning up."

"There are seven of them. The pups were born last spring, just before school got out."

"Coyotes are pretty private animals, with a keen sense of smell. I'm surprised they'd come out while you're anywhere in the vicinity."

Tyson shrugged. "I saw the dad sometimes — the male — before he had a whole family. He got used to me being around, I guess. I used to lie on this little hill at the edge of the woods for hours, watching the clearing because so many animals came through there on their way to the creek. I figured out his territory by watching where he peed, marking his borders, you know?"

Millard nodded. "Your mother told me you like to spend a lot of time in the woods."

The solitaire game froze up, even after the boy had run through his deck five times. He scooped the cards into a pile with a sigh of frustration. "Living all cooped up in houses is stupid. And school. I don't know why everyone thinks it's normal to live like that — with walls all around them."

"Come December you might think differently. Even the animals crawl in somewhere to keep warm." Millard buttoned another button on his gray sweater just thinking about it. "And school — well, that's just a necessary part of life. A young man needs an education. Why, you'll be a man before you know it. What do you intend to do with your life?"

The boy rolled his eyes and plopped his deck of cards onto the table. "I've got to take a pee." He pushed out his chair and headed for the bathroom.

Millard fumed. Disrespectful kid. Why did he bother with him? The boy had a good mind according to his mother. But he was wasting it. Kids nowadays took everything for granted. They had it too good. Back in his day, boys longed to go to school but too often got pulled out to till the family farm while their fathers traveled to any town that had work. Still, even during the Great Depression, when kids had so little in the way of material things, they seemed happier than the kids of today.

The phone rang again. So soon? Millard picked up, expecting to hear a robotic voice. "Hello."

"Mr. Bradbury? It's Mark Dane, Tyson's probation officer."

"He's in the bathroom. Can he call you back?"

"Sure. But while I've got you here, how's he been doing since we met last week?"

"Oh, all right, I guess. He comes and goes right on schedule."

"Is he keeping up with his schoolwork?"

Millard glanced at the backpack on the floor over by the couch. Books had been pulled from it that morning while Ty searched for his deck of cards and there they lay, untouched. "Oh, it's coming along." Millard was surprised by his blatant lie. If the kid didn't do the work, they'd toss his butt in juvenile jail. Millard would be free of him.

"Make sure his mother drops his assignments off at the school by Friday," Dane continued. "Principal Weston and I are keeping in touch. Now, on another matter: Tyson's community service. Deputy Sheriff Estrada has been in touch with me and has a project lined up. Since Tyson is on house arrest, he's going to have to be closely supervised. Will you tell him the deputy will pick him up from his home Saturday morning at nine?" Millard heard the toilet flush and the bathroom door open. "Here he is. You can tell him yourself."

He passed the phone to Tyson and watched him as he grunted one-word answers into the receiver, his head and shoulders in their perpetual drooping state like a begonia in desperate need of water. The boy glanced at the schoolbooks on the floor. "Uh-huh. Yeah. Okay." He listened some more. "I know." He hung up without saying good-bye and stared out toward his house across the road.

"Community service, eh? What does that look like?"

"Fixing a porch and building a wheelchair ramp."

Millard nodded in approval. "Good. They think that'll take up your required forty hours?"

"It'll take me forty years. I don't know how to do that stuff."

Millard wondered if the kid's dad ever showed him which end of a hammer to hang on to before he took off. "Oh, I'm sure someone will be there to oversee the job. You'll learn." He walked over to the sofa, stooping to pick up the carelessly strewn schoolbooks from the floor. "American history, geometry, English . . ." He tossed them one by one onto the coffee table. A packet of papers was clipped together. "These must be your assignments. Have you looked at them?"

"Yeah."

"How much have you got done?"

"Nothing." The kid dropped into Millard's blue chair.

Millard frowned as he took the liberty to ruffle through the pages. "Let's see what you've got here. 'Read chapter eight in your math book and work the problems on pages 52 and 57.' " He flipped to the next page. "Says here your English assignment is to write a one-page analysis of a poem you like."

Tyson scoffed. "Poetry sucks!"

Millard flashed back to a rebellious student he had tried to teach back in his days at Silver Falls High. Donald? Dennis? A kid who would write on his jeans, his hands, anything but a piece of paper. That boy had felt the same way about English, which had infuriated Millard. So many good minds going to waste while his feebleminded son struggled with telling his right hand from his left.

"You've got a problem, then." Millard dropped the packet to the coffee table. "You either have to wade through this *sucky* situation like a man or sit out your sentence behind bars. It won't be so bad, though. You've already done a week in jail. You'd have less than fourteen weeks to go. That's what? About a hundred days. In fact, you might as well be bored there as here. I say you just let it slide. Take a load off both of our minds."

Tyson scowled. "Maybe I will."

"You'd rather be locked up where you can't even see a bird fly by than exercise your brain a little bit?"

"Nobody's locking me up. They'd have to find me first and they never will."

"What is it with you? You think you've got it so bad; everyone's out to get you. You poor, mistreated boy. Everyone else — your teachers, the law, me — we're all idiots and you've got the world all figured out. You're pathetic!"

Millard snatched up his newspaper, swatting the air in front of Tyson. "And you're in my chair!"

15

Bradbury's door flung open before Sidney had a chance to knock. Tyson emerged, his backpack hanging from one shoulder, his face wearing the angry countenance that had become too familiar. Her father used to warn her when she made a face to be careful; it could get stuck that way. Perhaps that had happened to her son. She poked her head in the doorway. "Hi, Millard. How did it go today?"

The old man sat with both hands gripping the arms of his faded blue chair. His narrowed eyes spoke first. "Splendid. Like a tea party in the morgue."

"Mom, I'm going home," Tyson said over his shoulder as he stormed off the porch. She watched him push through the picket gate, letting it swing behind him.

"Not good, then." She stepped inside and closed the door to keep the cold night air outside where it belonged. "What did he do?"

"Nothing. Not a blessed thing all day. I tried to get him to do schoolwork but he's got his mind set on giving up. He lies around here like the King of Ham Bone eating and watching TV."

She dropped her head, shaking it sadly. "I'm sorry."

"No, don't do that. I'm just venting a little steam, that's all." He pushed himself out of the chair. "Why don't I get your food containers?"

She followed him into the kitchen, where the counters were clean, dishes washed and resting in a drainer by the sink. "Did you guys finish off that bread already?"

"That was the best loaf so far. I ate some for breakfast while it was warm and made a sandwich for lunch. Tyson did the rest. Good soup, too. My daughter, Rita, is getting jealous. You're a much better cook than she is."

Sidney laughed. "Ooh, now I'm really motivated. Let me know when she's coming again. I'll make a gourmet feast."

"Yeah, well, feel free to throw a little meat in there sometime."

She raised her chin. "Millard, I like you too much to do that."

He chuckled, shaking his head. "How's

the car running?"

"About the same. I pray over it every morning and it eventually starts. The only time it wouldn't kick in was the morning of Ty's hearing — which turned out to be a blessing for me and a curse for you. If you hadn't been there to save the day, Ty would be in jail right now."

Millard's lined face grew solemn. "Might be the best thing for him." He cleared his throat. "The probation officer called today."

"Yes, Mr. Dane called me at work, too. About the community service project." Sidney tucked a plastic container inside her slow cooker, and she and Millard walked together toward the front door. "I understand Deputy Estrada is going to pick Ty up on Saturday and actually work with him on the project." She shuddered. She longed for the day she would never have to deal with that condescending man again.

"Do they still suspect it was your boy that committed that other robbery?"

"I don't know. The man at the Sheriff's Department wouldn't tell me anything. Made me feel like a criminal for asking." Sidney paused at the door. "Ty has only three days to get this week's assignments done. Did he even look at them today?" Millard shook his head grimly. She sighed, a wave of fatigue washing over her, making even her clothes feel heavy. "I'll talk to him about it tonight." She hugged him with her free arm. "See you in the morning, Millard."

She ran across the road, not because she had the energy, but because the night air was chilly. She was anxious to be home with her children and there was so much to do. She hadn't prepared anything that morning for their dinner and she was running out of options. There would be no more groceries until after payday on Friday.

Rebecca greeted her at the door. "Mom, will you tell Sissy to stay off my bed? There's dirt all over my comforter."

"My day was just fine, thank you. How was yours?"

Rebecca rolled her eyes.

"Mommy!" Sissy ran out, wrapping her arms around her mother, almost tripping her.

"That's what I like. A little enthusiasm." She bent, Crock-Pot still in hand and her coat halfway off one shoulder, to kiss the top of her daughter's head. "Oh, Sis. What have you got in your hair?"

"Caramel apple. It was Willy Goodwin's birthday today. For my birthday I want caramel apples, too. No carrot muffins."

"Okay. Where's your brother?"

"In his room on the computer. He's mean. I just wanted to talk to him but he slammed his door."

Sidney set the slow cooker down in the kitchen, slid off her coat, and shuffled through the mail. No invitation to the prince's ball, no winning sweepstakes notice, not even a note from her mother. Just bills. "I'll talk to Tyson. That is not acceptable behavior in our house. Neither is getting your sister's bedspread dirty," she added just to be fair. "Tell her you're sorry and bring it out to the laundry room."

The phone rang. Sidney grabbed the portable from the kitchen counter. "Hello?" she said cheerily.

"Mrs. Walker, this is Deputy Estrada." The smile dropped from her face. "We don't need your diamond ring anymore. The burglary victim confirmed that it's not hers. I can drop it by tonight if you like."

Fat chance. She'd rather see Hannibal Lecter. The insult of the deputy's innuendos on the night he took the ring was still like a barbed hook in her skin. "No, thanks. Why don't you just leave it at the Sheriff's Department? I'll pick it up tomorrow." She didn't often hear such iciness in her own voice.

187

"All right. That will be fine. Just didn't want you to have to go to any trouble. Speaking of which, I guess Mark Dane called you today about the community service project."

"Yes, he did. I was surprised to hear that you'll be involved. I thought Ty could line something up on his own." She walked down the hallway into her bedroom, closing the door behind her.

"Well, Mark — Mr. Dane is ultimately in control of all that. He feels that as long as I'm there to supervise, this would be a good thing for everyone." She immediately wondered how it would be good for the deputy and how close his friendship was with the probation officer. "This way Tyson can start working off his hours while he's still on house arrest."

"And how does it benefit you, Deputy?"

There was a long pause. "I'll have the satisfaction of seeing your son make some retribution."

"Why do I get the feeling there's something personal here?"

"I can't speak for your feelings, Mrs. Walker."

"Is Tyson still a suspect in that burglary in town?"

Another pause. "Prime suspect."

The conviction in his voice chilled her. What if he was right? It would mean a new charge against Tyson, two strikes on his record, and another legal ordeal. She took a deep breath. "I understand you'll pick him up at nine o'clock on Saturday. We'll see you then."

She clicked the phone off and held it to her chest, willing her blood to slow to normal speed. She could not think about this tonight. For the sake of her children and her own sanity, she *would* not.

She decided on baked potatoes topped with meatless chili for dinner. While the potatoes were baking, she cut carrots, celery, and green peppers into strips, chatting with the girls about the upcoming marathon they had both chosen to compete in at school. It was a nightly ritual, this gathering in the kitchen where the kids could twirl on their bar stools at the raised counter while she cooked. Ty wandered through the kitchen, slicing off hunks of cheese and reaching over his mother's shoulder to nab strips of vegetables as fast as she could cut them. "Don't blame me if you lose a finger," she chided. "Anyway, we have enough finger food." She believed he was glad to be home, though he rarely showed any sign of it.

"Ooh, Mother!" Rebecca recoiled with her usual drama. "That's disgusting!"

Ty rolled his eyes. "That is so lame."

"But I *could* make you a knuckle sandwich." A laugh bubbled up from deep in her belly. Her older children humored her with half smiles.

"And the blood could be ketchup!" Sissy said.

Ty tossed a carrot stick, hitting his little sister squarely on the forehead. She tossed it back. He dodged and it landed on the floor. Rebecca snatched it up, launching the orange missile at Ty. "Food fight!"

"Hey, I don't think so." Sidney reached over to remove the carrot from her son's hand, but suddenly thought better of it. Instead she grabbed a handful of veggies from the cutting board. "There will be no food fighting around here," she announced piously, and then spun around, hurling a barrage of vegetables at her children.

At first they looked stunned. Sissy squealed with delight. Rebecca and Ty suddenly scrambled for the carrots and celery that had hit the floor, and it became an all-out war. "Sissy, help me out here!" Sidney cried. "Ouch! Not so hard, Tyson!" He chased his mother around the corner into the living room, the girls following, still pelting one another, all of them laughing, stumbling over furniture. Duke barked, lunging from one child to the next, clearly convinced that this game was all about him. Rebecca tried to push carrots down the back of Ty's pants, which led to a wrestling match on the floor. Rebecca ended up hopelessly pinned while Ty's assistant, Sissy, tried to push celery up her sister's nose. Since Rebecca clearly did not approve of the procedure, Sidney decided it was time to intervene. "Okay, that's enough. Whoever doesn't help clean this mess up has to eat that celery that's been in Becca's nose."

Sidney went back to the kitchen and began slicing carrots all over again. Wind spattered droplets of rain against the window, but it was warm inside. The kids bantered cheerily in the other room while the scents of baking potatoes and spicy chili nourished her soul. Normally the thought of throwing away all those organic vegetables would put ringlets in Sidney's smooth, dark blond hair. But nothing was wasted that night. All the beta-carotene and vitamins A, C, and E may have bounced right off her children's bodies, but they had laughed together as a whole family for the first time in weeks.

At the dinner table, Tyson went quiet

again. She and the girls carried the conversation, which was mostly about the events of their day at school. Both of her daughters loved school, but for different reasons. Rebecca was a real student, eager to please, always doing extra-credit projects. Her essays were accompanied by illustrations or magazine clippings whether required or not. For Sissy it was all about recess. That girl lived to kick balls and any boys who got in her way. At one point Sidney glimpsed Tyson staring at her. She smiled, wondering how long he had been watching her face, disappointed to see the familiar sadness back in his eyes again. He acknowledged her with a brief spreading of his lips, something between a smile and a frown, and went back to the business of eating his chili potato. When he was finished, he excused himself.

"Which subject are you working on tonight?" she asked, trying to sound positive.

He shrugged his shoulders and looked away.

"Tyson. Don't think about all of it. Just pick one thing. One manageable thing. I'll help you if you'd like."

"No, I'm okay. I don't need any help."

"*I* need help," Rebecca said. "I have to color in my state map and I can't find a yellow-colored pencil. That's for the goldfinch. I'm going to put our state bird and our state flower on the edges."

Sidney watched her son walk away, her heart heavy at the sight of his chronically sagging shoulders. "Try the junk drawer, Bec. There are some colored pencils in there, I think."

The phone rang. Sissy ran for the portable while Sidney began clearing the table. "Rebecca, will you bag up these leftover veggies for your lunches tomorrow?"

"Mom! It's for you. It's a man!"

Sidney sighed. What now? She took the phone from her daughter and walked into the living room. "Hello."

"Hi, Sid. It's Jack. How's it going?"

"Jack! Hi." She danced around in a joyful circle. "Things are good around here. What's up?"

"I've got a peewee game in Ham Bone on Saturday. You wanna come watch? We could go out for pizza or something afterward."

"I'll have the girls with me on Saturday."

"Bring them along. The more, the merrier. There will be lots of kids there."

Sidney found herself pacing on the sofa, lifting her knees high in a jubilant march. Jack was back! Everything was going to turn out fine.

"Mom!" Sissy whispered with her eyes bugging out.

Sidney stepped sheepishly from the sofa to the floor, caught in the act of committing a major crime in the Walker house.

"The game starts at one, but I have to be a little early. Do you want to meet me there?"

"Sure. How's your little team doing?"

He chuckled. "They bounce around the field like pinballs. I don't know if any of the rules are sinking in, but they have fun. The good news is that so far the other teams we've played don't seem any sharper."

She laughed just picturing them — little boys peering out from helmets as big as watermelons, their little legs scurrying haphazardly across the field.

"Hot dang, I love that laugh of yours."

She chortled again, not to show it off, but because it erupted from her naturally. She had apparently inherited her deep, spontaneous laughter from her father. It was a gift, probably one of the reasons she had enjoyed so many friends in school. Though it had gotten her in trouble with teachers more than once. She also suspected it was the sound that had lured Dodge Walker out of the forest of Christmas trees the night she first met him. "Yeah, well, just think twice before bringing me to a funeral."

"I'll do that. Hey, too bad Ty can't come. Tell him we'll have to go throw a ball around sometime after he's sprung."

Sidney smiled. "I'll do that." The clouds were lifting from her life.

After tucking the girls into bed and praying with them that night, she peeked in on Ty. His lights were already out, though it was only a little after nine. She leaned against the door frame, barely able to make out his still form beneath the blankets. She had wanted to see what progress he'd made on his poetry assignment for English — if any. The last time she checked, there was an open book on his desk beside a stark white notebook page, nothing more. It worried her. How could she motivate him? Maybe Jack could help. "Are you asleep?" she whispered. There was no answer. She had the urge to kiss him, but he was fifteen now so she slipped out, closing his door quietly behind her.

In her own room she ran a bath, sprinkling lavender bath crystals into the steaming water. Ray Charles sang love songs while she lit three dusty pillar candles and slipped into the water with a sigh. "Ah, romance. I've missed you so." She could see herself in the full-length mirror on the linen closet door, her hair pinned loosely to the top of her head, warm candlelight reflecting off her skin. It occurred to her for the first time in ages that she was beautiful. Not like a movie star, granted. But she was more than just a mom or a bumbling insurance agent. Jack's phone call had roused the sleeping woman inside her. They had talked for almost a half hour before she had to break off the conversation to help Rebecca with her map project. She knew now that Jack still had feelings for her; she was certain of it. A woman could sense these things. He had just been cautious in the beginning; that was all. At one time he loved her enough to want to marry her, but she had pushed him away. She had panicked. After all that Dodge put her through, she had been fearful to allow her feelings to run deep. All those years of gut-twisting emotions, of wondering and worrying while she lay in bed all night listening for her husband's car. Then, when a good man came along, she couldn't feel a thing. She'd gone numb inside.

She cranked the hot water on again with her toes. How long might it take for Jack to trust her again? As far as she was concerned, she was ready to start planning the wedding right now. It's not like they didn't know each other well enough. They had dated for almost two years.

God had heard her prayers. Jack was back. *Tell him we'll have to go throw a ball around sometime.* She smiled, sinking lower into the hot bath. Tyson was not out of the dark woods yet, but neither was he in jail. She had Mr. Bradbury to thank for that. Surely the Lord had orchestrated that series of events, too. The image of Jesus bending under the hood of her car to mess with her spark plugs came into her head. If her car had not refused to start, Millard would not have even been there to intervene with the judge. She remembered the grief she had felt as the corrections officer stepped forward to haul Tyson out of court and then the wonderful sound of Millard's voice as he offered to take her son in.

"Thank you, Lord." She tipped her head back and closed her eyes. "Thank you, thank you, thank you!"

She stepped out of the tub, dried herself, and donned her yellow flannel pajamas. As she yanked the top down on her body, the gold cross she always wore around her neck caught on the top button. She felt the resistance and then a quiet pop as the delicate gold chain broke. The cross fell to the floor at her feet. "Oh, no." She picked it up, suddenly remembering that the necklace had been from Jack. He gave it to her for her birthday but it had held so little significance for her at the time. She couldn't love him back then.

It could be fixed. There was no jewelry store in Ham Bone, but she could have it done in Dunbar. She went to place it in the jewelry box on her dresser for safekeeping.

Puzzled, she stared inside the box. Things were missing. The sapphire and diamond ring she had inherited from her great-aunt Louise was gone. She remembered seeing it just a few days ago in its usual slot in the red velvet lining. There was no doubt in her mind. The chiming refrain from "Some Enchanted Evening" playing from the music box became suddenly annoying. Where was the gold bracelet from her father? The rhinestone bracelet and earring set? Her silver locket?

Sidney's heart sank like a boulder in quicksand. She knew that neither Rebecca nor Sissy would dare get into her jewelry. They had used it for playing dress-up once and learned their lesson during a week of restrictions. She hugged herself, suddenly chilled. Deputy Estrada had seemed so sure that Tyson stole someone's jewelry, and now hers was missing, too. But what could Ty do with it? He was on house arrest; there was no way to fence it for cash. And what desperate need could he possibly have for cash in his current situation?

Her mind whirled. Ty was too smart to steal from his own mother where he was sure to be caught. Besides, she reasoned, he wouldn't do that to her. Ty wasn't like that. She went to the girls' room first, feeling as if Deputy Estrada were looking over her shoulder, his narrowed eyes shouting, *See? I told you so!* Her daughters didn't stir when she turned on a lamp or when she quietly opened and closed drawers. She didn't search hard. She knew the jewelry wasn't there.

In Ty's doorway she paused, fear and fatigue rooting her bare feet to the floor. "Tyson," she whispered. He didn't stir. She couldn't hear his breath. "Tyson, I need to talk to you." This time she spoke firmly. When he didn't respond, she turned on the light. The lump under his covers didn't look right. She made herself walk up to the bed, stretching out her arm, knowing before she touched the mound of pillows beneath his comforter that her son was not there.

16

Millard lay wide-awake in his bed, his thoughts jumping between his mole problem and the moody boy who had invaded his home. He knew there was a way to rid himself of the mole. In fact, the solution was tottering at the edge of his mind, so close to falling in that he held his breath. But then, uninvited, the image of that sad-faced kid would fill his brain again, scattering shadows of emerging ideas back into hiding.

Tyson had started to open up to him that day, but then had closed again like a threatened sea anemone. Millard had never known a kid so enthralled by nature, one who not only knew and understood the wild things around him but had relationships with them. A student he was not. But he was smart. And the kid had passion; Millard had seen it in his eyes as he stared out at the four-point buck and the woodlands beyond.

It was the phone call from his probation officer that caused the boy to recede again into his dark, secret world. If it was the threat of being taken back to jail again, why didn't the kid just get busy on his school-work? Millard had had no patience for students like that back when he taught at Silver Falls High. Kids that had good brains and wouldn't use them. He wouldn't even let a wrestler on his team compete if his grade-point average dipped below 2.0. There he had been struggling to raise a son with a brain the size of a marshmallow while others with healthy minds willingly let them go to waste. It made him angry, then and now.

When his phone rang, Millard's heart reverberated like a gong after being struck with a heavy mallet. He blinked in confusion and sat up, fumbling for the switch on his bedside lamp. Eleven-thirty. Nobody he knew would call him that late. Not unless it was an emergency. He stumbled down the hall, still shaking, to the phone by his easy chair. Oh, God. Not Rita. Not the kids. "Hello?"

"Millard. It's Sidney. I'm so sorry to wake you; I saw that your lights were out. It's just — well, Tyson is gone. I thought for some reason he might have gone over there."

"No." He turned on a lamp and looked around his living room even though his doors were locked. The boy couldn't possibly have gotten in. "Did you call the sheriff?"

"No. That wouldn't be a very good idea under the circumstances."

He felt stupid for suggesting it. "No. I guess not. I suppose he's off in the woods somewhere."

"That's what I was hoping." Her voice sounded deflated. "I thought maybe he was taking a little break from being stuck indoors. But then I found this note. It doesn't sound like he's planning to sneak back in his window tonight. It says: 'Mom, please don't worry about me.'" She started to cry.

"Is that all it says?"

She sniffed and seemed to be gathering herself. "'I love you. Ty.'"

She broke down again. He stared helplessly at his white knobby knees. He had turned down the electric heat before crawling into bed and was beginning to get goose bumps standing there in just his Fruit of the Looms and sleeveless undershirt. "Now, don't get all in a dither," he said, though he couldn't imagine why not. The kid was certainly destined for jail this time — if he could be found. "What did he take with him?"

"I'm pretty sure one of our sleeping bags is missing. Then again, it could have been left at someone's house after a sleepover for all I know. I don't do a regular inventory." She hesitated. "I'm also missing some jewelry."

Millard pondered this. What good was stolen jewelry to a fifteen-year-old kid in Ham Bone? Could he fence it anywhere around there? "What about cash?"

"Well, I don't think he had any saved up."

"Did you check your purse?"

"I didn't even think of that." She put the phone down while she rummaged through her purse. "I still have the $20 bill I came home with. There is one other place I should check, I suppose. My secret box. Can you hang on a minute?" She was gone for at least two. "Millard?" Her voice was weak. "My emergency fund is gone — $225."

He frowned. Stupid, selfish kid. "Doesn't sound like your secret box was a secret."

"I've had it since Ty was a baby. It's an oriental puzzle box. I thought only a genius could figure out how to open it without the directions."

"Well, I don't think he'll get far. He'd have

to thumb it all the way to Dunbar to catch a bus to anywhere and I think he's smarter than that. He'd be a sitting duck for law enforcement out on the highway at night."

She let out a long sigh. "Millard, I'm sorry to have disturbed you." She sniffed and then laughed dolefully. "I'll bet you rue the day you ever met me."

They said their good-byes and Millard made his way back to his bedroom, shivering as he crawled beneath the cold sheets. He lay flat on his back, eyes closed. This was really not his problem. Not a thing he could do about it. The kid could be anywhere. A guy wouldn't know whether to go north or south, east or west looking for him. The boy would surely keep under the cover of the trees, and there were woodlands spread around them in all directions. East was unlikely. The mountains were too cold this time of year; there had already been some dustings of snow on the foothills. Let it go, he told himself. Let the kid run. He'd survive. If anyone could make it through a cold October night in the Cascade foothills, Tyson could. He might just crawl inside that old stump with the skunk family since they all seemed to get along so well.

Counting sheep had never worked for Millard. He tried conjuring up comforting images of his dear departed Molly, but for some reason tonight her apparition appeared frowning, arms folded across her chest and foot tapping as if he had forgotten to clean his whiskers out of the sink again. He finally huffed in frustration and threw the covers off his body. What he needed was a big slice of Sidney Walker's zucchini bread, that and a glass of milk. Give his mind a chance to settle down so that sleep would come. He slid his feet into his brown slippers and grabbed the green flannel robe from the back of a chair. As he fumbled for the armholes, he paused by the bedroom window. The lights were still on in the Walker house. Then he noticed a small, single light bouncing off the trees at the edge of their yard. A flashlight. He opened his window a crack. Sidney was calling her son's name into the wind.

"Oh, for crying out loud," he muttered. Suddenly he yanked his arms from the bathrobe, turning it inside out and dumping it in a wad on the chair. He pulled on the khaki pants he had worn for the past three or four days and donned a shirt and the faded gray cardigan that Rita tried to replace every Christmas with gaudy plaid V-necks and the like. "That little woman is going to drive me to drink." He threw on a jacket and grabbed his keys from a peg on the kitchen wall before storming out the front door.

The Lincoln had not been out of the garage for a while. He sat inside trembling, waiting for the heat to kick in, waiting for a plan. A plan didn't come. He backed the car out slowly, looking cautiously both ways before backing across the road into Sidney's driveway. The car still running, he trudged around to the back of the house. There was no sound other than a faint murmuring in the trees, no flashlight beam in sight. He rapped on the back door.

"Oh, Millard!" Sidney was still dressed, wearing a pair of logger boots and a heavy jacket, her dark blond hair piled up on her head like she was going to the prom. She looked pretty like that. Her cheeks were red, and when she hugged him he could feel that they were still cold from being outdoors.

"Thought I might be able to help somehow," he said.

She sighed, letting her head drop back and her shoulders relax. "Thank you, Jesus."

Millard thought he was the one she should be thanking, standing out there in the cold at half past midnight when he ought to be getting his beauty sleep.

"Please come in."

"I saw you out there by the woods."

She shook her head. "It was useless. I know he's headed somewhere. I just can't figure out where. I don't know my own son anymore." She led him through the laundry room to the kitchen. "I was thinking of driving along the highway — just in case. I know it's a long shot, but he's got to get out of town somehow. He's too recognizable in Ham Bone. But I don't want to leave the girls here alone."

Millard pondered that while eyeing a plate of muffins covered with plastic wrap on the counter. She shoved it toward him.

"Have one if you like."

"Oh, well, all right." The muffin was quite moist, filled with raisins and shreds of carrot. She poured him a glass of milk before he had to ask for it. "You stay home," he said after washing down a mouthful. "I'll take the old Lincoln out for a spin and look around. He'd recognize the sound of your car a mile away."

"I didn't think of that. You're absolutely right." Her eyes followed the muffin from the plate to his mouth as if willing it to dissolve in his hand.

He reluctantly set the other half down, wiping his mouth with a napkin. "I guess I'd better hit the road, then."

She agreed enthusiastically, almost pushing him out the door.

The car was warm as he drove down Boulder Road toward town. He reached beneath the seat for his long-handled flashlight, clicking it on. Good. Still put out a strong white light. He turned it off and set it on the seat beside him, keeping his high beams on all the way down the hill. The only sign that he was not alone out there at that ridiculous hour was the set of red eyeballs, probably a possum or a coon, reflecting his lights from the grassy ditch at the edge of the road. The clock on his dash read 12:55 a.m. as he crossed the bridge over the creek, dropping into downtown.

Streetlights illuminated the doorways of the buildings he passed: Cascade Savings and Loan, Red's Barber Shop, Clara's Café, Art's Hardware (God rest his soul). The whole town looked as if its occupants had passed on; it had a ghost-town feel to it with not a soul in sight. Where would *he* go if he were a kid on the run? Certainly not Center Street. He shone his light down alleys between the old brick buildings that lined the street, then turned onto Spruce and drove around behind the Ham Bone Market. On a windy night like this, the kid would be looking for a way to stay warm.

Millard himself had scrounged cardboard and crates from behind the grocery in his younger days. When he and the Umquist brothers hopped the freight train up to Stevens Ridge to fish the alpine lakes, flattened cardboard boxes had made good insulation beneath their sleeping bags. Of course, logs were brought down the mountain by truck now. That spur of railroad had been shut down for years.

Millard cruised by the Dumpsters, panning the area with the beam of his flashlight. A skinny cat crouched and froze. Bundles of broken-down cartons protruded from a Dumpster labeled Cardboard Only. He stepped out of the car, leaving the door open as he looked behind and inside the metal containers. The cat, probably a feral, streaked into the darkness. But there was no sign of the boy.

He decided to head for the open highway, though uncomfortable with the thought of traveling so far from home on that desolate night. The kid was long gone by now whichever direction he had headed, whether he was bold enough to hitchhike or had taken the slow, safe mode of hiking through evergreen forests. But at least Millard could honestly report to Sidney that he had tried. It was not until he turned on his right-turn signal and began to crawl onto the main highway that another thought occurred to him. The railroad spur that led up the mountain pass had been shut down, but both the sawmill and Lipman's Fertilizer Plant still shipped their wares by rail. He recalled hearing the warning whistles of the freight trains in the wee hours of many mornings, usually around the time he needed to make a trip to the bathroom. He wondered for the first time if it was the biological urge that woke him regularly somewhere between 1 and 2 a.m. or the haunting peals of the train as it screeched into the yard at the bottom of Sparrow Hill. He glanced at the clock on the dash: 1:20. Did the kid know the railroad dispatch schedule? He had been on the run, sleeping outdoors all those nights before his arrest. He had surely heard the train whistles loud and clear. Yes, he knew. And being as smart as he was, he had probably assessed that riding the rails was the stealthiest option for getting out of town unseen.

Millard looped around to the northeast side of town, the back side, through a neighborhood of houses that were at least a hundred years old. Some showed their age with shabby siding and broken fences; others wore neatly painted shutters and window boxes with enviable gardens that he had observed when occasion drew him through that part of town. Most of the homes along the railroad tracks were smaller cottages, many occupied by Ham Bone's Mexican population, who had originally come to the area to work in the nearby fields but had since put down roots. He imagined how their houses must shake when the trains ambled through at night and wondered if they had somehow learned to sleep through the clanking clamor.

At the end of Digby Street, he turned onto an unnamed gravel drive. The Lincoln bounced through potholes as deep as apple baskets, the beams of his headlights dipping and rising violently as he approached the freight yard. If the train had already come through that night, he would have heard it, wouldn't he? He crossed several sets of tracks to an area of patchy grass and shrubs bordering the foot of Sparrow Hill. The road ended there, if one could call it a road. A string of railroad cars sat idle on a side track about a hundred yards off. Millard turned the car, sweeping its headlights over the lumpy terrain. No sign of life. Everyone in his right mind was tucked in his bed. Exactly what *he* was doing in this godforsaken place in the middle of the night was still a mystery to him. It was like he was in a dream, a bad one, and knowing it but waiting patiently for dawn and reality to come back to him. He coaxed the car toward a clump of small trees, riding the shocks like a rodeo cowboy until the nose dipped into a rut so deep that it scraped its chrome bumper on hard-packed clay that might as well have been concrete. Confound it! This was no way to treat a classic automobile! He'd never had a scratch on it until now.

The train whistle surprised him. He rolled his window down, listening. It must be coming up on Bodle's tree farm just south of town. There wasn't much time. He shut off the ignition, pocketed the keys, and stepped out with flashlight in hand. A breeze brought a damp, penetrating chill, part of the price one paid for living so close to the mountains. He stretched out his stiff knees and zipped his wool plaid jacket up to the throat. "Tyson!" he shouted. "Tyson Walker, I want to talk to you!"

The only response was another set of mournful whistles from the train.

Millard scanned the area as he swept the flashlight beam slowly across the landscape. He kept shining it back to the grove of trees. That's where the boy would be. The perfect place to lay out a sleeping bag in seclusion and still be close enough to the main track to catch a passing train.

He stumbled. The beam of light bounced wildly as he caught his balance. After that he kept the light aimed at the ground in front of his feet.

The trees were young alders mostly, and beneath them was a carpet of curled yellow and brown leaves. He directed his beam to likely hiding places among the undergrowth of huckleberries and bracken fern. The clamor of the approaching train vibrated the soles of his shoes. "Tyson!" He heard the bells clanging at the crossing over on Digby and knew that the bars were lowering to block traffic — not that there was any at this time of night. "Come on, boy. Let's talk about this man to man!"

He realized then that he was shouting to the night and nothing more. The kid had probably made it to Dunbar by now, thumbing his way down the highway. Maybe he got lucky and hooked up with a long-haul trucker headed for California, nothing but sunshine and palm trees on his horizon. Millard clicked off the flashlight and leaned against a tree as the freight train ambled into the yard, the powerful beam from its engine illuminating the tracks. California sounded pretty good to him right now, come to think of it. He hadn't been there since he and Molly went down to her best friend Wanda's twenty-fifth anniversary. He hadn't been anywhere in years. Standing here watching this old freight train lumber in and out of Ham Bone, Washington, was the closest thing he'd had to an adventure in a long time.

The freight cars ambled by slowly as the engine pulled onto a side track for loading or unloading. Millard watched for an open boxcar in the faint illumination from yard lights up ahead. All the cars so far appeared to be buttoned up tight.

At that moment it did not occur to him to head back home. All good sense left him, and in its place a case of nostalgia caused him to listen to the train's rumbles and squeals, to inhale scents of smoke and creosote as if through the ears and nostrils of his teenage self. Armed with a collapsible fishing rod and enough gear to survive in the wilderness for a few days, he and Art and the boys rode the freights up to the ridge several times each summer, hiking in to lakes and streams that they imagined had never been fished by another soul. Oh, those native trout could put up a fight! Millard's mouth began to water just from his remembering the delicacy of fresh trout dusted in pancake flour and fried over an open fire.

He heard a rustling in the leaves about twenty yards away. Maybe an animal, maybe not. He held still. The steps seemed tentative, stealthy, as if someone or something might be wondering if he was still there. Then he saw a shadow move into the dim light. Definitely human — the slouched figure of the boy with a large bundle on his back.

Tyson looked both ways, held still, and waited. He couldn't see Millard's car even if it were daylight; the train had blocked it from view. The end of the train was approaching yet there was still no open boxcar in sight. The boy had to do something now, Millard knew, like climb up into a gondola and out of sight before the train became bathed in the light of the electric yard lamps up ahead. A yard man would do more than just kick the kid off the train. Riding the freights was a federal offense.

Tyson made his move, scurrying across the uneven terrain toward the tracks. Millard followed, ignoring the complaints of his stiff knees, staggering as he tried to avoid clumps of hard earth and holes in his path. "Wait up!" he called.

Tyson's head jerked over his shoulder at

the sound of Millard's voice, then spun back toward the train. He hesitated as a loaded gondola approached. As it crawled past, he turned resolutely, walking in a swift gait alongside until he found something to grip on its tail end. A few more strides and he lunged upward, his feet flailing until finding a metal bar on which to rest them.

Millard caught up, grateful that the train was in slow motion, fighting to catch his breath. "You're going to freeze your tail off on that thing," he huffed. "Windchill! Come morning some yard bull's going to be prying you off with a crowbar!"

"I'll be okay!" They had to almost shout to be heard over the clatter.

"Have you thought this thing through?"

"Leave me alone, you useless old man!"

That did it. Millard stretched out his long arm, grabbing hold of the kid's pant leg. Tyson tried to shake him off, but Millard held tight, striding so close to the train that he was painfully aware of the steel wheels running along the tracks like can-opener blades. If he was going to pull the boy off, he would have to calculate well. Tyson kicked out violently, wrenching his pant leg from Millard's hand. The boy reached up to a ladder bolted to the side of the car, struggling with balancing the loaded pack and sleeping bag strapped to his back. Suddenly he lost his grip, his body lurching downward.

Instinctively, Millard grabbed a metal bar, yanking himself onto the train with strength that astonished him. His feet found a foothold and he threw himself against the boy's legs, his shoulder supporting the heavy load on Tyson's back until he felt the boy regain his grip. Millard stretched a gangly arm around him, gripping the ladder and maneuvering his feet until he could pull himself up to the boy's level.

"You can get out of town," he said into the boy's ear, "but you can't get away from your troubles. In fact, there'll be bigger ones waiting when you get back." Tyson struggled, but Millard had him pinned. "You think that sheriff is going to forget you? And what do you think the judge is going to do next time you get dragged into his courtroom? You're too old for a spanking; besides, that's all you got last time and that definitely didn't work. No, if you ride out this train, you'd better plan on never coming back."

One side of Tyson's face was plastered against the side of the metal gondola. "What do you care what I do?" he shouted.

"I care about your mother, you selfish little punk! Remember her? The one who wiped your snotty nose and held your head when you puked? The woman I saw tromping around the woods tonight calling your name?"

"Shut up!"

The car was approaching the well-lit area in the center of the yard. "Come on, boy. Let's get off this train to nowhere." Millard pulled his body off Tyson and began to feel with his foot for a lower rung.

The boy glanced around as if uncertain, clinging to the side of the train. "Go to hell," he finally said, his hand reaching upward.

He was going to do it. Out of stupid pride, the kid had just made a decision that might derail the rest of his life. Millard quickly scanned the ground below. Before Tyson's hand could grip another rung, Millard yanked him backward. "Throw your body or we're going to die!"

The boy tottered. Millard pushed with his feet, gripping the boy and hurling their bodies away from the train. His shoulder hit a clump of grass and he rolled like he had learned to do in the military. He heard the boy cry out. Terror shot through him. If Tyson was maimed, it was all Millard's fault. What had gotten into him to do such a thing? He scrambled to his feet, adrenaline pulsing through him. Boy and backpack were a lump on the ground next to the track. "Oh, God," he cried as he stumbled to where Tyson lay. His legs appeared to be intact, but he was curled up like a woolly caterpillar. "Tyson." He knelt beside him. "Are you okay, boy?"

"You crazy old fool! Are you trying to kill me? Just leave me alone!" Tyson jerked to his feet, pushing Millard away.

Millard reached out, grabbing a strap on Tyson's backpack for support as he pulled himself erect. The backpack gave way, sliding from the boy's shoulders, and Millard tossed it aside. Tyson wheeled back for it and Millard grabbed the front of his jacket. "I'm not going to leave you alone. I'm sticking to you like a porcupine quill; what do you think about that?"

Tyson tried to wrench himself free, swearing, pushing, and punching, but Millard's height and large hands helped him prevail. He wrestled the slight boy to the ground and though he twisted and turned, Millard had him pinned in five seconds flat. Millard was as shocked by this as the boy must have been. It was amazing what an old wrestling coach could do once he pried himself out of his easy chair.

What surprised Millard even more was

that Tyson was crying. The boy turned his face away as angry sobs tore from his throat. Millard slowly released the pressure and this time the boy didn't try to escape. There he was, his face pressed to the dirt, crying like he didn't have a hope in the world.

The old man thought to touch the boy's hair, to smooth a bit of grass from his wet cheek, but something held him back. Maybe the same thing that had paralyzed him so often when Jefferson cried. His wrestlers he had understood — mostly sharp, tough young men with goals that they were willing to fight for. The ones who couldn't cut it were cut from the team. Millard had never been one to coddle the mama's boys. Silver Falls High didn't take the state championship six years out of ten by being sensitive, that was for sure. He waited for Tyson's back and shoulders to stop convulsing, wondering about his next move. Finally, the sobs subsided and the boy lay motionless, though Millard was no longer restraining him in any way.

"Come on, boy," he finally said. He reached out, meaning to give the boy's shoulder a brisk pat, but his hand did not pull away. Instead it rested there for a moment. "Let's go on home. Your mom still had a plate of muffins and cold milk last time I checked."

Tyson rolled onto his back without speaking. Millard stood slowly, every muscle and joint complaining about the things they had been through that night, and reached his hand down. Tyson paused, pulled himself up on one elbow, and placed his smooth, fragile hand into the old man's. Millard pulled the runaway to his feet, slung the backpack over his own shoulder, and placed a guiding arm on Tyson's back as they trudged through the moonless night back to the old Lincoln.

17

On Saturday morning a ceiling of mottled gray spread above the foothills. Sidney stared out her bedroom window, cup of raspberry tea in hand, wondering if Jack's peewee football game would be canceled in the case of a heavy rain. If so, would their date be called off, too? But then it was not really a date, she reminded herself. Jack just happened to be coming to Ham Bone and had invited her and the girls to watch the game. In the past she would have called him. But things were different now. Jack was different. A little distant, sometimes aloof, and yet other times surprising her with his candid admiration. Perhaps he had other options and was being careful to keep them open.

She wandered down the hall, still in her bathrobe. The girls could sleep in for a while, but she would have to wake Ty. She entered his room softly and sat on the edge of his bed.

"Hey, Ty," she whispered. He needed a haircut. Tufts of dark hair spread in all directions on his pillow. "Happy Saturday," she said, knowing that for Ty it was not a happy day at all. His lips formed a frown; he blinked and closed his eyes again, rolling away from her onto his side. "Deputy Estrada will be here in forty-five minutes."

He groaned.

"Eggs and toast?"

"Okay," he murmured.

She went out to the kitchen, warmed her tea, and began cracking organic eggs into a poaching mold. Her conversations with Ty had flowed about as freely as cold lava since Millard brought him home during the wee hours of Thursday morning. He had come in head down, his face pink from the cold, eyes betraying the fact that they had recently shed tears, and headed straight for his room. Just like that. No "Sorry, Mom," no explanation at all for stealing from her and attempting to flee by freight train from her and his sisters, not to mention his legal responsibilities. His whole idiotic plan or lack thereof alarmed her. She did not want to think that her son had inherited his father's genes — that he was somehow pre-programmed to be a lying, thieving flake.

She didn't believe in that. Yet Ty was showing all the signs.

She hadn't confronted him about the cash and jewelry missing from her bedroom until Thursday night when he returned home from Millard's. That was another bad night. First of all, Millard informed her that Ty had still not cracked a book. Instead he had spent most of that day sleeping on the sofa, catching up from the sleepless night before. She had waited until after dinner before confronting him in the privacy of his room.

"Why did you steal from me, Tyson?"

His eyes had narrowed and his jaw went tight. "I did *not* steal anything."

"Well, that's really strange. At the beginning of the week, my jewelry was in my jewelry box where it belonged. I put it there myself. Then the same night that you stuff your bed with pillows and crawl out your bedroom window to head for Timbuktu, everything turns up missing. Even the cash from my secret box. It took me a long time to save that up, Ty. That was our emergency fund."

He had slammed his computer mouse on his desk so hard that it should have broken, then stood glaring down at her where she sat on his bed. "How about Sissy and Rebecca? Did you ever think they might have done it? Or are they too sweet and perfect?"

"I don't think so, Ty. I asked them and they both denied it. Besides, I don't think either one of them could figure out how to open that box. It's too complicated."

He had gone into a rage then. "I don't want your stupid jewelry or anything else! Somebody's lying to you, but it isn't me! Believe me or not — it's up to you."

Sidney sliced whole-grain bread and popped two pieces into the toaster. He had been so outraged that she had almost believed him. But when she questioned each of the girls again the next day, she was even more convinced that neither of them was the guilty party. She was thankful that they were still transparent with her. On the few occasions when one of them had tried to lie to her, her conscience still manifested guilt all over her face.

"Tyson! Breakfast is ready."

When he didn't emerge, she went back to his room to find him sound asleep. "Hey, come on! The sheriff will be here in twenty minutes."

This time he sat up, rubbing his eyes. "Why can't I just pick up trash from the side of the highway?" he mumbled. "At least I know how to do that."

"You'll figure it out. It's an opportunity,

really. A chance to learn a new skill. You know what they say: if it doesn't kill you, it's good for you." He gave her a sour look and she shrugged. "Throw some clothes on. Breakfast is getting cold."

She went to her room and began pulling clothes from drawers. For Jack's sake, she chose her tight-fitting jeans and a soft V-neck sweater, but before she could slip them over her naked body, there was a knock on the front door. "Tyson, will you get that?"

"I'm in the bathroom," he called.

"Oh, for Pete's sake!" She grabbed her yellow robe, tying it around her as she stomped to the door. She peered out the peephole. Deputy Estrada. Frowning, she opened the door slightly. "You're early," she said.

He glanced at his watch. "Is Tyson ready?"

"No. Not quite. He hasn't even eaten." She hesitated before swinging the door open. "Why don't you come in? He over-slept, but he's getting ready now."

The deputy nodded, stepping in and standing awkwardly on the square of vinyl tiles that was her foyer. He looked so different wearing faded jeans instead of his stiff green and khaki uniform. Like a regular guy — but with biceps that swelled from beneath the sleeves of his T-shirt. The way he looked at her made her hand go up to her chest, pinching the lapels of her robe together.

"Would you like a cup of tea?" she asked, immediately realizing that he was probably not an herbal tea kind of guy. "Or coffee?" She was sure she still had a bag of ground Sumatra in her freezer leftover from a summer evening when she had entertained Micki and some other women friends from the office.

"Coffee would be great." He glanced around the living room, shoving his hands into his back pockets and blowing out a stream of breath.

"Sit down, then. I'll get your coffee going and then see what I can do to light a fire under Ty."

Ty was sitting on his bed, tying his shoes. "Get out there and scarf down your eggs," she said. "Don't keep the man waiting."

She hurried down the hall, slipped her clothes on, and ran a comb through her hair, congratulating herself for taking the high road by not insisting that the deputy wait in his car. She had decided to be civil today. When she returned, the single cup of coffee had dripped through its filter into a mug. Ty stood by the sink, devouring an egg folded into a slice of toast. She delivered the coffee to the deputy in the other room. "Sorry about the wait. He's almost done."

"Thanks." He took a sip and seemed to relax. "No big rush. Except it looks like the rain's coming. We'll be working outdoors."

"You're working with him?"

"Yes, ma'am."

He sounded like he was from the South, addressing her like that, though she knew by his features and the name *Estrada* that he must be Mexican by descent. Even his dark eyes looked softer without the uniform. "Is that in your line of duty?"

He shook his head, averting his eyes over his shoulder toward the window. "No, it's my day off, actually."

Sidney didn't know what to make of that. "Your day off? Shouldn't you be spending the day with your family or raking leaves or flying a kite or something?"

The corners of his lips twitched. "I'll be seeing my dad today." He sipped his coffee. "I gave up flying kites. Too many trees around here."

"True. I heard that Ty's project is building a wheelchair ramp," she said tentatively. Ty was probably listening to every word from the kitchen so she didn't mention her concerns. She had never even shown her son how to nail two boards together and now here he was, fifteen already. So close to being a man. What else had she forgotten to teach him?

Sidney saw the deputy's face flinch, a shadow passing over his eyes as Tyson came around the corner, finishing off a glass of orange juice. "Yes. It's for a handicapped woman down on Digby Street. The one who was recently robbed."

His bullet hit its target. Ty glared back at him.

Deputy Estrada stood, passing Sidney his half-empty mug. "Thanks for the coffee. We'd better hit the road."

Sidney's heart began to throb in her ears. A handicapped woman. Estrada still thought Ty was guilty of that other crime, and now she had reason to believe that he was right. What would happen to Ty if the deputy could make a case against him? She followed them to the door. "Where exactly on Digby? I'd like to bring Tyson some lunch."

The deputy glanced at her sideways. She regretted saying it, knowing that she sounded like a doting mommy, some kind of airhead who thought her child could do no wrong even when the evidence against him was piling up and smelling bad. If Tyson wanted lunch, he should have gotten himself out of bed early enough to make it himself. "I could bring you some too if you'd like."

He shook his head. "That won't be necessary. It's a pink house: 2128 Digby. There's a little windmill in the yard."

"How long is this going to take?" Tyson asked as they stepped outside.

"I'll let you know."

Ty trudged behind him but stopped halfway to the patrol car. "I forgot my hat."

"Get in," the deputy said gruffly, jerking his head toward the car. Tyson obliged with a scowl. Estrada glanced up at Sidney where she stood on the porch, gave her a grim nod, and slid onto the seat, slamming the car door.

Rebecca and Sidney appointed themselves to be cheerleaders for the peewee football game. Rebecca already had pom-poms; Sidney couldn't remember when or how she acquired them. Sissy practiced her cheers noisily in the backseat of the car, using a pair of canary-colored feather dusters. After a bout of sneezing, Sidney asked her to refrain from slapping them together until they arrived at the field where they were to meet Jack.

"How come we have to bring Ty his lunch,

Mom? He should have just brung it himself."

"Brought," Sidney corrected. Sissy was right. Ty was old enough to take responsibility for himself. She had to let go, for his sake as well as her own.

"Mom" — Rebecca hesitated — "I know this doesn't sound very nice, but sometimes I wish Ty didn't live with us anymore. It was happier at our house when he ran away. I wish he could just live with Mr. Bradbury."

"Yeah," Sissy added. "We could wave at him sometimes from across the street."

Sidney laughed at the comment despite its deep connotations. "I know he's not nice to you lately. He's not very nice to me either. But we're a family. We're going to stick together and get through this. Ty is not a happy young man right now. Something has hurt him. Our job is to love him no matter what. Can we agree to do that for your brother?"

"Okay," Sissy chirped.

Rebecca didn't respond for a moment. "But what if he never changes? What if he gets worse?"

Sidney glanced over to where Rebecca sat in the passenger seat. She took her daughter's hand. "Love never fails, Becca. It's never wasted."

Here she was echoing her own mother, that wonderful, wacky woman of faith. It occurred to Sidney that she was passing on mere tidbits to her children instead of the smorgasbords of truth that her mother had served up to her. This world was a dangerous place to venture without it. Ty had blasted through childhood like a movie on fast-forward, and the girls were right behind him. She was running out of time.

She drove down Digby. It was easy to spot the house. It was the only pink one in the neighborhood, and a Sheriff's Department patrol car was parked out front. She pulled into the driveway of the modest little cottage. Tyson and Deputy Estrada looked up from their labors on the front porch. "I'll only be a minute, girls. Wait here, please."

She stepped out and walked up to the porch. "How's it going, guys?"

"Good." They looked as excited to see her as if she were an approaching rain cloud.

"Here's your lunch, Ty." She turned to the deputy. "What time should I expect him home?"

"About three. Maybe three-thirty." The deputy wiped sawdust from his brow with a bare forearm. It was a shame that he had the personality of an abused guard dog; he was an incredible specimen of a man.

The front door opened. "Hello." Sidney turned to see a pleasant-looking gray-haired woman.

"Oh, hi." She held out her hand to the woman. "I'm Sidney Walker." She gestured toward her son. "Tyson's mother."

"I'm sorry." The woman laughed. "I'd better not take my hands off this doorway. I'm Amilia. Amilia Vargas. Please come in."

The deputy dropped his hammer to his side and huffed, obviously displeased.

"My girls are in the car. I just came to drop off Ty's lunch." Amilia had already turned her back, leaving the door open as she gripped the handles of a rolling walker, and began shuffling away from the door. Sidney glanced over her shoulder. The car was bouncing, pom-poms and feather dusters shaking wildly. Ty passed the deputy a slat for the porch rail and the deputy grabbed it, a spray of nails protruding from between his lips. She followed Amilia inside.

"Sit; sit." Amilia wore blue jeans, suede moccasins, and a man's button-down shirt with the tails hanging out. Her silvery gray hair was swept into a neat French roll, sweeping across one temple like a swag valance. Amilia dropped into a brown reclining chair surrounded by baskets of books, yarn and knitting needles, mail, and magazines. "I don't suppose you have time for tea?"

Sidney smiled at the rosy-cheeked woman. "No. I'm taking my girls to a peewee football game."

"Oh, they play football?"

"Today they're just cheerleaders. We're meeting a friend who coaches the team." Sidney glanced around the humbly furnished room. Why would a robber choose to break in here of all places? She glanced at Amilia's hands. No rings. The only jewelry on her body was a dangly pair of colorful bird earrings. She leaned forward. "Amilia, I understand you were robbed."

She nodded. "A few weeks ago."

"Deputy Estrada thinks my son, Tyson, did it. I'm sure that's why he's got him here."

"Yes, that's what he says. Alex wants the boy to feel real bad about it." She chuckled. "Wants to rub it in good — even though they still can't prove anything. Alex is very protective of me. He doesn't like me coming out on the porch while they're working. I think I'm supposed to look all sad and pathetic, moaning about how I can't sleep nights anymore since my home was invaded." She clucked her tongue. "Truth is, I doze off during *Jeopardy!* and I'm a goner for the night."

"Alex? Are you related to Deputy Estrada somehow?" The strokes of the hammer outside rattled the windows.

"I've scrubbed his butt and cleaned wax out of his ears, but no. Not by blood. His papa lives next door. Rosa Estrada died of the cancer when Alex was eight. She was my best friend. We came and went between our places like Lucy and Ethel." She leaned her head back and closed her eyes. "For a couple of field workers, we had some good times."

Sidney was shocked. "You worked the fields?" She glanced at the books lining Amilia's shelves. American classics, theology, politics, a travel series. Though Amilia had Mexican features, there was no hint of a Spanish accent. "I had you pegged for a college professor or something like that."

"That was a long time ago. It's what our families did — about all they could do when they came up from Mexico, not speaking English. But God bless America, nobody held a gun to our heads and made us stay on our knees, cutting cabbage for the rest of our lives."

A couple of birds twittered and flapped in a cage suspended from a stand behind Amilia's head. Sidney watched as they scattered seeds through the cage bars onto the large, worn area rug. "Pretty birds," Sidney said. They were smaller than robins, with smooth, honeydew green bodies and peach-colored heads. "What kind are they?"

"Lovebirds. Kate and Spencer, after Hepburn and Tracy. I love old movies."

Sidney had been anxious at first. This was the woman that Ty supposedly burglarized, though he still denied stealing a thing from her. There were sparks of animosity crackling in the air out there on the front porch, her girls were waiting in the car, and it was time to meet Jack. But for some reason she wanted to linger. There was something about this woman that Sidney wanted to explore. She stood, glancing out the front window. Sissy was hanging out the car window now, dragging one end of her long knit scarf back and forth on the ground.

Alex Estrada glanced up from his work, and their eyes met. His darted away, and at that instant his hammer came down on his thumb. They heard a loud expletive. A giggle escaped unexpectedly from Sidney's throat. She spun back toward her hostess, pushing the laughter back with a hand over her mouth.

Amilia raised her brows in question.

Sidney let out a roll of laughter. "I'm

236

sorry. The deputy — Alex just hammered his thumb."

The older woman looked delighted. "Did he? Well, I think I'd better bring him chocolate. That used to be all he needed to fix his hurts. Chocolate raisins were his favorite." She rummaged through a basket under the table by her chair, producing a handful of wrapped chocolate candies. "This is the best I can do right now. Leftover from Easter." She made no attempt to get up, but stretched out her hand until Sidney took the candies from her. "You tell those boys that Amilia said it's time for a lunch break."

"Amilia, could I come back and visit you sometime?"

Amilia grinned. "I'd like that. Next time, you let me know you're coming and I'll make tamales."

She got Amilia's phone number, leaving her own with an offer to run errands for the handicapped woman, and they said their good-byes.

Out on the porch, Sidney was surprised to see that the pounding sounds were being made by Tyson now. Alex pushed a two-by-four through a whining saw blade, holding a flat pencil between his lips. "Wow. Look what you guys have done!" Tyson glanced up slightly, then went back to hammering.

He was trying, she realized, to duplicate the deputy's rhythm, one-two, one-two. She had been hearing it for the past ten minutes. Two hard strokes and the nail was home. Ty averaged four strokes, but when he sunk one in only three without bending it, his jaw softened and he looked up as if to make sure she noticed. She smiled proudly, then stepped down to where Alex stood, holding out her handful of stale chocolate. "For your boo-boo." She tried to keep a straight face. "Amilia says it's time for lunch."

Alex Estrada stood to his full height and took a deep breath, studying her. He had seen her laugh; she was sure of it. "I can only imagine what else Amilia said."

Sidney smirked as she placed the candies in his open hand. "I'll never tell."

18

Halfway through the peewee football game, it began to rain. Not the usual drizzle that Sidney was accustomed to, but shafts of steel shooting down from the heavens like a barrage of medieval spears. Jack blew a whistle and with a violent throwing motion of his arm sent the entire field of mini football players scurrying toward the parking lot. Sidney and the girls scrambled down from the small bleachers, laughing and dashing with the rest of the crowd toward the protective cover of their vehicles. The black sky above them made a blanket statement: the game was called.

The girls piled into the backseat of her car. Sidney watched through the streams of water on the windshield for Jack, using a napkin from the glove box to blot her face. "Mom, look at my pom-poms. They're ruined!" Rebecca dropped her wet head against the back of the seat with a dramatic sigh.

Sissy waved her feather dusters. "Too bad you don't have some of these." She glanced down at the clumps of wet crepe in her sister's lap and then brushed her legs with her wet yellow feathers. "But mine don't paint."

That comment made Sidney take a second look over her shoulder.

"Oh, no!" Rebecca wailed. Just as Sidney had suspected, the red dye in the pom-poms had bled into Rebecca's pale blue jacket and pants. "Mom, will it come out?" she whined.

The rain pounded on the car roof like hail. Sidney tried to peer through the downpour. Where was he? How long could it take to gather up a football? Surely Jack wasn't standing out there in the torrent discussing the game with the other coach. "Sissy, take your things out of that plastic bag and put those pom-poms in it before they touch anything else. Becca, stop pouting. You don't even like that jacket, remember?" Both girls looked like half-drowned cats. She pulled the visor down to look at herself. Her mascara had run, and her hair lay flat and dark, dripping like syrup from her head.

The knock on her window startled her. Water poured down Jack's forehead and cheeks. She cranked the window open, laughing at the sight of him. "Hey," he said.

"A bunch of us are going to meet at Jimmy's for pizza. Do you want to go in my car?"

She remembered that Ty was due back at about three and she would have to be home. Hopefully they had enough work to do under the cover of Amilia's porch roof to keep busy until then. "We'll meet you there."

He peered in at the girls, grinning, and slapped the car door. "Okay. See you there."

She watched him dash to his dark SUV and followed him for three blocks. Jimmy's Pizza was attached to the three-lane bowling alley on the west end of town. They parked around back, darting inside and heading straight for the circular fireplace in a sunken area in the middle of the restaurant. They were in luck. Some people who had been sitting by the crackling fire were just getting up. Sidney peeled off her wet jacket, running her hands through her wet hair. "Girls, hang your jackets on the coatrack to dry." She smiled at Jack. "I'll be right back."

In the restroom she wiped the mascara smudges from her eyes, ran a comb through her hair, and applied lip gloss. Another young woman slid in next to her, leaning over the sink to paint her full lips a deep rose. "I saw you at the game," she said, blotting her lips on a paper towel. "Aren't you Tyson Walker's mom?"

Sidney smiled. "Yes, I am."

The woman raised her eyebrows. "I heard all about what happened. God, you poor woman! I don't know what I'd do if one of my kids went off the edge like that. Luckily my boys don't have a mean streak in them." She shook her head. "They're both as good as gold. I hear you feel a lot safer now that he's in jail."

"Oh, really? Who told you that?"

She scoffed. "Well, who knows who told me first? This is Ham Bone, for God's sake." She put on a sympathetic expression. "How much time did he get?"

"My name is Sidney Walker." She didn't offer her hand. "What's yours?"

"Oh." She looked suddenly uncomfortable. "Patty Polanski."

"Well, Patty," Sidney said as she zipped her purse closed and headed for the door. "See you around."

Jack had saved her a chair next to him. The place buzzed with voices; kids whose spirits were not dampened by the rain begged their parents for quarters to play the video games in the back corner of the restaurant, and as always there was the distant sound of bowling balls striking pins in the alley next door. "What's wrong?" Jack said.

She tried to shake it off. It didn't matter what people said. She inhaled deeply, willing her face to soften. "It smells wonderful in here, and we got the coveted chairs by the fire where we can warm our toes. What could be wrong?"

Jack grinned. His blond hair had recently been buzzed down to about a quarter inch all the way around. The jock look. "Always the optimist. I ordered a veggie pizza for you and the girls." Sissy and Rebecca, along with a couple of friends from school, were revolving their bodies in front of the fire across from them like chickens roasting on a rotisserie. "I can't believe how big the girls are. Sissy was missing her front teeth the last time I saw her."

"She's almost eight now; Becca's ten."

"How are they at soccer?"

"Sissy is pretty good. That girl has no fear, and she's as tenacious as a terrier after a rat. Becca could be better if she wasn't so afraid of getting muddy."

He shook his head with a frown. "That's not good."

She chortled and slapped his leg. "Don't get all in a tizzy. There's more to life than sports, you know."

"Like what?"

"Well, drama, for one thing. I'll bet you anything we'll see Becca parading across our TV screen some day." *Our* TV screen. She hadn't meant it to sound like that. This was only their second date, after all, if one could qualify it as a date when she had driven her own car and had her girls in tow.

He shrugged his stocky shoulders. "Well, what if she stars in a movie about a soccer player? She's going to have to know all the moves to be convincing. You can't fake skill."

Sidney leaned toward his face, which was rosy from the weather and the fire. His blue eyes were like ice in contrast. She could feel the warm glow emanating from her own skin. "Thank God for doubles, or stunt women, whatever you call them," she said. "I don't care if my kids win any trophies. All I care about is that they have fun."

He shook his head, clicking his tongue. "You still don't have a competitive bone in your body." It was not meant as a compliment. A number was called from the service counter and he stood. "Number nineteen. That's us." He bent toward her face, placing his hands on the little table next to her. "Winning isn't everything, green-eyed lady, but if you're not doing it, you're the loser."

He leaned into her ear, repeating the word in a teasing whisper. "Loser."

She laughed and smacked his arm. It was as solid as a fire log. "Why don't you go get those pizzas before they get cold?"

What a perfect way to spend a rainy Saturday afternoon. Sidney kicked off her shoes, propping her stocking feet on the brick hearth. Within minutes steam began rising from her toes. What was taking Jack so long? She turned and stood to peer over a planter full of fake ferns behind her. Jack was still up by the counter, two pizza boxes in his arm, talking to, of all people, Patty Polanski. A nasty feeling ran down Sidney's backbone. Patty was all smiles, talking to Jack with animated gestures as if they were longtime friends. She kept touching his arm. Sidney looked at his face. He was definitely into the conversation, not just waylaid, no furtive glances toward the fireplace where Sidney waited. That little gossip was charming him so skillfully that even the scent of the pepperoni pizza just below his nose couldn't lure him away.

Sidney couldn't bear to watch the pathetic scene. She went back to her seat, returning Rebecca's wave from where the girls now sat at a table with friends. Was this a date or not? She had no idea. Jack had asked only if she'd like to come to the game. So maybe they weren't even officially *together* here. Should she pay for her own pizza? A thought occurred to her. She stood again for another peek. Patty's good-as-gold little boys had joined them, looking up at Jack like he was some star quarterback. And aha! Just as Sidney suspected, their charming mother was *not* wearing a wedding ring. Sidney saw right through Patty's little game. She plopped down in her seat again while an uneasiness seeped like heartburn into her soul. How was she different? Jack was probably every single mother's dream. She glanced around the crowded restaurant. How many more of them were out there drooling for the opportunity to share a slice of pizza from his box?

And then his words came back to her. *You still don't have a competitive bone in your body. Loser!*

She jumped to her feet. Sidney Walker was not a loser! She stepped up the two steps from the sunken fireplace area and walked directly up to Jack. "Hey, did you get lost?"

"Oh, sorry. Hey, Sidney, this is Patty Polanski" — he gestured then toward each of the boys — "and Jacob and Jason. I was their coach last year."

Patty faked a half smile, which Sidney

ignored. She smiled down at Patty's boys. "Was he a good coach?"

"Yeah!" they said simultaneously. "But now he coaches the Dunbar team," one said.

Patty pushed her stylish brunette hair upward as if to gain volume. "So how do you two know each other?"

"Oh, we go way back," Jack said, glancing at Sidney. "From when I lived here in town. I guess we met at Graber's Market, didn't we?"

"Yup. You were the produce manager back then."

"And you were what we called a melon-knocker. Sniffed and squeezed everything." He turned his head toward Patty. "I had to watch her like a hawk to keep her from bruising the avocados."

That brought a deep laugh out of Sidney, partly from embarrassment. There was an element of truth to it. "I do not abuse vegetables. I like them too much." She lifted the top of one of the pizza boxes in Jack's hand. "Speaking of which . . ."

"Yeah, hey, let's eat. It's getting cold." Jack patted the boys' shoulders. "I'll see you around, guys. Coach Petrie will let you know when we play each other again."

Sidney turned to head back to their seats by the fireplace, glancing over her shoulder, expecting to see Jack on her heels. Instead she saw Patty stretch out her hand to touch Jack's arm. Sidney read her lips. *Call me.* She saw the back of Jack's head drop in a quick nod. He gave Patty a midair salute before walking away.

19

On Monday morning, Ty arrived on Millard's porch with a Crock-Pot full of his mother's chili. The boy slid his heavy backpack from his shoulder onto the sofa on his way to the kitchen to plug the cooker in. "I guess you're stuck with me 'til about eight-thirty," the boy said in passing. "Mom has to go to open house at the school tonight."

Millard nodded. "That's right. She told me last week and I almost forgot." Tyson returned to the living room, where Millard sat in his chair with the *Herald* and his second cup of instant coffee. "I saw a man bring your sisters home on Saturday." Millard had planned to wait awhile longer before casually bringing it up, but the curiosity had tormented him like an itch on a palace guard's foot. "Was that your father?"

The boy shot him a strange look and

scoffed bitterly. "No."

Millard waited.

"That was Jack. An old boyfriend of Mom's. I guess they met him at Jimmy's because his game got rained out. He coaches peewee football. Anyway, Mom had to come back here because of me, but Jack took Sissy and Becca bowling."

One of Millard's legs was crossed over the other, his brown leather slipper bouncing rhythmically in the air. "Oh. Nice guy?"

Tyson shrugged. "He's okay, I guess." He kicked off his shoes without untying the laces and flopped onto the sofa, pulling his backpack close as if to open it, then apparently thinking better of it and pushing it to the floor. "But he's a sports junkie. That's all he can talk about."

"He stayed a long time."

"Yup."

Millard hoped that more information might be forthcoming. He really didn't like to pry. He pulled out the tail of his cotton shirt and began polishing his reading glasses. "I thought maybe that was your dad."

Tyson glared at him and looked away.

Apparently he was trespassing on forbidden ground. Millard slid his reading glasses onto the bridge of his nose. "How did the first day of your community service project go?"

"The stupid sheriff made me work in the rain." He dropped onto his back, staring at the ceiling with his hands under his head.

"In that downpour?" Millard unwittingly shivered, thinking for a moment that it was cruel and unusual punishment to make the boy work in that deluge until a memory crossed his mind. "My father sent me out to round up his horses in a squall like that once. I was about twelve, I think." He had been lost in his own pasture, pelted by watery bullets that stung his face. He remembered crying. "We had a farm on the Skagit River. The spring snowmelt from the mountains had swollen the river near the tops of its banks and then a storm came along to beat all. I'll never forget that one." He took a sip of lukewarm coffee, dropping his head to the back of the chair. "The rain was so thick that I couldn't see the horses."

"Well, what happened?"

Millard opened his eyes to see Tyson up on one elbow. "My father and the neighbor men were a half mile away filling gunnysacks with sand and stacking them into a wall along the dike. We'd never seen the river get that high and everyone was scared. We knew that if it got over the dike, it would wash our houses and barns clean down to Puget Sound. Anyway, my father was depending on me to get the horses to higher ground. The wind knocked me around like a battering ram, but I finally found our little herd all huddled together in a cottonwood grove. Seemed like I was half-drowned before I got a rope and bridle on one mare and managed to climb bareback onto the alpha stallion so that I could lead them out of there."

"Did the river flood?"

Millard dropped his paper to the floor. It had been a long time since anyone cared to hear any of his stories. "It seeped over the dike in places. Enough to turn the pastures into shallow lakes, a foot or two of standing water in the barn. The good news was that the rain stopped when the water was an inch or two shy of the top step on our front porch." He chuckled. "Caught an eight-pound steelhead trout out by the chicken coop the next day with my bare hands."

"Dude. I wish something like that would happen around here."

"I thought you didn't like the rain."

Ty rolled his eyes. "I wasn't exactly having an adventure out there. Estrada is a jerk. There was no reason for me to stand there handing him boards when I could have just stacked them up on the porch for him. He hates me."

Millard pursed his lips and wrinkled his brow into a thoughtful expression. "Why do you think that is?"

Ty scoffed, shaking his head. "For one thing, he says I stole this old lady's wedding ring and she's like some close family friend, plus she can hardly walk."

"Well, did you take her ring?"

"No!" Ty sat up and leaned forward, his eyes riveted plaintively on Millard's. "Nobody believes me, but I didn't take her jewelry or my mom's." His face went dark. "That's why I need to get out of here. Everybody's going to blame me for everything that goes wrong for the rest of my life." He kicked at his backpack where it lay on the floor. "It sucks."

Millard was struck by something in the boy's face, in his voice. Against all reason, he found himself believing Tyson. He suddenly wanted to, anyway. But he was puzzled.

"What about your mom's money?"

Tyson stared at the floor, slowly shaking his head. "If I wanted to steal her money, I could have done it a long time ago. I figured out how to open her stupid little box when

I was about eight."

That seemed like an honest comment. The logical stance would be to plead ignorance. While Millard pondered this, his eyes fell on the face of Molly's grandfather clock. Eight fifty-five. "Confound it!" He jumped to his feet. "Help me out, son. Rita's due here in five minutes!"

"What?"

"I have to make it look like I've been eating her crappy frozen dinners all week!"

Tyson joined him in the kitchen. "What do you want me to do?"

Millard was already frantically removing plastic containers from the fridge and freezer. "Dump the stuff in the garbage. I'll rinse the containers." Tyson pulled out the kitchen trash receptacle and began popping hard clumps of broccoli and bricks of stew from the plastic cartons. Millard snatched one from Tyson's hand and put it back in the fridge. "Not the squash. She'll get suspicious."

Just as Rita pulled into the drive, Millard dropped into his chair and reached for the paper. "Why don't you get some books out of that backpack and look busy?"

Rita bustled in, a lock of her red hair falling over one eye. She closed the door behind her with one foot as Millard stood to help her. "Here, let me take those bags," he said.

She glanced at Tyson's back where he sat at the dining room table with an open book and frowned. "Hello, Dad." Tyson glanced up, but she did not acknowledge him. "What's that I smell?" She followed the scent into the kitchen, opening the lid of the slow cooker. She sniffed, pulled a spoon from the drawer for a taste, and replaced the glass lid with a slight shake of her head. "Is she trying to kill you? That's too spicy for a man your age. It'll give you acid reflux so bad that you'll have to eat baby food for a week." She walked over and pulled the kitchen door closed. "How's it going?" she whispered, gesturing toward the door with her head.

He nodded as he pulled a fresh supply of frozen leftovers and a bag of store-bought bread from a sack on the counter. "Fine, fine."

"Have you had any trouble with him?"

The scene from last Wednesday night down at the freight yard flashed into his mind. The boy shouting, "Go to hell!" Millard remembered the pounding of his heart, the terror he had felt as he thrust their bodies from the moving train. His hand went to his left shoulder, which had pained him ever since. "No trouble that I can recall — other than motivating him to do his schoolwork."

Rita's lips clamped into a dissatisfied line. "Well, just watch him, Dad. You're so trusting of everyone, and believe me, there are a lot of people who can't be trusted out there. They're out to take advantage — and I hate to say it, but I'm afraid that's exactly what's happening here. This Sidney woman — you hardly know her. She lives in a trailer; she drives that broken-down old car; her kids are out of control. But she's not stupid. She looks out her window at your nice, well-maintained house and car, and it's like she's peeking right into your bank account. Has she asked you for money yet?"

Millard glared at his daughter before dropping his head in utter disappointment. Had he raised her to think like this? He sat at the small table, just big enough for two, which was pushed against the wall beneath a window looking out on the field and the woods. She didn't get this suspicious, critical attitude from her mother; that was for sure. Molly could find something good to say about an ax murderer. Perhaps Rita *had* learned it from him. He had always been one to speak his mind freely. Probably too freely, he thought with regret.

Rita misinterpreted his silence. "Oh, Dad.

You *have* given her money, haven't you." It was not a question. She sighed, turning her back and placing both hands on the edge of the counter. She took a deep breath. "Dan and I think it might be a good idea to sit down together and discuss your finances. I mean, I know you're secure, Dad. But we don't know any of the details. God forbid, if something should happen to you — if your health or mental condition should fail . . ."

Obviously she thought his mental capacity had already failed. He didn't fling out his usual retorts. He felt too hollow. Instead he waited, knowing the truth would leach out of her if he only held his tongue.

She turned to face him. "I should have power of attorney for you, Dad."

He studied the veins in his hand, the long, wrinkled fingers spread flat on the tabletop. It was about his money. She was terrified that it might get away from her. She had determined that his days were winding to an end, his useful life over, and now all that was left to do was to plan accordingly. She was full of advice, too full of her own to ever seek or accept any from him. She couldn't hear him, couldn't really see him, because he was fading away. He pushed himself up from the table. "Your containers are in the dishwasher. I'll be going to the market on Saturday. Don't bother bringing anything next week."

After Rita left, Millard sat in his chair with the crossword puzzle in his lap. He had felt fine that morning, but now it was as if someone had pulled a plug and drained all of his energy away. His daughter and her kids were all the family he had left, but they didn't need him anymore. He had become a useless burden. Rita came by only out of a sense of obligation. The frozen dinners were her guilt offerings. If he would no longer accept her frozen sacrifices, how would she purge her soul?

She had still been sputtering as he ushered her to the door, nervous and confused by his somber silence. He too felt confused. Was she right? Was his bank account and the real estate that he sat on more valuable now than he was?

"What did she say to you?"

Tyson's voice surprised him. The boy was no longer at the dining room table, but lying on his stomach on the sofa, dangling one arm to turn the pages of a book on the floor.

"Why do you ask?"

"Because you're just sitting there. I know you're not reading the paper because you don't have your glasses on." When Millard didn't respond, the boy rolled over, pulling himself up and hugging his knees. "Was it about me? I know she doesn't like me."

Millard shook his head. "No. It was about Rita."

Tyson seemed to study his face. "Are you sad or mad?"

An empty laugh crept from Millard's throat. "A little of both. Mostly sad, I think."

The boy nodded as if he understood. They didn't speak for about a minute, caught up in an almost reverent silence, both possibly aware that they were sitting on common ground. Millard wanted to ask about the pain behind Tyson's eyes, but held his tongue intuitively, knowing that neither of them was ready to go under the knife and allow their twisted guts to be exposed.

"What are you reading there?"

Tyson glanced down at his open book with disdain. "Poetry. Word slime."

Millard chuckled. "That was poetic. Maybe you're a poet and don't know it."

A corner of Tyson's lip twitched. "It's so stupid. I'm supposed to find one I like and try to make up a poem that's like it in some way. But I don't like any of them. They're all about love." He rolled his head, feigning a feminine voice. "And pretty leaves and daffodils."

Millard closed his eyes and dropped his head to the back of his chair. Could he still recite it? The first line came to him and then the next:

> There are strange things done in the
>   midnight sun
> By the men who moil for gold;
> The Arctic trails have their secret tales
> That would make your blood run cold;
> The Northern Lights have seen queer
>   sights,
> But the queerest they ever did see
> Was that night on the marge of
>   Lake Lebarge
> I cremated Sam McGee.

Millard paused, glancing over to see that the boy's eyes were riveted on his face. "That's the beginning of a poem written by a man named Robert Service. He wrote a whole slew of them, put them in a book called *The Spell of the Yukon.*"

"Say the rest of it."

Millard rubbed his chin thoughtfully. Should he give it to him or make him dig? "Let's see if I can recall some more.

> Now Sam McGee was from Tennessee,
> Where the cotton blooms and blows.

Why he left his home in the South to roam
'round the Pole, God only knows.
He was always cold, but the land of gold
Seemed to hold him like a spell;
Though he'd often say in his homely way
That he'd 'sooner live in hell.' "

Millard sighed, searching his brain for a tantalizing bit. "There's this one part further on; how does it go? Something like:

The flames just soared
And the furnace roared —
Such a blaze you seldom see;
And I burrowed a hole in the glowing coal
And I stuffed in Sam McGee."

Tyson was practically drooling, his head stretched toward Millard like a coyote poised outside a rat hole. Millard shook his head. "Wish I could remember the rest. I've got that book around here somewhere." He glanced around the room as if it might be in plain sight, his eyes falling on the clock. "Look at that. It's almost noon and I haven't even done the crossword." He shook his paper open. "You might want to get yourself some lunch."

Ty stood and stretched before heading for the kitchen. "Do you want me to bring you some chili?"

Millard looked up, surprised by the offer. Spring thaw. The ice had begun to melt the night he and the boy wrestled down at the freight yard. Ty's tears had fallen on the cold ground between them, and there had been a gradual thinning and cracking ever since. "Yes, that would be fine," Millard said. "There's some of your mother's bread in the freezer. Why don't you pop a couple of slices in the toaster, and I'll see if I can't find that book."

After dinner that evening, Millard took his garbage out, dropping the neat bundle into a can next to the back porch. The temperature had dropped to thirty-two degrees Fahrenheit according to the thermometer mounted by the door. Stars shone against the black sky like ice crystals. He inhaled the scents of mountains and woodlands, exhaling a fog of steam. A hoot owl called from the woods. Millard cupped his hands together at his mouth and blew out a mimicking call. He waited. A few seconds later the owl answered. Millard stepped up to the back door, pushing it open a crack. "Hey, Tyson. Come out here for a minute."

The boy joined him on the porch, shivering. "What's up?"

"Listen." Millard raised his hands and

wooed the owl again. A hollow answering call came from the darkness. Was it closer this time? He repeated the plaintive sound and waited until they heard the owl's response. "He's moving in," Millard said before blowing another note between his thumbs. The owl answered. "He's in the middle of the pasture now. Probably in that lone maple."

"Do it again."

Millard complied. This time they heard a distinct flapping sound and then saw the massive white wings gilded in moonlight. The owl lit in the spruce tree at the corner of the backyard, bouncing a limb like driftwood riding a wake of water.

"That is so cool," Tyson breathed. "Show me how to do it."

Millard took the boy's hands in his, shaping them into a sort of conch shell. "Make your lips like this," he demonstrated, "and blow from your cheeks." They worked on it for several minutes, but the strange sounds that came from Tyson did nothing for the owl. Disappointed by not finding the mate of its dreams, it soared down toward a fence post and then out of sight. "You can work on it tomorrow," Millard said.

As frigid as it was out there, Tyson seemed in no hurry to go inside. He stood staring into the glittered sky with his arms wrapped around himself, his breath dissipating like smoke in the glow of the porch lamp.

"You got a good lick in today," Millard said. "Two pages of math and the start of a poem. I knew you could do it."

Tyson shot him a sideways glance. "Thanks for the help."

"Anytime." Millard too was under the spell of the starry sky. "I'm proud of you, son." As soon as the words came, he felt an uncomfortable sensation, like pit gravel had just passed through his throat. Had he ever said them to Jefferson? Ever?

Ty looked up at him, seemingly surprised, and a guarded softness fell over the boy's face. It was the look of a battered dog on the verge of taking bread from a kind stranger, his heart pulling him forward, every muscle in his body reining him back.

Millard cleared his throat. "And I want you to know something. Maybe I'm wrong; maybe I'm just a gullible old man, but I don't think so. I can't figure it out, but I don't think it was you who stole from your mother — or the woman in town."

Moonlight glistened from the wetness brimming in the boy's eyes.

"I believe you, Tyson. God help us if I'm wrong."

20

Sidney forced a smile, giving her son a little wave as his head disappeared inside Deputy Estrada's patrol car. Ty had been ready on time that morning, his lunch packed and all set to go. Sidney had ushered him out the door to meet the deputy before the man had any reason to tread again on her front steps.

Just as the deputy reached for his door handle, Micki drove into the driveway. He pressed his body against the side of his car as she pulled around him, parking her boxy Ford SUV to one side. He opened his door and began to slide in.

"Wait!" Micki called as her blond head popped out of her vehicle. "I could really use some muscle before you guys get away!"

Sidney groaned. Oh, Micki. She trudged reluctantly down the steps.

"Hi, Sid!" Micki ran around to open the back of her Expedition while Ty and the deputy came around. "My husband helped me get this in here," she said. "It was a lot heavier than I thought." She turned to face the deputy. "I'm sorry." She held out her hand. "I'm Micki, a friend of Sid's."

He dipped his head as they shook hands. "Alex Estrada." He glanced back at his vehicle briefly, a subtle sigh and squaring of his shoulders indicating to Sidney that he really didn't have time for this. "What have you got here?"

"It was my grandmother's buffet." She tousled Ty's hair. "Sidney's going to help me paint it. You know, with birds and vines and things, although I'm thinking maybe a rooster theme on this one. She's never done roosters, but she's an artist. Have you ever seen any of her work?"

Sidney attempted to give her friend the glare that meant "Shut up," but Micki didn't look at her.

Deputy Estrada glanced at Sidney. "Did *you* paint that furniture in your house?"

"Oh, she did all of that," Micki answered. "I love the way she antiqued it by rubbing black over the red."

"I noticed that," he said without smiling. "Nice job." He pushed up the sleeves of his dove-gray sweatshirt, revealing solid, muscular forearms, then lifted and yanked the buffet toward him, acknowledging Tyson, who stood off to one side. "I'll slide it out. You get the other end."

Sidney could see that it was going to be too heavy for Ty. She stepped forward, reaching for a corner of the heavy piece.

"He doesn't need your help," the deputy barked.

Ty flashed an angry scowl at Estrada as Ty got between his mother and the end of the buffet. She stepped back, watching him hoist it with a strength that must have come from his hatred for the deputy, every visible muscle in her son's neck and even his face rigid. She wanted to step in to help if for no other reason than to defy the deputy, but something held her back.

"Where do you want it?" Estrada asked. He swung the furniture around as if it were made of Styrofoam and began stepping backward.

Sidney had hoped to work on the back porch, but she didn't want them to have to carry it that far. "It's not going to rain. Right here in the front yard is fine." Ty grunted as he lowered his end to the sparse lawn near the front walk.

"Thanks, guys," she said.

"You saved the day," Micki said. She tried to pull Tyson into a hug but he went as rigid as a totem pole. "What's the matter, tough guy? Are you too cool for me now?"

He gave her a patronizing half smile, obviously embarrassed, his eyes darting toward the deputy.

Estrada dipped his head toward Ty. "Okay, let's go." He turned back toward the car and Tyson followed.

"I'll pick him up today," Sidney called after them. "What time?"

"Three o'clock." The deputy gave a slight, almost indiscernible wave, slipped into the car, and pulled out of the drive.

The sight of her son in the patrol car still made her stomach clench.

"Oh, my gosh," Micki breathed as the car rounded the bend. "He is an absolutely beautiful hunk of man!" She idly ran her hand over the smooth top of the buffet. "I saw him in uniform that one day, the day Ty got arrested, but of course I didn't notice then. I was too busy trying to hold you together. I noticed he's not wearing a ring."

"Oh, for Pete's sake! I can't believe you're even going there. He's a jerk, Micki. I don't care what he looks like; it's what's inside that counts. He's a dark and bitter man. Can't you see that? I don't know what his problem is, but it runs deeper than this thing he's got against Tyson. It emanates from him — like when you eat too much raw garlic and everyone around you knows it for days." She shuddered. "I don't want him around here. Ty has to deal with him, and so be it. This process is supposed to be painful. But I don't want the girls exposed to the man's negative aura. I can't wait 'til Ty's community service hours are fulfilled. After today he'll have done twelve out of forty."

Micki shrugged. "Any word from Jack?"

Sidney raised an eyebrow as she pushed herself up on top of the buffet. "He called last night and I invited him over to watch football on Sunday. We talked for a long time and he was so sweet. I feel like he's opening up more, starting to trust me again. Up until now he's been smart, like a big fish that's been caught before and thrown back. A little wary. I could tell he was keeping his options open." She flashed a wry grin. "You'd be shocked by the number of manipulative single mothers out there who would do just about anything to get Jack Mellon walking behind their lawn mowers."

Micki snickered. "But you have a prior claim."

"I have no claim. All I know is he was great with the kids last Saturday. He insisted on taking the girls bowling after his peewee game got washed out, and then he brings them home and plays Sorry! with them while he watches the sports channel. He even got Ty to sit out in the living room with us for a while. He was certainly in no hurry to leave." She raised her eyebrows. "And I got *the look*."

"The look?"

Sidney nodded. "You know what I'm talking about. The way Richard Gere looked at Julia Roberts in *Pretty Woman* when she wore that classic polka dot dress with the white gloves and wide-brimmed hat."

"Oh. What were you wearing?"

"My jeans and a T-shirt. But that's not the point. It's that look of appreciation — and longing. That's it. Lancelot and Guinevere. Did you see the original *Camelot*?"

"Okay, I think I've got the concept. But he hasn't kissed you yet."

"He hasn't so much as held my hand. I've considered sticking a slice of pepperoni on my forehead to speed up the process."

Micki snickered. "Give it time. If it's meant to be, it will happen. Where are the girls?"

"At soccer this morning and then skating over in Dunbar this afternoon. Gena Denton picked them up. It's Kayley's birthday."

Sidney's eyes swept the panorama of blue-green mountains and blazing fall leaves against a clear blue sky. Autumn had always been her favorite time of year. She made a mental note to snap some fresh branches from the red vine maples along the east fence to replace the ones on her dining room table, which had curled into crisp fists on spindly arms. With a deep breath of cool mountain air, a rush of joy tingled through her body. She stood, lifting her face to the sun and twirling. "Woohoo! It's Saturday! No work, no kids, no nasty sheriff. It's just you and me, girlfriend. How about a cup of hot spiced cider?"

They brought a tray of cider and sliced pumpkin bread out to the small porch, setting it on a wooden step a safe distance away from the paint project at hand. Micki brushed the worn and slightly battered oak buffet with a watermelon green base, while Sidney practiced painting colorful roosters onto a piece of board with her acrylic paints.

"My landlord agreed to buy some shrubs for this place as long as I'm willing to plant them. I tried for a real lawn, but he claims that all these patches will eventually fill in." Sidney dabbed rusty red onto her current rooster's flowing tail. "What I really want to do next spring is get some used brick somewhere and make a little patio. Then I'll get some of those sawed-off oak barrels for planters."

Micki stood back from her buffet, paintbrush in hand. "Does this need two coats?"

"No; let it dry. We're going over the whole thing with a glaze after I get the roosters on, remember?"

"Okay. So what are you going to plant in your barrels?"

"Geraniums, sweet alyssum, cherry tomatoes, basil. I like marigolds, but so do the slugs. I swear they even get into my hanging baskets somehow." She pushed the board away to critique her work. "We must have jumping slugs around here." A vision of the slimy creatures springing like jack-in-the-boxes from the damp ground on a moonlit night made her laugh. "If I could catch them, they'd make a great circus act. The Leaping Slugs of Ham Bone and their daring trainer, Ms. Sidney Walker."

Micki guffawed. It was never hard to get Micki chortling right along with her, even when something wasn't all that funny. Sidney held her rooster sampler up for her friend's inspection.

"I love it!" Micki pointed at the one in the middle. "This is my favorite. I like the shading."

"Okay. I'll make that the large one in the center." She wiped her hands on a damp towel and tossed it to Micki. "The cider's cold. You want some anyway?"

They sat on the porch, sipping spiced cider while crumbs of moist pumpkin bread fell between their legs. "You know what else I'd do with my trained slugs? I'd take them over to Deputy Estrada's house, wherever that is, in their fancy custom-made circus slug carrying case and command them to slime his windows."

Micki's giggle burst out in a spray of cider and she began to choke.

"Really," Sidney continued after patting her friend on the back. "Being highly intelligent, above-average slugs, they would write in cursive 'Bad cop' on every windowpane, even the windshield of his car." Now Micki's titters had Sidney chortling, too.

"What is your problem with him?" Micki asked when she could catch her breath. She was still snickering, wiping tears from the corners of her eyes. "You haven't told me one thing that he's done that's outside the line of duty."

Sidney's laughter was subdued as she searched her brain. "I don't know how to explain it. I guess it's not so much what he does as how he makes me feel."

"How does he make you feel?"

"I don't know. Bad. Mad. Sad."

"Do you think he's hurting Ty in some way?"

Sidney pondered. "No, not exactly. He's terse and bossy with him, though. Ty says the deputy hates him."

"Why would an officer of the law hate a fifteen-year-old kid who is basically guilty of shoplifting and pulling a gun that shoots little plastic balls? You would think he's had to deal with worse criminals in his career."

"Well, for one thing, the deputy still seems convinced that it was Ty that broke into Amilia's house and stole her wedding ring — and Amilia is like the guy's adopted mother. She lives right next door to the house where he grew up and she helped his father raise him after his mother died. There seems to be quite the bond between them."

"You told me yourself that you suspect Ty did it now that your own jewelry and cash are missing. So maybe Deputy Estrada isn't out of line."

"Whose side are you on here?" Sidney asked.

"Yours. I'm your therapist and we're not dropping this until we get to the bottom of it. Why does the deputy make you feel bad, mad, and/or sad?"

Sidney sighed, staring off at the mountains without really seeing. "He makes me feel ashamed of who I am." Where did that come from?

"Aha. Now we're getting somewhere."

Why would that be? Sidney was not a bad person. She knew that about herself. She was honest, worked hard, and cared about people. And yet whenever Deputy Estrada was around, she felt like she had to prove something. Maybe it was the condescending way he looked at her that caused her to cling defiantly to her self-respect. "It has to do with Dodge. It's the way I felt the whole time I was with him — in the shadow of his shadiness. You don't know how many times I answered the door to find some police officer or officers there, Dodge usually off who-knew-where, sometimes for days, me standing there barefoot with a baby on my hip in a run-down place with broken vehicles in the yard. I tried to cover for him." The levity was gone. She was tapping into a deep vein of grief and shame. "What an idiot I was. And now, look what I've done. I've raised a son who seems to be sliding right into his father's ways." She shook her head. "I should have moved somewhere that Dodge could never find us. I should have done it before the damage was done."

Micki took Sidney's hand and rubbed it like she was smoothing on hand lotion.

"You're doing fine. Keep it up."

"I also should have kept going to church. For my sake as well as the kids'. Things were different then."

"What was different?"

Sidney sighed. "I started taking the kids to the community church after Dodge left us the first time. I was pregnant with Sissy. Ty was about seven, I think. He and Rebecca loved it, and I was glad they were learning about God. And to me, the wonderful people and the words I heard — it was like finding an oasis with cool, clear water in the midst of the dry, destitute life I'd been exiled to. They gave me hope." She twisted a loose thread hanging from a slit in the knee of her favorite jeans, which fit like an old friend — too many memories to throw away. "If only I had taught Ty that there's hope for this sometimes dark world, that God cares about him even when it seems no one else does." Duke had been loping freely through the tall grass in the field next door. He returned, panting, and dropped his chin on Sidney's knee. She stroked the fur on the top of his skull. "Dodge kept popping in and out of our lives, and in all the turmoil, church attendance got pretty sporadic. By the time I got around to praying with the kids at night,

Ty wouldn't cooperate. He didn't have any faith. My own has dwindled so much. I forget to pray until things get really bad. It's not the way I was raised." She glanced at her friend. "Did I ever tell you that Dad and Mom prayed together every night?"

Micki's eyes softened. "Really? How beautiful. No wonder they stayed in love all those years."

"Sometimes I listened. There was a heat vent in the hallway just outside their bedroom door. I liked to sit on it and let the warm air inflate my nightgown like a balloon. It was my peaceful place. I remember hearing one prayer in particular. It was my senior year in high school and I had just come home from the football game where Spencer Horn asked me out, so I was happy. I wanted to tell Mom all about it, but didn't want to interrupt their conversation." She raised her eyebrows and shot Micki a twisted smile. "It's bad to be rude to God. Anyway, while I was patiently waiting, I heard my dad say, 'Lord, I pray that Sidney will keep her eyes on you and never look away.' "

Sidney stared off toward the blue heavens. "Out of all the prayers I heard over the years, that one just got stuck in my head."

Micki was reverently silent for a moment.

"So what's stopping you from going back to church now?"

There was no point in sidestepping when Micki was zeroing in. "Habit and lack of discipline."

Micki seemed satisfied. "All right. What have we learned from this session?"

Sidney gave her a closed-lip smile. "Get back to church."

"And?"

"Alex Estrada is only a mirror reflecting my own self-deprecation."

"In which case, what will your circus slugs write on his windows?"

"Have a nice day?"

Micki cocked her head and smiled, patting Sidney's knee as she stood and stretched. "Good for you. Our time is up, Ms. Walker. That will be $200."

"And worth every penny of it. Put it on my tab."

Millard Bradbury had come out his door. He waved as he swung the picket gate open and headed for his mailbox.

"Mavis hasn't come by yet, Millard!" Sidney called. She stood and walked up to the edge of the road. "She tends to run late on Saturdays."

"Oh, fine, then," he said. "I'll check the mail when I get back."

"Are you enjoying your day off?"

"Yes, I'm getting some things done around here. I see you have a project of your own." He gestured toward the green buffet, and Micki waved. "I'm going down to Graber's. Do you need anything?"

A car with a rattling muffler approached and sped between them. Sidney waited until it rounded the bend and was swallowed by the trees. "No, but thanks for asking."

He nodded and turned back toward his garage, his long arms dangling at his sides, head down as if to monitor the progress of his feet. She wondered if he had adjusted yet to living alone. When he spoke of his wife, Sidney had the feeling that he still held her close to him, as if she were merely locked in the spare room where he could converse with her only through a bolted door.

"Hey, Millard! Why don't you come over and watch the Seahawks game with us tomorrow afternoon?"

He froze in place. Sidney knew he was processing this new development in his neatly ordered life. It would mean changing his Sunday routine. He turned slowly. "Well, that would be fine. Just fine. We're playing the Dallas Cowboys, you know."

Sidney didn't know and she didn't care.

The important thing was that Jack would be there. "Yes. One o'clock!"

He winked as he turned away.

"The paint's dry," Micki said. "Give me some roosters, girl."

By early afternoon, Micki's grandmother's oak buffet wore a single proud bird on the carved oval medallion on its front. Less is more, Sidney had assured her friend. The rooster's feathers ranged from a rich burnt red to violet to black. A squash vine trailed along the curves of the buffet's carved accents, and even Sidney agreed that the almost finished product was a masterpiece. "The final glaze will give it an antique look," she said as they admired their work from the porch steps. Sidney had brought out egg burritos and the last of the hot cider. She glanced at her watch. "I have to pick up Ty in a little while."

"Let's just put a tarp over this tonight. I'll have Dennis load it up tomorrow and I can finish it at home."

They heard a car laboring its way up the hill. It emerged from the trees, a dated two-door sedan, its hood painted primer gray and the rest a well-oxidized black. The same car that had passed by earlier. Sidney became curious when the vehicle slowed to a crawl in front of the field next door.

Maybe the driver had spotted a deer or some other animal. It pulled onto the shoulder and almost stopped, but then accelerated back onto the road. It turned into her driveway. Sidney's burrito dropped to the ground. "Oh, God. No."

Micki gasped. "Is that Dodge?"

An alarm rang through every nerve in Sidney's body. She didn't get up. She watched her ex-husband get out of the car, stretching his arms and legs as if he had been driving for a long time. He cocked his head, flashing a stage smile her way, that cocky grin his way of saying that she was blessed above all women by his presence today. She reached for Micki's arm.

"Don't worry. I'm not going anywhere," Micki said in a resolute whisper.

Duke lapped up the remains of the fallen burrito and raised his head slightly. He didn't bark; he didn't growl. He and Dodge had met before. Still, the German shepherd eyed the infrequent visitor warily.

"Afternoon, ladies!" Dodge strode toward them. He looked thinner. His black pants were tight, studded with silver on the outside seam from below his knees to where they covered the tops of his black boots. A faded T-shirt had some sort of emblem on it, but was partially covered by the open cotton shirt he wore over it.

Thank God the kids were not home. They had not seen their father for more than a year and they were better off for it. Sidney raised her chin. "What are you doing here?"

"I just finished a gig in Seattle — Jackson Street Tavern in Pioneer Square." He glanced at the house and around the yard. "Where's my little rug rats?"

"You missed them. They're gone for the day." She recoiled inwardly at the sight of a blue demonic claw reaching from beneath the collar of his shirt toward his throat. That was new. She had no desire to see the rest of the tattoo. "Maybe you should call next time."

"Yeah." He stretched his hand toward Duke. "Hey, big guy." Duke sniffed tentatively and lowered to his haunches, still watching Dodge with what Sidney surmised was cautious intuition. "What's his name again?"

"Duke."

"Yeah, I knew that. And yours?" he asked, looking down at Micki. Sidney had made no polite effort to introduce them. Her friend had apparently recognized him from the old family photos on Sidney's wall, despite the fact that her once handsome ex looked so different now. His brown hair had gone long and scraggly; creases had formed around his mouth and chin, and red rims on his lower eyelids made him appear as if he had a bad cold.

"Micki." She crossed her arms, not bothering to fake a smile.

He placed his hands in his back pockets, then glanced with disinterest at their paint project and then up at the evergreen mountains and their snowy peaks, inhaling deeply. "Ah, I miss it up here. Woke up this morning to a blue sky and the next thing you know the old Chevy was headed north." His eyes darted toward his dilapidated car. "Actually, that's not mine. I borrowed it from a friend; I usually drive my '69 Camaro, totally restored. She's a classic. Even old ladies turn their heads when I drive by."

Especially old ladies, Sidney surmised. "Oh, you must be doing well, then." It occurred to her to call the sheriff while Dodge was standing here in her yard. He owed her enough child support that she could own that spiffy car and a few more like it — if it really existed. But it was too complicated. The most urgent thought in her mind at the moment was getting rid of Dodge before he could plunge another dagger into Tyson's vulnerable soul. "You must be leaving town soon. Where's your next gig?" Russia would not be far enough away. She wondered if rockabilly was popular in Moscow.

"Well, actually, the band sort of broke up." He tried to puff his chest but he had lost so much weight it seemed almost concave. The proud feathered cock of the barnyard he was not. "You know how I am. I'm a perfectionist when it comes to music. If you can't do it right, then don't do it at all. I kept trying to get Sammy and Rondo to kick it up a notch, throw their guts into it, you know? But we just couldn't see eye-to-eye. I finally had to fire them all." His eyes narrowed into slits. "Every stinking one of them."

Yeah, right. Sidney knew better than to believe one word he had said. She envisioned two *L*s on his forehead. Loser and Liar. If anyone got kicked out of the band, it was Dodge. He had become a serious druggie; there was no doubt in her mind. His eyes had not yet become as adept at lying as his tongue.

"Actually, the road isn't all it's cracked up to be. The fans, the glory, the miles of highway crammed into a bus with the same five guys." He shook his head. "It gets old. I'm thinking of settling down for a while. Some place quiet and off the beaten path." He crossed his arms over his chest, pulling his T-shirt downward and causing the demonic blue claw to reach from beneath his collar. He grinned down at her. "I guess I'm really a family man at heart."

Sidney's blood froze in her veins.

"I've given it some thought," he said. "I'm moving back to Ham Bone."

21

Sidney's cloudless Saturday had gone awry. She drove to pick up Tyson, Dodge's statement resounding in her mind in a relentless, heart-shattering clanging, like a demonic alarm clock that could not be shut off. *I'm moving back to Ham Bone. Moving back to Ham Bone. Moving back. . . .* "God, no!" she screamed into the interior of her car. Where had her prayers gotten her? Had God even heard? She pounded the steering wheel. "How could you let this happen?"

As she turned the car onto Digby, the engine began to sputter, making an unfamiliar sound. She felt the car lose power, then surge, then cough and limp again. She was already late. Alex Estrada had said to pick up Ty at three and it was twenty-five after. It had taken a while to get rid of Dodge. She did *not* want their father there when the kids got home.

"Come on, car. Please." The deputy would

not be pleased that she had kept him waiting. At least she was within a couple of blocks of Amilia's house. She urged the car onward. Two houses away, the engine spit and then died. The car coasted down the slight incline, and she pulled onto the side of the road in front of the pink house. Alex, Amilia, and an older man in a cowboy hat were sitting on the porch. Tyson, elbows on knees and chin in hands, slouched on the porch steps. She pulled on the brake and got out of the car.

"Sorry I'm late!"

Amilia waved. "I've been waiting for you!" She wore a long, colorful skirt with a loose-fitting gauzy blouse and looked like an old hippie except for the white crew socks and Adidas. "Come on up here and have some tea. I've made tamales for everyone."

The deputy did not seem at all excited about the idea. Sidney avoided his dark eyes as she approached. "Oh, Amilia. Thanks for the offer, but —"

Amilia pushed herself up from her folding lawn chair, gripping the metal bars of her walker for support. "Oh, I don't want to hear it. We hardly had time to visit last time you were here." She glanced at Alex and the other man. "There's something special about this girl and I'm going to find out what it is. Alex, where are your manners? I don't believe these two have been introduced."

"Well, it's not like I've had all day to do it," he retorted. "Sidney Walker, this is my pop, Enrique Estrada."

The old man's face crinkled into a smile. He dropped a knife and the hunk of wood that he had been whittling to his lap and pushed the straw cowboy hat up from his broad brown forehead, revealing a handsome lined face with a slim gray mustache. Except for the warmth in his eyes, he could have been Alex in thirty or forty years. A guitar leaned against the side of his chair. He stretched out a dark, weathered hand. *"Mucho gusto,"* he said. "Happy to meet you."

"El gusto es mio," she replied, pleased to think that she had not sat through two years of Spanish in high school for nothing. So far the only good it had done her was to be able to impress friends when ordering at Mexican restaurants. The only problem with that had been waiters who assumed that she was fluent and began conversing with her so fast that she couldn't keep up.

"Ah, hablas español," he breathed, glancing over at his son as if the fact that she could speak his language should come to

288

him as good news. *"¡Y que bonita!"*

Now she was embarrassed.

"Yes, very pretty," Amilia agreed. "I could use your help, Sidney, if you don't mind." She scooted her walker toward the open door.

Sidney glanced at Ty. His dark, choppy hair hung on his forehead and over his ears. His eyes widened, silently imploring her to get him far away from there, fast. "Ty, I'm going to help Amilia for just a little bit."

His shoulders dropped.

"You can work some more if you want to," the deputy said. "You might as well knock off more of your time." He stood, pushing up his sleeves and turning to Sidney. "I think I'll take a look at your car. By the way it sounded when you pulled up, you might not be going anywhere for a while."

"Oh. Well, if you don't mind . . ."

"Come on, Pop." He reached for his father's arm, helping him to his feet. "Give me a hand."

Ty followed the women into the house, veering off down the hall toward the bathroom. "Something smells wonderful in here," Sidney said.

"That's apple pie. Enrique's apple trees keep me busy this time every year." Amilia leaned on the stove top, turning the oven dial to 350 degrees. "I didn't want to warm the tamales until you got here. They're no good all dried up."

Sidney wondered how long it might take and then realized it didn't matter. Alex was right. If he couldn't get her car running again, she would be stuck — or have to impose on someone for a ride home. "What can I do to help?"

"Get that pitcher of tea from the fridge." Amilia produced a couple of tall glasses. "I've been waiting for this visit all week," she said as Sidney poured. "Female company is rare around here." She pushed her walker out to the living room, backing into her chair.

Ty came down the hallway, sighing as he saw Sidney pass Amilia her tea and sit opposite her. "I guess I'll get some more work done," he said.

Sidney smiled at him. "Good for you."

"We'll call you when the tamales are done," Amilia said. "You like my tamales, don't you, Tyson?"

Ty began to nod, his head freezing in midair. His eyes widened and blinked before locking on Amilia's.

"Come here," she said. He hesitated, then approached cautiously. She reached up to cup his cheek in her hand. "Nobody can resist my tamales," she cooed. "Grown man or boy, the aroma pulls them off the street, out of the woods. It was silly of me to put them out there on the back porch to cool." Her thumb caressed his jaw before she let him go.

He straightened and backed away. Sidney wasn't sure what was happening but the look in her son's eyes told her he wanted to run. He turned but stopped with his back to them before reaching the door. His head dropped. "I took the rope out by the backdoor," he murmured, "plus a tarp and a machete. Also a sharp knife from your kitchen drawer." Sidney watched her son's shoulders rise as if a burden was being lifted from them. He turned, his eyes going from Amilia's to his mother's. "I can get everything back — everything but the tamales. It's all hidden in the woods."

Tears flooded Sidney's eyes. Come on, Ty. Get it all out. She waited, holding her breath. Amilia smiled patiently.

"I don't know who stole your jewelry, but it wasn't me."

Amilia's head dropped momentarily, her chest and gauzy blouse rising as she filled her lungs and lifted her face to Ty's. "All right, then." She sighed. "Perhaps I had two burglars on the same night."

Ty's face went cold again. "I guess you did."

The porch floorboards creaked as he stormed outside.

Sidney was shaken. He should have said he was sorry. She should make him come back and say it, but what good was a forced apology? And as much as she wanted to believe that her son had stolen only those few items, logic told her that he was not coming clean. Was it because he knew that admitting to taking the diamond ring would be the confession of a felony as opposed to petty theft? "Amilia" — her voice faltered — "I'm sorry." The tears came then. She dropped her face in her hands.

She heard the creaking of Amilia's chair and felt the older woman place her hand on her head. "Cry. It's good for you."

"I'm sorry," Sidney sobbed when she could catch a breath. "I'm just having a rotten day." Amilia passed her a tissue and she blew her nose. "He's not really like this." She looked up into Amilia's understanding gaze. "He's a good boy at heart," Sidney said. "But he desperately needs something that I can't seem to give him. Something is just eating away at him; it has been for a long time. Please sit down, Amilia. I'm okay now."

Amilia complied, supporting her weight on a lamp table and dropping back between the arms of her brown overstuffed chair. "Maybe that's why I'm drawn to him so," she said. "He's got that wounded look in his big brown eyes, like Alex did after his mother died. Sometimes I wondered if that boy's heart would ever heal up."

Sidney was not encouraged by her words. From the looks of it, Alex was still brooding after all those years.

"It did, though," Amilia continued. "It just took time and a lot of love."

Sidney leaned forward until she could see out the front window. Alex and his father were draped over the front of her car, peering beneath its hood. A red toolbox rested on the gravel beside them. Ty had just begun pounding nails into what must have been the framework for part of the wheelchair ramp, though it was lying unattached on the lawn. She was surprised by the confidence in her son's movements. He seemed to know exactly what he was doing. Alex glanced over his shoulder at him and then back to his task at hand. Apparently he too believed in Ty's competence. "*Did* his heart heal up, Amilia? I hate to say it, but sometimes he seems so . . ." She grappled for an inoffensive adjective. "So cold. I don't know; maybe it's just me."

"He's afraid of you," Amilia stated with a slightly annoyed tone as if Sidney should have been able to discern that for herself.

Sidney laughed despite the tears still dampening her face. "Afraid of me?"

"Because you're so pretty. It automatically makes you suspect for a thousand crimes."

"I don't get it. What's the story?"

Amilia took a deep breath before looking away. "I'm not supposed to talk about it." She clammed up, but Sidney suspected that Amilia wanted to talk about it in the worst way. "Maybe he'll tell you about it someday."

This made Sidney chortle again. "Fat chance. The only thing Alex and I have in common is that we both like you."

Amilia grinned. "Well, that's a good start. And I like you. I knew it for sure when you tried to stifle that laugh after Alex smashed his thumb."

They both chuckled. "It's not good to delight in another man's adversity." Sidney's eyes fell on the dust bunnies peering from the shadows beneath the TV console by the window. She wondered if it would be rude to offer to help Amilia clean her house. They hadn't known each other that long.

"That old TV doesn't work anymore.

Hasn't in years. I just use the console for holding up my plants." There were a lot of them — African violets, a spider plant, and several small ferns. Amilia tipped her head back for a long swallow of the sweetened iced tea. Layers of beaded necklaces hung over her orange blouse, and dangling turquoise earrings picked up the color from her paisley skirt. "So what made your day so rotten, Sidney Walker?"

Sidney stared at the water droplets on the outside of her tea glass. "My ex-husband showed up. We haven't seen him in a long time." She didn't know how to wrap up the sordid details of their past and offer them in a neat little bundle. She shook her head. "He's bad, Amilia. He's done nothing but lie to Tyson and my girls. He'll charm them all when he visits, make all kinds of promises about the things they're going to do together, and then just disappear. He doesn't call them; he doesn't write." She turned her head away, embarrassed by a new flood of tears. "He's moving back to Ham Bone. All of a sudden he wants to be a family man — or so he says."

"Are you sure he hasn't changed?"

"Oh, he's changed. For the worse." Sidney glanced up at an old framed print on Amilia's bookshelf. Jesus the Good Shepherd.

She averted her eyes. "The thing that breaks my heart is that Tyson is so vulnerable to Dodge. No matter how many times the man has disappointed him, or how angry Ty gets, when his dad comes around again, he eventually lets his guard down. He wants to trust him. Tyson needs a father so bad." She shook her head. "That's what I've been praying for."

Amilia leaned forward. "Well then, things are certainly going to get better."

Sidney tried to laugh. "I don't know, Amilia. I'm not sure of anything anymore. It feels like my life is spinning out of control."

Amilia dropped her glass to the cluttered table beside her with a loud thunk. "Well, there's your problem. You need to decide. Are you going to go by your feelings? If so, then you're absolutely right. Your life *is* spinning out of control."

Sidney stared at her, utterly confused.

"You said you prayed. Are you going to trust God to guide you or not?"

They heard Sidney's car trying to start. The engine fired up for a moment and then stopped. She watched as Enrique stuck his head out the driver's window to say something to his son. Alex answered in Spanish, grabbed another tool from the bumper, and went under the hood again. All she could see of him were his faded blue jeans. Tyson was hard at work on the ramp, working at a speed that belied his supposed intention of just whittling off some of his required time. If Sidney hadn't known better, she'd have sworn her son was enjoying himself.

Lord, I'm sorry I doubted, she prayed silently. Save my son. I don't care how you do it. Just save him from Dodge and heal his heart.

"Well, I'm sure those tamales are done." Amilia pushed herself up just as they heard the engine kick in. It wasn't exactly purring, but it was a definite improvement over the grumbling sounds it had made earlier. *"¡Ya está lista la comida!"* she called from the front door.

While the men washed their greasy hands in the laundry tub on the back porch, Sidney helped Amilia fill a cloth-lined basket with the hot corn-husk bundles. They gathered paper plates and other supplies along with chips and bowls of fresh green chili peppers and salsa, setting them on a small patio table on the front porch.

Sidney wondered if her eyes were still red from crying. It didn't matter. She felt more peaceful now, actually glad that Sissy and Rebecca would not be home until much later so that she and Ty could relax there on Amilia's porch for a while, enjoying this mid-October afternoon with the scents of corn masa and wood smoke wafting through the air.

Sidney scraped the beef from her tamale, which Ty scooped onto his own plate, hopefully before Amilia noticed. She piled chili peppers and homemade salsa on the remains and enjoyed the result thoroughly. Alex conversed off and on with his father in Spanish, while Amilia pumped Sidney with questions about the girls. The older woman spoke of Enrique's grandchildren as if they were her own, and Sidney couldn't help but wonder about this strange relationship between two neighbors, specifically why they had never married. By the sound of it, they were all just one big happy family, with Amilia playing the role of mother to Enrique's four children and even cooking most of his meals.

"Your sister called me today, Alex," Amilia said. "She said to tell you not to forget about Manuel's school play."

"I already forgot," he replied. "When is it?"

Amilia huffed indignantly. "Oh, I don't know. In two weeks, I think. She said she already told you."

"The fall play at the elementary school?" Sidney asked. They nodded. "It's not this Thursday, but the next one. The twenty-seventh. Rebecca and Sissy are in it, too."

"Oh, how nice." Amilia smiled, seemingly pleased that they had yet another thing in common.

"Tyson," Alex said, leaning forward in his chair so that he could make eye contact. "You got a lot done out there today. Have you ever formed up concrete?"

Ty shook his head. "Nope." He was demolishing his third tamale.

"You'll like that part. What we'll do is form a sidewalk between the base of the ramp and Pop's porch. If I can get the rest of the ramp built this week, we can start that next Saturday. We'll pour it in sections." Sidney could see that the worn gravel path that currently existed between the two houses was definitely not wheelchair- or walker-friendly. With all the rain they got around there, the low yard was probably prone to puddling.

Ty reached for a handful of chips. "Don't we have to set the posts in concrete?"

"Yes. But I'll have the framing done, so all we'll have to do is clamp the ramp sections together and dig some holes. Then we'll pour those along with the sidewalk."

Ty nodded as if he understood. "We'd better cut the posts then. I can do it if you want."

Alex nodded. "Sure. That'll be great."

The little exchange may have meant nothing to a stranger passing by, but to Sidney it was significant. Tyson had become interested in this project. Her son, despite himself, was beginning to participate, growing, learning about being a man. Amilia noticed, too. They exchanged subtle smiles.

Alex went into the house, returning with a bottle of *cerveza* for his father and a fresh pitcher of iced tea, which he poured into glasses all around. As he refreshed Ty's empty glass, Sidney saw them speaking but couldn't make out the words. Amilia had been making her laugh, and once she got started, it was hard to throttle the volume back. Ty stood and headed down the steps with Alex.

"Whoa," Amilia said. "Where do you two think you're going?"

"He's going to show me how to fix Mom's car in case it happens again," Ty said.

"Oh, poo! That can wait." Amilia reached for the guitar leaning against Enrique's chair.

Alex shook his head, still avoiding Sidney's eyes. "Not today, 'Milia."

"Yes, today. You promised if I made you tamales —"

Alex looked at Tyson and shrugged. "Women rule the world, you know." He obediently trudged back up the steps. "Pop, where's your violin?"

"It's just inside against the bookcase," Amilia answered. "You've walked by it ten times today."

As the men tuned their instruments, Ty finally pulled up a folding chair, joining them on the porch instead of the steps, where he had sat through most of their meal. Alex began to pick out a song on the strings of his guitar, a melody that immediately caused Sidney to relax into the cushioned back of her chair. Enrique removed his straw cowboy hat momentarily to wipe his brow, revealing a surprisingly thick head of silver-streaked black hair. He replaced the hat and began to slide his bow across and down the strings of the violin, melting into Alex's melancholy tune. Sidney closed her eyes, feeling as if she were slipping down into the healing mineral waters of a hot spring. The sky was fading to violet-gray, and without direct sun the chill fell quickly in the shadow of the mountains. When goose bumps appeared on her arms, she slipped into the house, found a fleece throw and an afghan, and returned to the porch. Amilia's eyes were half-closed, a smile of contentment softening her ruddy face. She squeezed Sidney's hand when she tucked the fleece blanket around her.

Sidney snuggled back into her own chair with the colorful afghan, the music itself a bright and intricate weaving of sounds that enveloped her in comfort. Alex's deep brown eyes narrowed in concentration as he watched his father's hands and vice versa, both of them skilled, their rhythm so tight that Sidney knew intuitively that they had been doing this together for a long time. The next song was a ballad in a minor key. Alex began to sing with a voice so deep and buttery that she had to catch her breath and look away. The song felt hauntingly sad. Enrique's clear tenor harmony blended in with his son's voice on the chorus. Sidney didn't recognize all the Spanish words, but she knew it was a love song. The melody was plaintive, Alex's voice conveying a lonely longing as if the words came from his own heart. Crinkles formed around his closed eyes, his white teeth flashing between full, smooth lips. And then she saw it. She saw what Micki had seen earlier that day when Alex had met her in the driveway. Alex Estrada was an absolutely beautiful specimen of a man.

The bow of the violin sliced through her soul like a sharp blade. It was almost too much to bear.

Oh, where was that love? Where was the passion that could fill her like this, so intensely beautiful that it almost hurt? She tried to think about Jack. She would see him tomorrow. But at the moment all she could envision when she closed her eyes was the mysteriously brooding face of Alex Estrada. Music could do that to people. Any woman would be drawn to him at this moment in this perfect atmosphere, she reminded herself. She knew better than to succumb to fleeting emotions. This attraction was physical just as it had been with Dodge. And the music. Another common thread. Dodge had been incredibly gifted, with a voice and mannerisms that wooed women like smooth, rich chocolate. Unwelcome tears began to gather at the corners of her eyes.

The song ended, leaving Sidney swaying near the edge of an emotional cliff. It was time to go home; she sensed it with a sudden urgency. Reaching for a lunch napkin from the table beside her, she dabbed at her eyes in an attempt to blot up the evidence before anyone could see what a sap she was.

The gentle strumming of Alex's guitar

caused her to cast a covert glance his way. His gaze was locked on her face — the first time their eyes had met all day — and for a long second, neither of them looked away.

22

Millard showed up on Sidney's doorstep at precisely one o'clock. The Seattle Seahawks/Dallas Cowboys game was already tuned in on the television. She hugged Millard, took his jacket, and steered him toward her most comfortable chair, the green wing back. Rebecca and Sissy had already claimed the sofa, saving the middle section for their new hero, Jack, who had not yet arrived.

"Hello, young ladies," he said as he lowered himself into the chair. He sat erect, his hands placed awkwardly on his knees.

"Hi, Mr. Bradbury," they replied politely almost in unison. They quietly stared at him as he glanced around the room, nodding from time to time at nothing in particular. Apparently the girls had never made conversation with the old man before.

Sidney wasn't sure how to put him at ease, but food seemed like a good icebreaker. She brought out a tray of spiraled cream cheese roll-ups. "How about being my first taste-tester, Millard?"

"Oh, glad to." He plucked one from the tray, but an edge unraveled and it fell to the floor. "Oh!"

"My fault, Millard." She bent to snatch it from the carpet. So did Millard. Their heads bonked together and Sidney, losing her balance, landed on her backside. The girls, of course, found this hilarious. Sidney chortled too as she and Millard rubbed their heads. "I'm sorry," she said amid gales of laughter as she picked herself up off the floor. Millard's face went from startled to the slow spread of an unnatural smile. He forced a couple of chuckles, obviously still grasping for the humor in it all.

"I forgot the little plates!" she said in apology as she left the room.

"Where's Jack, Mom?" Sissy asked when she returned.

Sidney presented Millard with a plate and napkin along with a glass of cold cider. She was wondering the same thing, more uncomfortable with every passing moment that she did not see Jack's dark SUV in the drive. It didn't seem like him to miss the opening kickoff of the game. "Well, I don't know. He must have been held up in traffic." There was little traffic to speak of on the highway between Dunbar and Ham Bone on a Sunday afternoon unless somebody's cows got out and were playing chicken with the cars on the road.

"Our friend Jack is supposed to join us today, Millard," she said. "I think you'll like him. He's a big Seahawks fan. Actually, he likes any game that involves a ball or a puck."

"He took us bowling," Sissy said. "My ball went backward," she added with a giggle, "so he made me do push-ups."

"If you get a gutter ball, he makes you kiss his feet." Rebecca seemed fine with that concept. Fortunately, there was still plenty of time to shape her little mind before it sank in too far.

"Oh, well," Millard said in mock alarm, "I don't know that I'd like to go bowling with him." He leaned forward to look down the hallway. "Where's Tyson today?"

"He'll be out in a minute." Sidney hoped, anyway. "He just wanted to finish up a computer game."

The football players on the screen had begun their usual scrambling and tumbling. Sidney had little interest, though it occurred to her that she had better develop some if she ever wanted to have something in common with Jack. Sissy asked which players they were rooting for and Millard pointed out the dark blue Seahawks uniforms. Rebecca shared her mother's lack of passion for the game. She started reading her latest girl sleuth book while craning her neck toward the window every minute or two looking for Jack.

He showed up at the end of the first quarter. Sidney acted nonchalant, accepting his grocery bag full of chips and soda cheerily with no questions. It was something she had learned to do during the Dodge days. No questions, no arguments or lies. Besides, she had no claim on Jack Mellon's life. He and Millard introduced themselves, and the girls eagerly beckoned him to his assigned seat between them on the sofa. He sat down, knocking the girls' heads together as they protested with loud giggles, and then he flashed a wink at Sidney.

Sissy patted Jack's arm. "Can you come to our play? I'm a pumpkin in the pumpkin patch. Becca's just a bus driver. She has to talk and stuff, but the pumpkins dance. You wanna see?"

While Sissy twirled, shooting her arms dynamically back and forth across her chest, Sidney went into the kitchen, pouring Jack's bag of greasy potato chips into a bowl, warily regarding the log of summer sausage in her hand as if it were a grenade that some suspicious stranger said was disarmed and perfectly safe. She sighed in resignation, sliced the log into disks of fatty, hormone-fed beef and chemicals, and arranged them on a plate around a ramekin of mustard.

At the sound of shouts and yelps from the other room, she smiled. A football game on a Sunday afternoon. It brought comforting childhood memories of her dad. This was what life was all about. Family, friends, and fun. But Tyson was still in his room.

She marched down the hall and peeked into his doorway. "Hey, why don't you come out and join us?"

His swivel chair twisted toward her. "I don't really like football, Mom."

"I know. I don't either — yet. But I think I'll learn to like it. I just haven't taken the time."

"Well, I already like this game." The primitive characters on his computer screen were busily building their own civilization, harvesting resources, constructing houses and fortresses with the ultimate goal, it seemed, of going to war.

"Millard has been asking about you. And Jack is here now. He'd really like to get to know you again."

At this he swiveled his chair so that his

back was to her again. "Why? Is he planning on sticking around for a while this time?" There was a bitter edge to his question.

She didn't know how to answer that. "Maybe. I really don't know, Ty. We're good friends. Let's just see where it goes."

"Not interested."

"Tyson Holyfield Walker! Snap out of it! I'm not asking you to do anything weird here. Just come out and be a part of this family." Her anger surprised her. She turned on her heels and started out the door, pausing at the threshold. "For heaven's sake, there's food out there. Come out for that if nothing else."

He did wander out about five minutes later. Jack stood and leaned across the coffee table with an extended hand. "Hey, buddy. How are ya? Man, you've grown!" Ty shook his hand and Jack slapped him lightly on the shoulder. "You look like you could take me now."

Ty glanced fleetingly at Millard as if somehow embarrassed by the comment and scoffed. "Yeah, right."

Rebecca and Sissy had lost interest in the football game, so Ty took the empty spot on the end of the sofa nearest Millard, propping his sock-covered feet on the edge of the hand-painted red coffee table. Sidney was on the other side of Jack, her feet pulled up and her chin resting on her knees. She caught Ty's eye, giving him a subtle Mona Lisa smile. His mouth did that thing that was supposed to be an acknowledging smile but couldn't seem to get the corners of his lips to pull into anything but a straight line. In their own dysfunctional communication style, Sidney knew they had just made amends.

Millard leaned forward, slapping the arm of his chair. "Oh, for crying out loud!"

"Let's get some defense in there!" Jack shouted. A minute later, both men were laughing and hooting as a Seahawks player intercepted a Cowboys pass.

Sidney tried to stay focused. She could learn this game. She knew she could. Normally she would be baking and cooking on a Sunday afternoon, getting healthy foods ready for the week to come. But Jack was beside her, the answer to her prayers, right where she wanted him. What would it be like to have him there every Sunday afternoon? Sissy and Becca adored him; there was no problem there. And Ty — he would come around. She imagined the comfort of coming home to a husband at night. A good man at the head of their dinner table. A man in her bed. It had been so long.

She glanced at his profile. His eyes were so blue, set into a pleasant face with an easy grin. He was not a head-turner, not until you got to know him. But she was not the only woman drawn to him. It was a miracle that he had made it to thirty-two without being snatched up. She liked to think it was because of her. Maybe he compared other women but they just couldn't measure up. Then again, maybe God had put an invisible fence around him to save him for when Sidney came to her senses. He had been meant for her all along.

An unsettling sound permeated her reverie. A noisy car laboring up the hill. Her heart went cold. Dodge? Oh, please, not today. Not any day. She had hoped that his vow to move back to Ham Bone to be a "family man" was as empty of true intention as all his other promises, but there had been something in his tone. She was afraid he meant this one. Well, he was not welcome in this house. She glanced at Jack, wondering if he could take her ex-husband. He was buff, but a bit of a teddy bear. He'd probably invite Dodge in, sit him down, and proceed to update him on all the plays he had missed.

Sidney sighed as the unfamiliar car rattled

by without stopping.

Jack placed his hand on her knee, leaning into her. "I have something to show you at halftime."

She perked up in anticipation. "What is it?"

His eyes were suddenly riveted back on the game. He leaned forward as a blue uniform pushed its way down the field, and then leaned back with a disappointed sigh as the player was crushed and buried beneath an avalanche of bodies. "You'll see," he mumbled as if he had that quickly forgotten about her.

"How much math did you get done yesterday, Tyson?" Millard asked.

Ty shook his head, swallowing a mouthful of cream cheese pinwheel. "Nothing. I had to work all day. I put in almost eight hours." He reached for a handful of carrots. "Got the ramp almost done. We're forming up concrete next week." Sidney noted the pride in his voice.

"I've got some tools if you need them. I poured my walkway years ago and haven't used them since." Millard's brows drew together in thought. "I think I've got an old tool belt out in the garage that you could use, too."

Ty nodded. "Yeah. That would be great. I

won't have to stand around waiting so much if I have my own stuff." He spun a coaster around and around on the top of a pen. Ty's hands were usually busy doing something — anything. "My history assignment is so stupid. I hate history."

Millard scoffed indignantly. "No, you don't. You don't even know what history is."

Ty reached under the coffee table and grabbed his history textbook from the lower tier. He opened it at random and started reading. "On July 12, 1812, General Hull's forces crossed into Canada at Sandwich. The invasion was quickly stopped and American forces were forced to withdraw. By August 16, Hull surrendered Detroit." He snapped the book closed as if confident that he had made his point. "Boring. The only interesting thing is the sandwich."

"That's history as I remember it," Jack added. "Boring with a capital *B*." Sidney elbowed him and he grimaced apologetically.

"Ah, the War of 1812," Millard said. "That was between the United States and Great Britain — ended in a stalemate." He tapped his large foot on the floor. Sidney hadn't realized they made Velcro-closing shoes for adults. "Does anyone here know how Ham

Bone got its name?"

"No," Sidney said. "I've always wondered that."

Jack peeled his eyes away from the game, slathered mustard on a cracker laden with two slices of sausage, and leaned toward the old man.

"Back in 1879 there wasn't much more than trees here. It was just miles and miles of wilderness spreading from Winger Valley up and over these mountains and beyond. A man named Bill Dangle heard there was gold up this way — everyone called him Silver because his hair went pale gray when he was twenty-one. He came upriver by canoe and started sluicing over there on Wolf Creek. He did okay, but it turned out that the trees were his gold mine. He bought land and timber rights and started his own logging business, cutting down native cedars as big around as school buses. I imagine that when they dropped, the ground shook like buses were falling out of the sky." Millard stared off at the crack in the ceiling, bushy brows drawn together in thought, his watery eyes as blue as the sea off a desert island. "Silver built himself a sawmill and then a house. His sawmill provided railroad ties to the rail line, which brought more and more people up this way. Silver Dangle, being the businessman that he was, built the Silver Dangle Hotel and Saloon — you may have heard of that — and then a general store. In the meantime, other houses and businesses were popping up all around him."

Sissy and Rebecca had been lying on their stomachs on the dining room floor and playing a board game. Rebecca rolled onto one elbow, regarding Millard with interest. Duke rested near the sofa, enjoying a back massage from his young master's feet. The second quarter of the Seahawks game had ended but nobody moved.

"Well," Millard went on, "old Silver Dangle had just about everything, but he was lonely. His friends kept telling him he should find himself a wife, but there were no unmarried women to speak of around here at that time." He raised his brows. "No *good* women anyway, if you know what I mean. So he got himself a dog, a big, multicolored mutt that turned out to be useless for hunting and did nothing but sprawl out on the board porch between the store and the saloon all day. He wasn't good company either from what I hear. The only person he'd wag his scraggly tail for was Sara Jenkins, the cook at the saloon who tossed him a bone every now and then."

"Were you there?" Sissy asked.

Ty snickered. "That was back in the old days. He'd have to be about 150 or something."

"No, I wasn't there, but I got all this from a good source."

"Was Silver Dangle still lonely?" Rebecca asked.

Millard nodded his head with a sad frown. "Terribly. You know what he finally did? He sent away for what they called a mail-order bride."

"I know what that is," Rebecca said.

"Yeah," Jack laughed, "a blind date that never ends."

"Exactly. In Silver's case it was the blind date from hell. Actually she came from West Virginia. A little bit of a spinster woman named Victoria, all decked out in ruffles and ribbons and curls. Silver was immediately smitten but Victoria made no attempt to hide her contempt. It seemed that she had assumed a man who owned as much real estate and business holdings as William Dangle would greet her in proper businessman's attire instead of worn canvas pants and a plaid shirt with red suspenders." Millard leaned toward the girls dramatically. "And those were his Sunday best." He shook his head as if the whole thing was a shame, and Sissy mimicked him, the same concerned expression on her face. "I guess Silver hadn't sent a photo with his ad, because Victoria was shocked by his long white hair and mustache. She accused him of lying about his age in the newspaper ad that said he was only thirty-six, which he swore was true. She never did believe him, though. She wouldn't call him Silver like everyone else, either. Mr. Dangle, it was, even after they were married."

"What does this have to do with Ham Bone?" Ty asked with his arms folded warily across his chest.

"Oh. Well, with the population of the village growing the way it was, it came time to set up a post office. But he had to give his little town a name. Dangle seemed right to him, especially since he was the founder. But Victoria was fit to be tied. Dangle, she said, was a silly name with no beauty or sophistication to it at all. Victoria, on the other hand, was regal. She insisted that the town be named after her. The woman went so far as to sneak into Silver's desk one night and scratch the name Dangle from the petition to the postal service and fill in her own. Then she sealed up the envelope."

Rebecca gasped. Sidney and Jack exchanged amused glances.

"But when the permit arrived from the government — it came through a post office in a neighboring town — everyone was shocked to learn that the official name of their new town was Ham Bone. Ham Bone, Washington."

"Why?"

"It seems Silver opened the envelope to the Postal Service just to make sure before he sent it off. Ham Bone was the name of Silver Dangle's mangy old dog."

There were titters of laughter around the room. Ty smirked.

"Apparently the dog was better company than she was," Jack said.

Millard sat back, placing his arms squarely on the arms of his chair. "Now that's history," he said, looking squarely at Ty.

"Do you know any more histories?" Sissy had crawled up to the foot of Millard's chair.

He laughed. "Honey, I'm a walking, talking history book. I've lived through the Great Depression; my father saw three men murdered during the lumber industry strike in the mid-1930s. I can tell you stories about presidents and politics and war. I fought in the Korean War. Have you studied about that?"

"He flew an F-86 Sabre," Ty added. "Tell

about shooting down those MiGs."

Jack pulled Sidney to her feet. "Come outside with me."

Sidney followed him outside, down the front steps to the back of his Suburban. He opened the hatch to reveal an antique oak chest. "A little present for you."

"Oh, Jack. Where did you get it?"

He clicked his tongue. "Off the side of the road with a Free sign on it. It's not perfect, but with a little sanding and some wood glue, I think you could paint it up to look pretty good."

There was no doubt in her mind. And she already knew exactly what she would do with it. "Is that why you were late?"

"Yeah. I couldn't maneuver the thing in there by myself. I had to call Petrie to come help."

A stiff breeze blew from the north, causing the golden arms of Millard's trees across the street to wave triumphantly, strewing leaves into the air. It felt like a celebration, confetti and all. Sidney's hair whipped wildly around her face. She pulled it back so that she could see Jack's grin. This was good. Life was good. She beamed back at him. "You're so sweet."

"Yeah, that's what they say. I'm just a *sweet* guy."

She smirked at his sarcasm. "Okay, how about cool? Rad? What would be appropriate here?"

"Sexy." He posed with an inflated chest and hands on his hips.

She put on a thoughtful expression, chin in hand. "Hmmm." She studied him up and down, acknowledging to herself that the description fit. He wasn't tall, and he had thick, stubby hands, broad shoulders, and a buzzed head that resembled a mailbox, but the whole package somehow worked together quite well. "Well, okay. I can see where you might get that."

He winked, brushing a wild strand of hair from her forehead. "Come on. Let's get back in there before the third-quarter kick-off."

Micki's SUV pulled into the gravel drive, Dennis at the wheel. They jumped out along with their son, Andy. "Hey, we came to get our beautifully painted buffet!" Micki said. "Dennis always falls asleep after the game, so we decided to get it at halftime."

Dennis scowled. "*You* decided to get it at halftime." He put on a friendly face, reintroducing himself to Jack. They had met only briefly when Jack and Sidney dated before.

Jack shook his hand. "Hey, let's make a deal. I'll help you get yours loaded and you help me unload mine."

They agreed, starting with the chest in Jack's vehicle. "Do those duffel bags go in, too?" Dennis asked as they slid the furniture toward them.

"Oh, that's my laundry."

Sidney peered in. Both canvas bags were stuffed to overflowing. She wondered how long it took for one man to dirty that many clothes. "Jack, do you need help with your laundry?"

He raised his brows. "Are you offering?"

"Well, yes. I didn't realize you don't have laundry facilities in your apartment. I don't mind at all." Her subconscious feelings didn't form words in her mind. There was just something about having his socks and underwear churning in her machine that seemed right. She couldn't get it all done today, of course. He would have to come back for it. "Why don't you put the chest on the back porch so that I can paint it even if it rains? You can toss the laundry bags just inside the door."

The men disappeared around the corner of the house with their burden. Micki leaned against the vehicle, arms locked across her chest, scrutinizing Sidney as she pushed the back hatch closed.

"Why are you looking at me like that?"

Micki shook her head. "What are you do-ing, Sid?"

"What do you mean?"

"Offering to do his laundry."

"Is that a bad thing?"

"I don't know. It seems a little early for all that. You're barely even dating the guy. I suppose you're going to string it all out on the clothesline so that Jack can enjoy the fresh scent of mountain breezes on his skiv-vies."

Sidney was perplexed by her friend's disapproval. "I might if it wasn't so darn windy and cold. I could get whipped to death by a gang of frozen T-shirts." Sidney thought that was funny but Micki, for once, didn't even smile.

"Something just feels wrong here. You already do laundry for four. There's only one of him and he has a lot more time on his hands than you do." She sighed. "I think you're trying too hard. Trying to please."

"Last time I checked, being nice was an attribute, not a crime."

Micki grabbed Sidney by the sleeve, pull-ing her toward the front of the car. She took Sidney's head in her hands, forcing Sidney to look into the side-view mirror. "Take a good look, girlfriend. What do you see?"

"Ooh. Fine lines around my eyes."

"Okay, so back up a couple of inches." Sidney complied. "That's Sidney Walker. Beautiful, intelligent, kind Sidney Walker. She is not desperate. She does not need to take in a man's laundry or eat ground round to win his approval."

Sidney stared into her own green eyes. She knew what Micki said about her was true. She was pretty enough, not a genius but well read, and able to carry on a keen conversation. Micki was just being analytical again. Overly analytical. Sidney knew she was not desperate and she didn't need to be told as much. Nor would she ever take up eating hamburger.

She blinked. *Trying too hard. Desperate.* It was unusual for Micki to be so wrong.

23

The auditorium of Ham Bone Elementary buzzed with the sounds of voices, chairs scraping the worn hardwood floors, and Mrs. Beatty warming up on the piano to the right of the stage. Rebecca and Sissy were backstage donning their costumes for the fall play. Sidney spotted two empty seats in the middle section. "Excuse me." She sidestepped past four sets of knees, threw her coat over the back of one of the folding metal chairs, and sat in the other. Jack would be late. He had just gotten off work and still had to make the long drive from Dunbar.

She glanced around looking for Micki and Dennis, finally spotting them in the first row. Micki turned, making eye contact with her and raising her hands in a helpless shrug. She had clearly tried to save Sidney some seats but failed miserably. Sidney gave her an understanding shake of the head.

Parents of children in plays could be vicious when it came to securing front-row seats. She pulled her camera from her pocket and held it up until Micki understood, gesturing for Sidney to bring it up to her. Sidney inched past the two couples beside her toward the aisle. "Sorry."

Up front, Dennis grabbed the cheap little camera from her hand. "I'll do it. She's taking video."

"Put it on telephoto," Sidney advised. "I want to see every dimple and the sparkle in their eyes. Sissy's a pumpkin and Becca is the bus driver." She already knew that Dennis and Micki's son was one of the dancing scarecrows. "I want shots of Andy, too."

She headed back for her seat, surprised to see Alex Estrada enter the back of the auditorium in his stiff khaki and green uniform. What surprised her even more was the surge of adrenaline that this sighting triggered in her body.

His presence there confused her until she remembered Amilia reminding him on the porch that day that his nephew had invited him to the play. They walked toward each other, meeting awkwardly midway down the aisle.

"Hi, Alex." She smiled casually. On one

hand, he was her son's arresting officer, breathing down Ty's neck and watching almost expectantly for him to make another mistake; on the other, they had spent a sunny autumn afternoon together on Amilia's porch. She had heard him sing.

"Sidney." He nodded. His proud, broad-chested posture and serious, piercing eyes gave him the look of an eagle. She had the sensation of his acute vision boring into her until she was as vulnerable as a mouse in an open field — but to what, she didn't know. He paused for an uncomfortable moment. "Where's Tyson tonight?"

Didn't the man ever take a night off? "He's with Millard — Mr. Bradbury. Doing homework, I think."

"Good."

Another awkward pause. Sidney took a breath. "Well, enjoy the play."

He nodded. "You too."

She returned to her seat just as the piano began to play loudly and a gentleman walked onto the stage. He introduced himself and said something about the play, but she couldn't really hear. Her heart was throbbing in her ears. In her peripheral vision she saw Alex slip into an aisle seat two rows ahead on the opposite side of the aisle. Why did that man do this to her? Was she afraid of him? No. Why should she be? He certainly couldn't do anything to Ty that he hadn't already done. Not if Tyson kept his nose clean, as her father used to say. But there was still the issue of the missing jewelry. Amilia's and her own. Sidney certainly wouldn't press charges against her own son, and she couldn't imagine Amilia doing so. After all, Tyson reminded her of her darling Alex when he was just a boy. "Maybe that's why I'm drawn to him so," she had said about Ty. "He's got that wounded look in his big brown eyes, like Alex did after his mother died. Sometimes I wondered if that boy's heart would ever heal up."

If Alex's heart was still broken over his mother's death, Sidney was sorry. She really was. But it seemed that by the time a man had reached thirty or forty he might have gotten over it. Sidney's father had died only a few years ago, but despite the waves of grief that still rose up from time to time, she didn't keep all her smiles packed away in mothballs.

The faded curtains parted in jerks, revealing a brightly painted backdrop of a farm scene with a red barn and receding rows of pumpkins narrowing to a **V** in the background. "The Pumpkin Patch" was painted in bold letters above the barn door. Stage left, two large crows sat atop a rail fence, dangling orange legs and three-toed crow's-feet.

"Maybe they're not comin' today," one crow said. Judging by his size and voice, he must have been a fifth-grader.

"Don't get your tail feathers in a knot, Melvin," the other crow answered. "They'll be here. They've got to get their pumpkins, don't they?"

"Are you sure about the sack lunches?"

"They bring them every year."

Sidney finally let her eyes wander to where Alex sat across the aisle. An attractive woman sat beside him, also Mexican, it appeared. His head began to turn toward the aisle and Sidney swiftly averted her eyes straight ahead.

"Hope someone's got tuna," Melvin said.

"I'm a bologna guy myself."

"Brownies are good, but you gotta have milk." The crow shook his head. "I hate those boxes with the straws. A guy can hardly get his beak into them."

There were titters of laughter from the audience.

"I once knew a guy who could open Tupperware with one wing tied behind his back."

More chuckles. Sidney snuck a look at Alex. He wasn't laughing. Suddenly he glanced over his shoulder and their eyes met. Both sets of eyeballs jerked away. Her face went hot. Oh, how junior high was that? Her heart was racing again. What had made him crane his neck to look at her? She determined to focus on the crows and avoid making the same mistake again. The big black birds got another laugh, but she missed the cause of it. Who was that woman? Alex's sister?

She looked at the empty seat beside her and then her watch. Shouldn't Jack be here by now? This silly fascination with the deputy sheriff made no sense at all, especially when she had the chance to have a meaningful relationship with Jack, who was not only positive and pleasant but the mentor she had asked God to provide for her kids. Alex Estrada, on the other hand, could hardly be called engaging. She had never heard him carry on a decent conversation with anyone — not in English, anyway. He and his dad had a somewhat enthusiastic exchange that Saturday they all sat together on Amilia's porch; she was pretty sure it had something to with deer hunting from the bits and pieces she could understand. But he had hardly acknowledged her, and from what she observed, his dialogue with Ty had been clipped and limited to the construction project, their only common bond. She was pleased that her son was showing more respect for the sheriff, though that probably had more to do with Ty's new-found pride in doing a man's work than any personal connection.

Bottom line: Alex Estrada was neither a decent companion nor a family man. She demanded that her mind accept this ridiculous attraction for what it was: naturally occurring sensual magnetism based on physical appearance and a certain aura of mystery. Nothing more.

Pumpkins poured onto the stage from both sides. Sissy took her place in the front row. Her pudgy legs were a little shorter than most of the second-graders. The kids wore stuffed orange flannel sacks with holes for their green leotarded arms and legs. Their heads emerged through drawstring necklines and were topped with pumpkin-stem hats. The costumes were so easy to make that Sidney had volunteered to stitch up a half dozen of them. Sissy grinned out at the audience as comfortable, it seemed, as if she were in her own living room. Sidney leaned to the left, hoping to catch her daughter's eye.

The piano began to plink out the tune Sissy had hummed for three weeks straight and the pumpkins began to dance. Sissy had many attributes, but so far grace was not among them. Her legs couldn't quite keep up with the choreographed steps; her arms shot out in jerky motions while others, but not all, swept theirs across their bodies in long, fluid strokes. What she had going for her, Sidney thought, was that she was the cutest, most enthusiastic pumpkin in the patch.

The people to Sidney's left adjusted their legs and pulled in purses as Jack made his way down the row. Sidney grinned up at him, whisking her coat from the back of his chair. "Sorry," he whispered as he sat. "Traffic."

"Sissy's up there now," she whispered back.

"Pick me!" a pumpkin shouted. "Pick me! Pick me!" others cried, jumping like popcorn from their squatting positions on the stage floor.

Jack chortled, reaching over to take Sidney's hand. His touch filled her with an instant sense of tranquillity. She threw her head back and laughed along with the crowd.

Sissy waved good-bye to no one in particular when the pumpkins exited the stage. She probably had not been able to pick out her mother's face in the crowd. Now a school bus entered stage right. It appeared to be made of huge panels of cardboard, and instead of wheels it had legs, lots of them, giving it the appearance of a monstrous yellow centipede. In each window was the face of a child. Rebecca was the driver, staring straight ahead, her dark blond hair stuffed inside a billed cap. She took her role very seriously. Sidney was sure that if there were a rearview mirror, her daughter would have been checking it. She'd probably go to Hollywood someday.

Suddenly one set of legs stopped as a girl mid-bus waved at someone in the front row. Bodies compressed like an accordion. One boy fell to the floor and was immediately stepped on. The audience gasped. The back end of the school bus, apparently held up by handles mounted on the inside, dropped to the floor. The little boy on the stage curled up, holding his stomach and moaning.

Several adults leapt up the side steps as the boy cried out in pain. Including Alex. He pushed his way to the boy's side, his hands running over the child's stomach and ribs. In all the commotion no one in the crowd could hear what he said to the boy as he scooped him into his arms. People parted as they left the stage. Sidney supposed that if there was not a doctor in the house, a sheriff was the next best thing. Certainly he must have some kind of training for medical emergencies.

After the bus was righted and the play resumed, Sidney was surprised to see Alex return to his seat along with the dark-haired woman who had been at his side. The boy was still in his arms. The woman opened her arms, but the child shook his head, snuggling closer to Alex and resting against Alex's broad chest. It must be his nephew, Sidney thought. Surely, Amilia would have mentioned if Alex had any children of his own. Alex rested his chin in the boy's tousled hair, tenderly stroking his back. They looked so much alike. Could the woman beside him be Alex's ex-wife?

"She's good," Jack whispered in her ear.

It was then that Sidney realized Rebecca was almost through her lines. Perhaps after hearing her daughter practice so often, she had learned to tune the girl out.

"And don't forget your sack lunches," Becca the bus driver announced. She drove the bus offstage with the help of one set of legs at the rear, leaving a crowd of kids behind. As the children sat on the hardwood stage and had an imaginary picnic, the two crows reappeared on the rail fence.

"What a smorgasbord!" Melvin said. "I don't know where to start."

"I'm going for the Twinkie," the other crow answered.

Melvin shook his head, crossing his black wings across his chest. "Oh, I don't think you should. Dessert is supposed to be last." Black-gloved fingers resembling the feathers dripping from his wing tapped an orange beak that was somehow strapped over the boy's nose. "I think I see a couple of tunas, but do I want whole wheat or rye?"

When the crows swooped down, children screamed, including some in the audience. There was havoc on the stage until a band of scarecrows came to the rescue. They waved their hay-stuffed arms in unison, chasing Melvin and his partner in crime in a circle around the picnicking children. The spectators guffawed and giggled; Jack whistled. A peal of laughter rang out from Sidney at the scarecrows' hilarious antics. She rocked forward, holding her side, tears squeezing from the corners of her eyes.

And then she looked at Alex. He too was laughing. The boy had twisted around in his lap to see the play but had not yet found the humor in it. Alex said something in his ear and tickled him until the little guy was writhing with giggles. The scene took her breath away. Was this the same austere deputy sheriff that had repelled her so? Alex's beaming face was like the sun coming up over the mountains, his teeth as white as porcelain, shockingly so against his brown skin. She had known the man was physically attractive; that would be hard for anyone to miss. But this — this was almost too much to bear.

"What's wrong?" Jack said in her ear.

She jerked her head away from Alex to the man on her other side. "Nothing!" It came out a little too adamant, a lot too guilty. She hadn't realized that her laughter had frozen in her throat. "I saw my boss." That was not a lie. Leon Schuman was in there somewhere; she hadn't noticed where he sat. "Reminded me of some things I've got to do at work."

Jack squeezed her hand. "No thinking about work tonight."

She smiled. "Good idea."

For the remainder of the performance, Sidney silently counseled herself back to her senses. She pretended her mind was an Etch A Sketch and shook it until there was a blank screen to work from. Alex Estrada had nothing to do with her goal; he was merely a distraction, one that she would not allow. She knew that Jack was right for her and, more important, right for her children, and nothing else mattered. So she etched the pictures in her mind that had been there before the dials went crazy superimposing wild, confusing images over her dream. Jack was the dream. A happy, healthy family complete with a dad.

After the play, Jack walked her to her car, which was parked against the south side of the school. The girls were already inside, buckled up and waiting, when he pulled her back around the corner of the old brick building. "I have to ask you something," he said.

The light in the eaves cast deep shadows on his face. She touched his arm. "Ask me anything."

"Is it different this time?"

"What do you mean?"

He shrugged and looked away, stuffing his hands into the back pockets of his pants. "Am I just an old friend, someone kind of fun to hang around, or what?"

She felt a smile warm her heart. "It's the 'or what.' You *are* a fun guy, but to me you're more than that. Much more."

He still looked unsure, but it was awkward. She didn't know how much of her guts to spill. Pride warned her to definitely stop short of grabbing his ankle and pleading for an engagement ring.

"Because I can't handle that 'just friends' line again," he said. "Not down the road, anyway. If that's what we are, I think I'd like to know right now."

She moved closer, letting her slender fingers intertwine with Jack's thick, stubby ones. "I want more than that."

His forehead dropped against hers. They were almost the same height. A perfect fit. He sighed. "Did I change somehow? Why was I all wrong for you before?"

"It wasn't you. It was me. I'm sorry it took so long for me to come to my senses."

He chuckled. "Touchdown." He lifted her chin and kissed her.

24

For once, Tyson didn't complain about going to work at Amilia's. In fact, he seemed anxious to get there, loading the tools that Millard had given him into the backseat of the car before Sidney and the girls had finished their breakfast. The trunk was already full and Tyson *had* grumbled about that as he and Sidney wrestled a freshly painted dresser into it the night before. "Come on!" he said impatiently from the open front door. "Estrada is a pain in the butt if I'm late."

Sidney held a piece of toast between her teeth as she grabbed her coat and bag, locked the front door, and rushed out to the car. The sky was a rumpled gray fleece blanket spreading as far as she could see. Ty sat in the front seat, Rebecca and Sissy in the back. Sidney backed out of the drive. "What's this for?" Sissy asked, leaning forward and waving a handled metal blade dangerously close to her brother's cheek.

"Give me that." He snatched it from her. "Are you trying to cut my ear off or something?" He ran his hand over the flat surface. "It's a trowel. You use it for finishing concrete." He made a few smooth swipes in the air as if practicing the movements that he had learned the previous week when he and Alex poured their first two sections of sidewalk.

While the kids bickered lightly over tools and the imaginary line dividing Sissy's side of the backseat from Rebecca's, Sidney's mind left the interior of the car and wandered back once again to the shadows of the old brick school building where Jack had kissed her on Thursday night. The thing she had been praying for had finally happened. He had called her twice the next day and planned to come over for dinner that night. She had no idea what to serve. He would want some kind of meat, of course. Chicken? But she didn't want the kids to develop an appetite for that kind of protein. Should she make two separate meals?

"Mom, you forgot to turn!" Rebecca whined.

Sidney's eyes darted to her mirrors before she pulled a U-turn. She had been heading straight for Amilia's, forgetting all about dropping the girls off at the park field for their soccer match. They met Dennis in the parking lot where he and Andy were unloading jackets and a cooler from the back of their Expedition. The girls piled out, calling, "Bye, Mom! Love you!" as they ran toward their friends on the field.

Dennis slapped the lid of her car's gaping trunk, which was tied down with bungee cords, and leaned into her open window. "Hey, Ty. Ever think of going into the furniture-moving business?"

Ty scoffed. "Yeah, I could make a living just off my mom — if she'd pay me."

"I pay in muffins and kisses." She reached out to tousle his hair, but he tipped his head away.

"I'll be back to watch the game after a while, Dennis. Can you keep an eye on the girls?"

He tossed a bag over his shoulder. "You bet. See ya." He threw an arm over his son's shoulder and walked away.

She drove back onto Center Street, passing Red's Barber Shop, the post office, Leon Schuman Insurance. She glanced toward her office on her right, relieved that Mr. Schuman had no jurisdiction over her on Saturdays. Tyson's head was turned that way too. Was he remembering the day of his arrest, when Alex Estrada tackled him, pushing his face into the gravel of the parking lot? Her son's eyes had burned with anger or terror, maybe both, like a captured wild animal being forced inside the bars of a cage.

"How are you and the deputy getting along now?"

Tyson shrugged. "I can handle him."

She waited as she often did, hoping that was just the opening sentence of a paragraph.

"What does that mean?" she finally asked.

"Nothing. This job will probably be done by next week. I can put up with him until then. He said after this I can finish up my community-service hours somewhere else. Like a church or an old-age place or something."

"Oh, I didn't know that. Maybe we should talk to the pastor at the community church where we used to go. He might have something you could help with."

He shrugged again. "Estrada said just going to church counts. Pretty weird, huh?"

"He said that? Yes, that surprises me." It made sense, though. The Winger County juvenile legal system was geared more toward rehabilitation than punishment, it seemed. "Actually, I've been thinking we all should start going to church again. I miss it."

Ty didn't respond. She drove down Digby and backed into Amilia's driveway. There was no one in sight. Ty jumped out, opening the back door to get his bucket of tools. "Hey, don't forget we need to unload this chest," Sidney said.

He heaved a sigh. "Is this the last time we're going to move this thing?"

"Well, that depends. Amilia might hate it, you know. Not everyone likes red furniture. Just help me get it out of the trunk for starters."

They began to pull. The short dresser didn't budge. One of the curved legs kept getting caught on the side of the trunk opening. "Try wiggling it." Ty wrestled it from side to side, grunting and butting his shoulder beneath it for support. The tendons in his neck became visible and his face turned red. Sidney pushed in, trying to take some of the weight off, accidentally bumping his trembling arm.

Suddenly he swore, a barrage of explosive words hitting her in the chest like buckshot. She recoiled in shock. "Damn it, Mom! Just get out of the way!"

"Ty! I was only trying to help you."

"Well, don't! You're just making things worse!"

A big hand reached between them, grabbing Ty by the shoulder and spinning him around. "Don't you ever talk to your mother like that." Alex Estrada's voice was restrained, but the words rolled from his mouth like boulders. "Ever."

Ty tried to jerk his shoulder free of the deputy's grip to no avail. "This is none of your business! I didn't do anything against the law, in case you're thinking about arresting me."

"This isn't about the law. It's about respect. A man who doesn't respect his own mother is no man at all."

Ty rolled his eyes and looked away.

"What if those were the last words you ever got to say to her?" Something in Alex's hushed voice made Sidney quiver and drew Ty's eyes back to the deputy's sober face. "Let me tell you. You'd regret it the rest of your life."

At that Alex began to turn away, then seemed to remember the thing that had kindled the blaze he'd just stomped out. He studied the position of the chest, then hoisted it up and to one side, freeing one leg and then the other. "Okay, Tyson. Let's get this thing out of here."

Tyson didn't speak. He took one side and together they slid the chest up and out, placing its legs on the cracked concrete driveway. Alex's eyes met Sidney's as he let out a low whistle. "You've done it again."

"What have I done?"

He nodded toward the piece of furniture. "This." He shook his head. "I don't know why you're selling insurance when you have this kind of talent."

Sidney's laugh was subdued. She was still in awe of the way Alex had come to her defense. Tyson's eyes fluttered sheepishly toward her in what she interpreted as remorse for the horrible things he said. Cursing had always been taboo in her house — at least since Dodge left. She still felt chilled, not just by her son's words and blatant disrespect but by that brief glimpse of the anger that still resided just beneath his skin. Ty picked up his bucket of tools, head down, and started toward the sidewalk project.

"I'd love to do it full-time," she said, noting Alex's steadfast gaze on her face. "I daydream about being my own boss, having my own little store." She smiled softly, still feeling sad. "I've even picked out my shop. It's that little space between Art's Hardware and Red's Barber Shop where the frame shop is now. I hear they're going out of business."

"So, are you going to do it?"

She laughed, pulling the empty pockets of her jacket inside out. "I have zip in savings, three kids to feed, and a car that surprises me every time it starts." She paused, giving him a quirky smile. "I could go on."

Alex ran a hand through his thick dark hair, his other hand fondling the carved detail on the antiqued dresser. He hadn't shaved that morning. "Well, shop or no shop, I'd really like to buy this from you."

She tipped her head, smiling softly. "Thanks. I appreciate the gesture, but this is a gift for Amilia." He made no attempt to leave, but stood there running his hand over the intricately painted design. "I don't have any more pieces to paint right now, but when I find something —"

"What do you have there?" Amilia called from the porch, leaning on her walker. Today she was dressed like a hunter: red and black wool jacket, jeans stuffed into laced boots.

"Oh, Amilia!" Sidney waved. She turned back to Alex. "I don't know if she's going to want this. It was just a whim I had."

"Trust me," he said as he jockeyed the chest into his long arms and hoisted it against himself. "She'll love it."

Tyson was inspecting the braced boards that Alex had apparently installed during the week to form the sidewalk. The boy began to straighten as if anticipating being called into slavery again, but Alex didn't so much as glance his way.

Alex's jaws flinched slightly as he bore his burden up one step at a time. He dropped the red chest under the covered porch while Amilia raved excitedly. Once she calmed down, she ran her fingers reverently over the birds in the painted design. "Lovebirds. Just like Kate and Spencer. Did you take a picture of my birds?"

Sidney grinned. "Nope. I just memorized them. I always study birds. They're my favorite thing to paint."

Amilia hugged her. "I can't believe you did this for me."

"Well, I was looking at your old TV console last time I was here and thought if it wasn't good for anything but holding up your plants, you might like something a little cheerier."

"Just leave it here for now, Alex. I have a mess to clean up in there." Amilia took Sidney's arm. "Come on inside, honey. It's cold out here."

"Oh, Amilia, I can't stay. I need to go

watch my girls play soccer today."

"Just one cup of tea?"

Alex backed away before turning and stepping down from the porch. "Thanks, Alex!" Sidney called after him. He had helped her with more than one burden in the past five minutes.

He threw up one hand. "No problem." He joined Ty and began explaining the sequence of events for their sidewalk project.

Once inside with a cup of tea in her hand, Sidney stood at the living room window and watched the man and boy at work. Tyson had to look up at Alex, who stood a head and a half taller and whose shoulders were twice as wide as her son's. Despite their earlier conflict, they were working side by side, dumping concrete mix into a wheelbarrow and chopping water from the hose into it to make a lumpy gray batter. Someone driving by might mistake them for father and son.

Enrique ambled across his lawn toward them, the brim of his straw cowboy hat shading his eyes. "Here comes the superintendent," Sidney commented to Amilia.

"Enrique?"

Sidney nodded.

Amilia clicked her tongue from where she

sat in her big chair. "Men! He didn't feel good this morning. Never even touched the chorizo and eggs I sent over, but now here he is out in the cold."

Sidney giggled. "All you've got to do is pop the hood of a car or mix up a batch of concrete. Men appear like ants. I guess somebody's got to stand there with their hands in their pockets and give advice."

Amilia chuckled. "Is he wearing a jacket?"

Sidney shook her head. "Cotton shirt rolled up at the cuffs." Enrique must have said something funny. The men laughed, even Ty. Alex gave Ty's arm a playful slap with the back of his hand. Ty said something back to him and they grinned again. She had loathed Deputy Estrada in his stiff khaki and green uniform, the man who searched her home, questioned her integrity, and treated her son with such disdain. But this smiling man in faded jeans with concrete spatters dappling his heavy sweatshirt — he was different. "I saw Alex at the school play the other night," she said casually.

"Oh, yes. He went to see our little Manuel. Poor little guy got run over by a bus, from what I hear."

"Yes. Is he okay?"

"Oh, sure. He's tough. His mother took it worse than he did. Got all worried that his psyche was bruised from becoming a spectacle in front of everybody. Alex calmed her down, though."

Sidney didn't know quite how to ask this, but for some reason she had to know. "So . . . is Manuel Alex's son?"

"Oh, heavens, no. Nephew. His sister Carmen's boy. Her husband, Paul, is a merchant marine. He's gone for months at a time so Alex fills in for him sometimes."

A wave of relief washed through Sidney at that news.

"I hear you were there with a man."

Sidney almost choked on her tea. She walked over to the sofa facing Amilia and sat, though she had promised herself she would not linger. "Did Alex tell you that?"

Amilia shrugged innocently. "It came up in conversation. Would you like to tell me about him?"

Sidney was usually comfortable with Amilia, but for some reason this felt awkward. "Well, his name is Jack. We dated a couple of years ago and we're seeing each other again."

"Is he the answer to your prayer?"

"Well . . . yes. I mean, I think so. My kids need a man like him. He's great with them. Always playful, upbeat. He's like a kid himself, really. Always has to be going somewhere, doing something. Especially sports. He loves any kind of sport."

"Is he good to you?"

"Oh, sure. He's a nice guy. Nice to everyone."

Amilia rocked gently in her chair without speaking.

Sidney's eyes wandered to the useless TV console beneath the window. Curled brown fern leaves were scattered around plant pots and some had fallen to the floor, commingling with dust bunnies. She would have liked to help clean the area before moving the new chest in, but the men were too busy to move furniture right now. Besides, she had to go.

"Are you in love with him?"

Sidney's head jerked back to Amilia. This series of blunt questions had her rocking like a weighted punching bag. How dare Amilia ask such a question? They had known each other for only a few weeks. Her cheeks were suddenly warm. "I think . . ." She looked at a spot above Amilia's head. "I think it's too soon to know." Why did she say that? She was only waiting for Jack to pop the big question. The sooner he was a steady fixture in her home, the better — ideally before Dodge moved back to town. Although she was seriously doubting that her ex-husband would really follow through with what may have been one of his fleeting whims.

"Good answer," Amilia said. "Be careful about trusting yourself. Sometimes we ask God for something and immediately get busy trying to answer our own prayer. If you feel yourself sinking, chances are you've taken your eyes off the Lord."

Tears came to Sidney's eyes. She tried to blink them away, staring at the last inch of tea in her cup. She had been treading water for days, fighting to stay afloat, all the while telling herself that she was walking on water. Her faith had not been in Jesus. It was all riding on Jack. And then he had kissed her. She had lain awake thinking about that moment for the past two nights.

She hadn't felt a thing. It was like ordering pasta primavera and being served a greasy burger on a bleached white bun.

She lifted her head. "Amilia, I don't know what I'm doing."

The wise woman in hunter garb smiled softly. "Practice. Listen and obey. You'll see. And every time you see how your prayer is answered, your faith will grow stronger."

Sidney smiled, remembering the faith of her mother. "I think I need to spend a lot more time with you, Amilia." She stood, gathering their teacups. "But right now I'd better get to the soccer game in progress."

As Sidney returned from the kitchen, she heard a loud shout from outside. It was an alarming cry, spraying adrenaline through her veins like fireworks. Amilia frantically pushed herself up as Sidney rushed to the front door, throwing it open. Outside, Enrique lay on the cold grass, his hat lying upside down on a nearby shrub. Tyson scrambled up the porch steps, breathless. "Call 911!"

Sidney spun around, but Amilia was already punching the number into her phone.

"What happened?" Amilia's hands were shaking and she missed the numbers the first time.

"Enrique had a heart attack or something. He just doubled over. He's grabbing his chest."

Sidney looked around helplessly. Alex was at his father's side. She grabbed a blanket from the back of the sofa and ran down to the yard, but Alex was already scooping his father into his arms. "Hang on, Pop. Let's get you in where it's warm." Sidney walked alongside, draping the blanket over Enrique and tucking it between him and Alex's chest. "Can you find an aspirin?" Alex asked.

She ran to Amilia's medicine cabinet, scanned until she found a small bottle of Bayer, then rushed to the kitchen for water. She returned to where Alex had laid his father on the sofa, passing him a single pill. Amilia hovered over them, leaning heavily on her walker. Her knuckles were white. Sidney caught Tyson's eye and gestured toward an armless chair against the wall. He brought it quickly, awkwardly helping the woman transfer her weight into it. Sidney took her hand as the siren at the volunteer fire department across town began to blare.

"Here you go, Pop. This will thin your blood. Lift your head a little." Alex took the water glass from Sidney's hand. Enrique gasped, turning his head away. "Pop, you've got to get this down."

"Mijo," the old man's voice was raspy. *"Juramelo antes que me muera."*

"You're not going anywhere, Pop." Alex forced the aspirin between his father's cracked lips and brought the glass to his mouth. Water spilled down his chin. "Swallow it."

Sidney couldn't tell if the pill went down. Veins stood out on Enrique's dark hand as

354

he clutched desperately at his chest; his face twisted in pain.

"Perdona a Ernesto," he rasped.

Who was Ernesto? Pardon him for what? Sidney wondered.

"I don't want to talk about this now! We'll talk tomorrow. Did you swallow the pill?" Suddenly Enrique's face relaxed. "Pop?" Alex cried, shaking him slightly.

The eyes fluttered. "Promise me, *mijo.*" His voice was so weak.

"I'll do anything you say, Pop. I promise. Just stay with me. Stay with me, Pop!"

The muscles in Enrique's lined face slowly relaxed even more. His hand went limp and slid from his chest. Sidney's breath caught in her chest. Amilia gasped, falling forward and dropping her head on her old friend's shoulder as all signs of life drained from him.

The sirens grew louder. They were coming down Digby now. Tyson, who had been standing off to one side, backed away. His eyes were wide and troubled. He had never witnessed death before. Sidney gave him a straight-lipped smile through her tears. Ty inhaled deeply before turning bravely toward the front door to wave in the aid car.

Alex moved the limp body to the floor and began performing CPR. His back was to

Sidney as he attempted to breathe life back into his father's lungs. He raised his head, murmuring, pleading in Spanish between sharp compressions of Enrique's chest. The only word Sidney recognized was *Papa.* Amilia bent over one lifeless hand, which she held to her lap, stroking it like a sleeping cat while silent tears ran down her ruddy cheeks.

The emergency crew swept in, relieving Alex and displacing Amilia to another chair as they dropped their equipment to the floor. Sidney placed her hands on the older woman's shoulders, watching and praying as technicians hooked up a heart monitor and other devices, turning away when shock paddles were applied to Enrique's chest.

When they had done all they could do, Alex stood tall, following the gurney out the door. He paused to glance back at Amilia where she sat rocking silently in her chair. A long look of understanding passed between them. "I'll stay with her," Sidney said.

He looked at Sidney without a sign of recognition, his features like chiseled stone. It was the face of the deputy who had once stood ominously on her porch, sending shivers down her spine. Now she understood. It was just a mask. A hard mask to hide his pain. She wanted to touch him, to brush the dried concrete spatters from the hair at his temples, but she knew at that moment in time he could barely even see her. "Alex, I'm so sorry."

He nodded gravely before turning to head down the steps. He crossed the yard to the driveway next door, where his patrol car was parked, and ducked inside. The blue lights began to flash as he backed out, but he must have changed his mind. The lights went dead and he followed the ambulance bearing his father's body down Digby Street.

"It was weird," Ty said, sweeping a trowel across the top of the wet concrete. "One minute he's gibing us about doing a bad job on his sidewalk, and the next minute he just croaks."

Millard frowned. He too was on all fours, smoothing a section of the sidewalk that was to run between Amilia's pink house and the gray one next door. It didn't make much sense to finish the project now, he thought. After all, the guy wouldn't be passing this way again. But it seemed important to Tyson, who had called Millard immediately after the ambulance had taken the deceased away. Now they were fighting the elements to level and smooth at least the section that had already been poured before it dried. "That was the way it was with Art Umquist down there at the hardware store. I went in to get a mole trap from him one day, and the next day he was gone." Millard had regretted his little tirade about the price of mole traps ever since. At least he could have asked about Art's wife and kids before he let the battered and poster-plastered door of the store slam behind him. "Art and I used to fish and hunt up in these mountains." He sat back on his haunches, scanning the hills and stretching his achy back. "Death is a fact of life, they say. I guess you just can't take anybody for granted. They might not be there when you turn around." With Molly he'd had some warning because of her sickness. He knew death was coming for her, but still its arrival had hit him like a truck barreling through a red light.

Ty got quiet on him for a while, their screed scraping the top of the gritty mixture and making a sound like long, slow strokes of sandpaper. Sissy and Rebecca were playing beneath the trees in the adjacent yard. Millard had picked them up from their soccer game on his way to help Ty. Cute kids. They had nearly chattered his ears off between the sports field and Digby Street.

"That would just suck to have someone in your family die."

Millard glanced over at the boy. "Yes. It does." He had hated the term when he first heard Ty speak it, instructing him that it was an offensive perversion of the English language. But at the moment he couldn't think of a phrase more suiting. "It really sucks!" He was surprised by Tyson's laugh. The boy grinned at him like he had just gone up a notch or two in status. Well, hell's bells. If that was all it took, he should have taken up shallow street slang a long time ago.

The little girls ran up, pinching multicolored leaves together at their stems. "Look what we made," Rebecca said. "Fans." They fanned their faces, Rebecca like a haughty queen and Sissy as if her face were on fire.

"Oh, beautiful," Millard said. "Look at all the bright colors. Yellow oak, red maple, green rhododendron."

"They're for Amilia," Sissy said. "To cheer her up." Sissy leaned against Millard's shoulder and surveyed the concrete project. "You guys are doing a good job."

Millard chuckled, exchanging a glance with Ty. "Are you sure?"

She nodded. "Yup."

The next thing he knew, her pudgy fingers were playing with his hair. "I can see your skin all over. You don't have much hairs on your head."

He thought to pull away or to stand. It felt strange having someone touch him in such a personal way.

"I wish you were our grandpa, Mr. Bradbury."

Rebecca plopped onto the cold grass beside them. "Me too. Our grandpa died when we were little. Ty remembers him but we don't. Mom has pictures of him, though."

Millard stared at the fan in Rebecca's hand. Living and dying leaves overlapping in a truly beautiful design. His boy, Jefferson, died on a cold fall day like this. The leaves always made him remember. They were lovely now, but soon they would be brown and mottled, tapped down by winter rains into the soil beneath the trees. Dead for a season. But new life would come in spring. Molly was gone, yet he knew in his heart she still lived. She knew God. She and Jefferson had prayed together every night.

At that moment he wondered if they were up there in heaven, still praying for him. He had thought it was his autumn — but it was beginning to feel more like spring. He glanced at Tyson, who was still working the top of the sludge while regarding the conversation with apparent interest. The boy had thought to call him. "I need your help," he had said. Millard couldn't recall the last time someone had needed him prior to the Walker family's invasion of his safely structured life. He let his arm reach around little Sissy's back and gave Rebecca a wink. "Well, I suppose we could pretend I'm your grandpa."

"Then what should we call you?"

Millard pushed himself up from the ground to relieve the burning sensation in his knees and rolled his head to stretch a cramp from his neck. "Well, let's see. I'm not your *real* grandpa. I suppose — if it's all right with your mother — you could call me Grandpa Bradbury."

"Can I write my name in the sidewalk, Grandpa Bradbury?" Rebecca asked.

He chuckled. "That's probably not a good idea, seeing as how this is not our sidewalk."

The front door opened and Sidney stepped down from the covered porch with a tray in her hands. She was such a pretty girl, Millard thought once again. Funny — she had not struck him that way when they first met. He had thought her cheekbones were too prominent, her nose a little sharp. But those green eyes of hers, whether laughing or crying — and he had seen a lot of both — were mesmerizing. She was intelligent, too. That young man Jack had better get his head in the game, and Millard wasn't thinking football. Judging by what had come out of the guy's mouth during that Sunday afternoon and evening together in the Walker home, he had never read anything more literary than the sports page. A woman like Sidney was bound to weary of that real soon.

"How's it going, guys?"

Ty sat back on his heels, lifting his eyes to Millard's.

"I think we're about done here," Millard said.

"Wow. It looks perfect." Sidney balanced the tray of sandwiches and cookies on top of Tyson's ten-gallon tool bucket. "Your reward." She turned toward Rebecca. "Honey, can you go in and get the juice pitcher and cups from the kitchen counter?"

"Wait for me," Sissy said, heading off behind her sister.

Her mother used her arm as a roadblock. "Not now, Sis. Amilia's resting on the couch."

"But we made fans for her!"

While the men rinsed their hands under the hose, Sidney admired the girls' leaf bouquets, saying they looked like Technicolor peacock tails and suggesting that Rebecca arrange them on the table beside Amilia for when she awoke. A minute after she went into the house, Rebecca returned.

"Sissy, come on in!" Apple juice sloshed and dripped down the sides of the pitcher as she delivered it into her mother's hands. "She was already awake, Mom. I tiptoed — I promise. She wants to visit with us!"

Sidney shook her head as the girls scrambled away. "She's a strong woman. Enrique was more than a neighbor. His wife was her best friend, and when she died, Amilia helped him raise his kids as if they were her own." Her eyes grew tender. "I can tell she really loved him." She stared at the poured section of sidewalk, which stopped abruptly at the border of the yard next door. Two-by-four forms continued to extend like train rails to the front stoop of the silent house. "I wonder if Alex will still want to finish this."

"He never told me what to do," Ty said through a mouthful of fried-egg sandwich. "He just took off. I didn't think it would be good to let it dry the way it was. Nobody could walk on that mess."

"You made the right decision," Millard offered. "Worst-case scenario, it can be jack-hammered out. I guess it'll depend on who moves in next door." He ate only half of a sandwich and began scraping and hosing down tools. Fried egg, no ketchup, white bread. Definitely not the fare one would expect if it was coming from Sidney's own pantry.

Millard had grown fond of his neighbor's cooking. It seemed to surprise Rita that he could prefer hot potato-leek soup and apple bread fresh from the oven over the bricks of frozen entrees that she delivered. Of course, Rita was probably thinking that Sidney was slowly poisoning him while wooing her name onto his will. Rita's suspicious thoughts revealed more about his daughter than he wanted to know.

It grieved him. He had been a good teacher but a lousy father. He raised an intelligent daughter, pouring into her every bit of information that she could receive. Perhaps he had dumped Jefferson's share in too to make up for what the boy lacked.

If only Millard had understood the truth before it was too late. Jefferson's loving, joyful heart was of greater worth than the national archives stored in a brain. He was the teacher, and Millard had been the mindless pupil shooting spit wads in class. Now, Millard knew that his own values had been perverse lies. Where Jefferson was now, in a place where a person's honor had nothing to do with knowledge or physical appearance or wealth, Jefferson Bradbury wore a crown.

If Millard had been wiser, he would have taught his daughter to value what was eternal more than achievement. She would not be capable of such suspicion — of what he reluctantly recognized as downright greed — if she had learned to embrace the substance of her brother's innocent heart.

"I'm going to stay with Amilia until the family arrives," he heard Sidney say over the splashing sound of the hose. "Alex's sister called to say they'll be here soon. Ty, you can go home with Millard whenever you guys are ready."

Rebecca and Sissy burst out the front door. Sissy tripped on the steps, diving headlong onto the grass. She jumped to her feet without brushing off the front of her grass-stained pants.

"Amilia wants us to put this in the side-walk!" Rebecca announced. She held out a brass oval with the raised pattern of a violin. "It's a belt buckle. It belonged to the man who died."

"She showed us some animals he carved out of wood with a knife, but they made her cry." Sissy tipped her head sympathetically. "She doesn't want them in the sidewalk."

Millard tested the concrete. Might be too set. They had finished their job in the nick of time. "Try it in this corner," he suggested, passing the buckle to Ty. The boy pressed it into the stiff mixture, working it gently. His sisters knelt beside him, watching intently.

For some reason Millard's eyes stung as he observed the children, and it wasn't because of the wind that swept down from the mountains and tossed autumn leaves into the damp air. The knot in Tyson's face had loosened and his brown eyes were soft, wondering. He had momentarily forgotten to be tough and cool. Tyson was being a boy.

The kid that had invaded Millard's home four weeks ago was arrogant, angry, and lazy. Millard could go on — and he often had as he lay awake in bed at night, regretting the obligation he had imposed on himself like a suicide bridge-jumper in midair. What a waste for a young man of obvious intelligence to be content with doodling skulls and graffiti around the frayed holes in his jeans. The boy had been impossible to like — let alone love.

Millard raised his eyes above the mountaintops, beyond the hazy clouds to what he perceived might be heaven. Perhaps he had been given a second chance to love an unlovable boy.

26

Enrique Estrada was buried beside his wife on a hillside overlooking the winding trail of Sparrow Creek. To the south, a thick soup of fog rested in the bowl of the mountains, obliterating the town of Ham Bone from sight. Sidney shivered, wrapping her black coat tightly around her slender body.

There was no priest, which surprised Sidney; she had assumed that Enrique was Catholic. Instead the eulogy was delivered by the minister of the small Reformed Episcopal church where Amilia attended along with Alex's sister Carmen's family.

Alex had two sisters and a brother; all of them gathered around the grave site with their spouses and children. A dozen or more friends of the family, mostly of Mexican descent, were scattered about. Sidney felt like an intruder, though Amilia had begged her to come. Alex had pushed her wheelchair up the slick, grassy slope to where it leveled off. He tucked a blanket around her, kissing her lightly on the cheek before stepping off to one side. The rest of the grieving family clustered close to Amilia, alternately resting hands on her shoulders and bending to whisper into her ear or pass fresh tissues. Carmen, the daughter that Sidney had seen with Alex at the school play, knelt beside the wheelchair and clasped Amilia's hand. Sidney had met Carmen briefly the day of Enrique's death, when through her tears she had expressed gratitude to Sidney for staying with the distraught Amilia until they arrived. The children called their surrogate grandmother *"Mi-Ma."* Truly she was the matriarch of the family.

As the short ceremony progressed, there were muffled sobs among the crowd. But Sidney's silent tears were not for Enrique. She had hardly known him. It was the sight of Amilia that wrenched her heart. The love of her life lay a few feet away in a sealed box, soon to be lowered into desolate, solitary silence. No more shared meals, or sunny afternoons on the porch, or dreamy melodies wafting from his violin. She would never adjust his collar again. The finality of it all seemed more than the woman could bear. She suddenly looked like an old lady, stooped and frail. The hushed children stared at her, wide-eyed, apparently frightened by the stifled sobs that tore from their Mi-Ma's throat, lingering echolike in the cold, damp air.

And then there was Alex. He stood alone, his narrowed eyes as hard as black marbles, not trained on the minister's face but staring straight ahead toward the distant foothills. "Stay with me, Pop!" he had pleaded. She had heard his frantically murmured Spanish prayer. And then, as his father's body was wheeled away, she had watched Alex's face turn back to stone. Had he allowed himself to cry?

Sidney averted her eyes. She couldn't look at him. If she were to break out in audible wails of sorrow, it would definitely not be good. She was an outsider there. They would all think she was out of her mind and maybe she was. Alex was almost a stranger despite the recurring intersections of their paths. Serious thoughts of her may never have crossed his mind, yet she found herself at that moment longing to be at his side. No one should bear pain alone.

Why did he stand apart from the rest of them? She remembered that Enrique had begged Alex to forgive someone — Ernesto. Was he here? Surely it had to be a family member if Alex's forgiveness was so important to Enrique on his deathbed. Sidney discreetly blotted her eyes and began sorting through the men in the family cluster, leaving one that might qualify. He was not as tall as Alex, but the facial structure was strikingly similar. Judging by his expensive-looking black wool coat, shiny shoes (probably Italian), and red silk tie, he was definitely not from Ham Bone. The tall woman beside him had dark hair in a short designer cut that could be pulled off only by a beautiful face, which she had. She too appeared to have just walked out of Saks Fifth Avenue. Her eyes roved from the minister to the polished wood coffin and then, without moving her head in his direction, came to rest on Alex.

Sidney was intrigued. Alex stood off to the left while the graveside service was taking place directly in front of the rest of the family. Sidney stood on the right with a half-dozen or so friends of the clan. The woman's intermittent gazes at Alex's profile were furtive. The man, on the other hand, never glanced Alex's way. He only turned his head from time to time toward the woman beside him, his left arm resting around her back.

When the service was over, Alex wheeled Amilia to a blue minivan that happened to be parked next to Sidney's little red car.

She lingered behind them awkwardly until Alex and Amilia were on the far side of their vehicle. Carmen caught up with her just as she got to her car, giving Sidney directions to her house, where a reception was being held. "Oh, thank you." Sidney stared down at the printed half sheet in her hand. "I appreciate the invitation, but honestly, I feel a little out of place."

Alex's sister touched Sidney's arm and smiled. "We'd love to have you if you can make it." She turned to leave, commenting over her shoulder, "We're usually not such a dreary batch!"

"Sidney!" It was Amilia's voice, but Sidney couldn't see her. She circled the back of the minivan. Alex had put her in the passenger seat and was folding up the empty wheelchair. Sidney smiled tenderly at him and he nodded.

"Hello, Sidney. Thanks for coming." She wondered if he meant it.

"Sidney?"

"Here I am, Amilia." Sidney reached through the open passenger door and took her hand. For a moment only their eyes spoke. "I want you to come," Amilia whispered.

"All right." Sidney gazed at her face. She had beautiful skin for a woman her age, soft, round cheeks, and eyes that even in her dark hour were full of love. Sidney wanted to be more like her. "I'll do anything for you, Amilia."

"Sidney, why don't you follow me out to the house?" Alex slid the side door briskly until it latched. "My sister lives way out in the woods. It's easy to get lost."

Carmen and her husband had built their log home on five acres in a bend of the Boulder River. Between two wings, the main living area boasted windows that stretched dramatically to a sharp peak. Sidney paused on the sprawling wraparound porch to glimpse the river between evergreen trees at the outer edge of the mowed yard.

She followed Alex and Amilia into the house, which was still filling up with people, seemingly more than the number who attended the graveside service. Amilia squeezed Sidney's hand before Alex wheeled her down a long hardwood hallway. "I'm just going to take a short rest. Alejandro, don't you let me sleep too long."

After piling her coat along with others on a bed in a room down the hall, Sidney returned to the main room, warming her backside by the blazing fire in a floor-to-ceiling river-rock fireplace. The interior walls were the same as the exterior — stripped cedar logs the color of honey. Cozy furniture groupings were anchored by a huge oriental rug, the kind Sidney dreamed of owning someday. She may have lived in a run-down rental — what Millard Bradbury innocently referred to as a trailer — but in her heart she was the queen of an elegant, perfectly decorated home.

The atmosphere was considerably lighter there away from the bone-chilling fog and tears of sorrow at the cemetery. Children giggled. Comfortable, familiar sounds of clanking and conversation came from the kitchen along with the unmistakable scents of onion and garlic mingled with spices. Sidney tried to eavesdrop on two older women sitting nearby in folding chairs, translating their Spanish into English just for practice. She wished they would slow down and enunciate their words. Though Alex's generation spoke fluent Spanish, his family chose to speak English. Amilia said it was important that they keep their own culture while blending for social and economic reasons with their American culture. After all, unlike their immigrant farm-working parents, they were born U.S. citizens.

Carmen approached, carefully stepping

over a little boy who lay on the floor, building a boat out of Legos. "Hot cider?"

"Yes, thank you." Sidney accepted the glass mug. "Please, Carmen, don't think you have to wait on me. In fact, if there's anything I can do —"

Carmen shook her head. Her thick hair was pulled back in a barrette at the nape and she wore no makeup. She didn't need it. "The meal's already made. It's what we do in times of crisis. Food therapy. My sister and aunts have been in my kitchen for two days. All we have to do now is warm it up and spread it out on the buffet. This family knows how to take it from there."

"Carmen, I haven't had a chance to tell you how sorry I am about your dad."

She nodded a soft smile. "Thank you." Carmen sipped her own cider and gazed around the room. "It's been a rough few days. A whole lot of crying going on. None of us expected this. He was taking something for high blood pressure, but the doctor hadn't sent up any red flags. Alex is enraged about that. He's requested all the medical records for his review."

Alex was sitting in a stuffed chair near the tall windows, conversing quietly with a gentleman Sidney had seen at the grave site. A little girl leaned against Alex's legs for support while playing a board game on the floor. Alejandro, Amilia had called him. He didn't look so fearsome at the moment. "I imagine he's taking it pretty hard."

Carmen's eyes misted slightly. She tipped her head, gazing tenderly at her brother. "Yes. He feels things deeply. He always has."

Ripples of laughter came from a group standing around the food table with hors d'oeuvre plates in their hands. All eyes in the cluster were on the man Sidney had deduced was Alex's brother. She had been watching him. His facial features were the only things that resembled Alex in any way. He was definitely Type A: confident, outgoing, eloquent, and charming. His gestures were loose and exaggerated; he was probably a great dancer. Everyone seemed to like him. Even the glamorous woman on his hip, whose fashionable boots Sidney couldn't help admiring at the graveside service, perfected the image. She had worried that the woman's spiky heels might sink into the damp soil and be ruined. Sidney's own boots had sensible heels, were two or three seasons old, and had come from the Wal-Mart in Dunbar.

"That's our brother, Ernesto," Carmen said. "He and his wife, Isadora, flew in from San Francisco for the funeral. He has an architectural firm down there." She nodded toward the little boy who had wandered off, leaving his Legos strewn on the floor. "And that's their son, Max."

"Oh." Sidney didn't think it was appropriate to ask, so she let her question slip out in disguise. "Your father begged Alex to forgive Ernesto just before he died."

Carmen's mouth dropped open. "He did?"

Suddenly Sidney felt she had made a mistake. If Alex wanted his sister to know that, he would have told her.

Carmen sighed. "So that's what's plaguing him." She shook her head slowly. "Alex vowed he would never forgive Ernesto for what he did to him. What happened between them was horrible, but it was seven years ago. I can't blame Alex for being bitter, but I wish he could let it go. It's destroying him."

"Oh, poor Alex." Sidney knew it was not her place to ask what that horrible event was. But the need to know was torturous.

"How did Alex answer Papa?"

Sidney felt like an informer. "Oh, Carmen, I wish he had told you this. I don't want him to be angry with me."

"Please. Alex eventually tells me everything. We're very close. But I wasn't there when Papa died and I need to know what really happened in those last few moments — for my sake as well as my brother's."

Sidney's eyes teared up, remembering the scene. "He kept saying, 'Stay with me, Pop!' He was trying to get him to swallow an aspirin because that can sometimes stop a heart attack. When your father tried to make him promise to forgive Ernesto, Alex finally said, 'I'll do anything you say.' He promised him."

Ernesto made eye contact with Carmen and broke away from his fans. "Carmen," he said loudly as he approached. "Who's your friend?"

"This is Sidney . . . I'm sorry, Sidney. I don't know your last name."

Sidney held out her hand, which Ernesto gripped firmly. "Walker. Sidney Walker."

"She's Alex and 'Milia's friend."

Sidney laughed. "Actually, the first time I met Alex, he was tackling my son and stuffing him into his patrol car."

Ernesto chuckled. "Oh-oh. You've got a bad boy on your hands, huh?"

Sidney had asked for that. She was the one who brought it up. "No. He's not a bad boy. Just temporarily confused." Ernesto finally let go of her hand.

"Her son has been working with Alex on

Amilia's porch and wheelchair ramp. Alex says he's a good worker," Carmen added.

Sidney was surprised. "He told you that?"

"Oh, yes. Alex says Tyson has an uncanny ability to figure things out. He shows Tyson something once and he pretty much gets it. And I'll tell you what, when Alex came back to 'Milia's and saw that piece of sidewalk finished, it blew him away. He thought he was going to have to break the whole mess out and start over."

Sidney glanced across the room toward Alex. He sat erect in his chair now, his piercing eagle glare aimed directly at the three of them. When Sidney's eyes met his, he slowly rotated his head to the window. Had he heard them speak his name?

Ernesto laughed a little too loudly. "Well, that would hardly be a disaster. Now, if something were to go wrong on the foundation of one of *my* projects, we could be talking millions of dollars. That would qualify as a really bad day." Unlike the rest of the family, there was not a hint of Spanish accent in his speech. He must have worked very hard to accomplish that. "I own Ernest Estrada Associates Architects." He passed Sidney a card from his pocket. So he went by Ernest. She glanced down at the glossy card, not because she was interested but because he was staring at her face. What kind of man passed out his business card at his own father's funeral reception? "This girl has beautiful eyes; have you noticed, Carmen?" He reached toward Sidney's temple, brushing her hair aside. Her head reflexively drew back.

Suddenly, Alex shot to his feet, firmly dropping his drink to the lamp table beside his chair. Sidney could see the muscles in his jaw flinch from across the room. He maneuvered his way through guests and furniture until he reached the front door, jerking it open like the house was on fire, and stormed outside. To his credit, he did not slam the door behind him.

"What's his problem?" Ernesto asked.

His sister glowered. "Ernesto, why don't you go sit in a corner and think about that?"

He held out both hands defensively. "Hey, I didn't do anything." He looked at Sidney. "My brother doesn't like me very much. The old sibling rivalry thing, I guess. I gather by his actions that there's something going on between you two. Believe me, I didn't mean to offend you — or Alex. I'm a happily married man, just appreciating the scenery, that's all."

"Sidney." Carmen took her by the arm. "You haven't had anything to eat. You must be starving." Carmen led her away while Ernesto wandered off to bestow his charms on another group of guests.

Sidney glanced over her shoulder. Through the window she could see Alex halfway across the wide lawn, headed toward the river, wearing only a cotton shirt with a light crewneck sweater.

Fifteen minutes later, he hadn't returned. Sidney couldn't stand it anymore. She slipped away from the kitchen, where she had been visiting with some of the women, wrapped up some tortillas from the buffet table, and retrieved her wool coat along with Alex's brown suede. When she stepped out a side door, a damp cold seeped through her clothes like ice water, chilling her bones to the marrow. Her shoulders clenched as she trudged across the lawn toward the river. She might not find him. By now he could be a mile up- or downstream. When she got to the perimeter of cedar trees, two paths lay before her. She took the one that seemed to be a more direct course to the river, and as she came around a bend, the smell of wood smoke filled her nostrils. Alex had his back toward her. He sat on his heels on a sandy spit littered with smooth rocks, blowing on a pile of thin branches, which suddenly ignited into a weak flame.

"Hey, Boy Scout," she said.

He turned, startled.

"Thought you might need this." She passed him his jacket as he stood.

"Thanks." He glanced at her face briefly, sliding his arms into the sleeves, immediately snapping the front closed and hugging it close to him. "It was getting a little nippy out here." He turned back to the fire, stooping to throw on a few larger sticks from a pile of gathered wood.

She stood there awkwardly, staring at his back. "Are you okay?"

He snapped a thick branch in half as if it were a mere chopstick and poked silently at the fire. "I'm not very good company right now."

Her face warmed. What was she doing there? "I'm sorry. I should have respected your privacy." She placed a bundle of tamales on the sand beside him and turned to leave. "My condolences to you and your family."

"I just said I'm not good company. You don't have to go."

She stood frozen. Was that an invitation to stay? "It's a long river, Alex. Unless you *want* me to stay, I can certainly find another place to watch it run by."

His profile softened and the corner of his

lip moved slightly. "Okay. I *want* you to stay."

He walked away for a moment, returning with a saw-cut log and placing it near the fire. "Take a load off." He pulled up a log for himself. "I guess I made an ass out of myself back there."

"Did you? I thought it was your brother who did that."

His eyes darted to her face. "What did he say?"

She shrugged. "It's not so much what he said. It's just what I perceived about him. Women have a way of knowing what a man is really saying even though the words don't actually come out of his mouth."

He huffed a bitter laugh. "Not all women have that gift."

"Well, come to think of it, I had to learn it the hard way. It's taken years to perfect the skill. I'll revise that statement to 'women who have been burned.' "

"Do you want to tell me about it?"

The flames leapt high and strong now, dancing hypnotically like a charmer's cobras. "Young, naive girl meets charming older man who seduces her, and the next thing she knows, she's a college dropout with a baby on her hip and a husband who comes and goes like a migraine." She kicked

383

at a rock in the sand. "Whenever he came home after one of his disappearing acts, he'd just turn on the charm and lie, lie, lie. No offense, but your brother reminds me of my ex-husband."

Alex's eyes lingered on her face. She thought he was about to say something, but he clamped his lips into a straight line and returned his gaze to the fire.

She removed her black leather gloves, placed them in her coat pocket, and leaned forward to warm her hands. An eagle cried overhead. They watched it soar just above the treetops, eventually joined by its mate. "Tyson would love it here," she said.

His eyes swept the curve of the wide stream. "Yeah. I know *I* do. I come up here a lot." He pointed downstream. "There's a hole right down there — I should bring Ty up here sometime. He'd catch a steelhead for sure."

Sidney's heart fluttered. "Oh, Alex. He'd love that! I bought him a little trout rod when he was small. He could catch fish in places where you'd swear he was just wasting his time. Trickling creeks, even a deep ditch out by the road. After his rod broke he'd wade into ponds with his hands poised above or in the water and stand there like a heron. People don't believe me when I say this, but that boy can catch fish with his bare hands."

Alex chuckled. "Sounds like me when I was a kid. I lived for the moment when the final school bell would ring and I could get down to Sparrow Creek. Amilia had me reading authors like Mark Twain, Jack London, Melville, so my imagination ran wild. My favorite fantasy was that I was Huck Finn." He smirked. "Sparrow Creek was the Mississippi. My dog played the role of Tom Sawyer — or Moby-Dick or White Fang as the need arose." His eyes scanned the river. "I miss those days." He glanced at her. "Being a kid."

She smiled. "Me too. Though I still pretend a lot."

He raised his brows questioningly.

"I'm Barbie all grown up with a fabulous wardrobe and a pink Cadillac that starts every time. I pretend I like my job; I live in a beautiful home of my own. Things like that."

He laughed. "And what about Ken?"

"Okay, he's in my daydreams, too. But he's not plastic."

As the words came from her lips and they shared a gaze of amusement, she was awed by the transformation of Alex's once hard, expressionless face. His dark hair ruffled in the wind; his eyes sparked like ripples in the stream. He was no longer a stiff figure without words or emotions. He was real. Her last comment embarrassed her, though she didn't regret saying it. She turned her eyes to the spots of autumn color among the evergreens across the river.

"It's fly-fishing only up here. Does Ty know how?"

She shook her head. "Doesn't that take a lot of expensive gear?"

"I can set him up. I think he'll learn the skill quickly. He's sharp."

There was something about a snapping fire. It seemed to anchor them there, even when there were no words between them. Sidney wished the flames would never die out.

Alex tossed a small log on, sending sparks flying. "Is your ex still around?"

She gave him a condensed version of her history with Dodge right up to his last visit when he cheerfully threatened to move back to Ham Bone. "Haven't seen him since. That's a good sign."

"You must hate him."

She thought about that. "I hate what he's done to the kids — Ty especially. Ty claims to hate Dodge, but deep inside he loves him. He's always tried so hard to get his father to love him back. Every boy needs a dad."

Alex nodded. "I was lucky. I never doubted that my father loved me." He looked away for a while and she respected his reverie. After some time he spoke again. "I'm sure that's the root of all of Tyson's trouble. He's a very angry young man."

So he got it. Maybe he was once out to take vengeance on her son, but it seemed now at least that he was sympathetic. "And what about you, Alex?"

"What? Am I angry?"

She nodded. "Do you hate your brother?"

He stared at his hands as he rubbed them together. "I guess you could say that." She waited. "It was about a woman."

She knew that. She knew the instant Ernesto had tried to touch her, if not before.

"I was married once. It lasted only three years. I was a cop down in Seattle and worked nights. I asked my brother to go check on her sometimes." He scoffed. "I knew he was a womanizer, but it never occurred to me that he would cross the big line. Family loyalty. That means something to most people."

"Oh, Alex."

"I came home midshift one night and caught him in my bed. Turns out they'd been having an affair for more than six months right under my nose."

She shook her head. What could she say? The betrayal would have been bad enough if the woman were Alex's girlfriend, let alone his wife.

"What did your family do?"

"Oh, they ostracized him for a while. But my family — all but Ernesto — is fiercely devoted. He eventually charmed his way back in and they forgave him. Of course, he seemed like a different person once he had a baby in his arms."

"A baby?"

"He's about six and a half now. His name is Max."

Suddenly it all came together. She gasped. "Is Isadora your ex-wife?"

He nodded, poking at the glowing embers, his jaw muscles flinching again.

It was no wonder he was bitter. First his brother defrauded him in the worst imaginable way, and now Ernesto flaunts his conquest — and Alex's loss — probably at every major family function. "And Max?"

"Ernesto claims he's his. I'll never know for sure."

She took a deep breath to keep from crying and scanned the gray November sky. The last thing a man like Alex would want to see in her eyes was pity. "Oh, Alex. I understand why it's so hard to forgive your brother. I wish I had slapped him when he tried to touch me. I wish I was still standing there slapping away."

He laughed. "Me too. I'd sit on my badge and eat peanuts until you were good and done."

"What about Isadora? How do you feel about her?"

His head moved slowly side to side. "I don't feel anything anymore. I didn't blame her so much. She was lonely and she got scared at night. She was vulnerable and to Ernesto that made her fair game. He knew what he was doing. He knew exactly what he was doing. My brother has no boundaries. Anything that gets between him and what he wants — he just tears it down like one of those apartment houses sitting where he wants to design a condo tower."

"You have to forgive him, you know."

He scowled. "Why is that?"

"Because your eyes are all squinty again. You look like Clint Eastwood in that movie where some guys hang him and leave him to die. Now that I know you a little better, I realize that's not the real you. But I've got to tell you, sometimes you look real mean."

"So, you're saying my face is going to get stuck like that?"

"I'm saying you're putting your head back in that noose every day — every time you dwell on what happened. You're letting your brother's twisted character choke the life out of you. You're the one suffering while Ernesto's off on his own merry way."

"I can't forget what he did."

"I don't think you have to. It just seems like you have to find a way to let it go somehow. Let God deal with Ernesto in his own way, in his own time."

He laughed bitterly. "I've heard it all before. Not just from Pop — my sisters, and now you. Believe me, it's easier said than done. I can't stand to be in the same town with him, let alone the same room. I just want him gone before I do something I'll regret."

"But you promised your dad —"

He fired a glare that shut her up instantly. She had gone too far. "I'm sorry. This is none of my business."

He hurled a small rock, which shot like a fastball to the middle of the stream. "Did my sisters put you up to this?"

"Oh, no." She blew out a slow breath, shaking her head. "I don't need anyone's prodding to say the wrong things at the wrong time. It just comes naturally." She leaned forward, doodling in the sand with the end of a dry alder branch, wishing that the sound of the rushing river could wash her preachy words from the air. The silence became uncomfortable. "I like Carmen and Linda. They went out of their way to befriend me back there in the kitchen." She chuckled. "One minute they're hugging and crying; the next they're spanking each other with wooden spoons. It made me miss my sister."

"Where is she?"

"Cleveland. My hometown. When I came out west to go to college, Alana was only in ninth grade. We didn't really become friends until much later because of the age difference. Even now we see each other only about once a year — if we're lucky."

"Why didn't you move back there after your divorce?"

She sighed, looking up at the tree-covered hills. "It turns out I'm a small-town girl. I love the mountains, the farms, the slower-paced life. Besides, I think it's safer here for the kids. Ty has been fascinated with nature since he was a little squirt. I could never have let him roam back there in the city like I have here." She raised her eyes to the river and a half-naked vine maple leaning over the opposite bank. "He could disappear into those hills with a backpack for days and I wouldn't need to worry."

"You're a good mom." His brown eyes had softened. He was sincere.

"Thank you."

Alex tossed another stone, following it with his eyes. "Do you think you'll ever get married again?"

The directness of his question startled her. "Yes."

"To that guy you were with at the play?" He was still gazing over his shoulder at the spot where his rock had plunged into the river. "He looked like a nice guy."

"He is a nice guy. He's been great with my kids." She pondered how to answer. "I don't know about marriage. We really haven't discussed it." As her words lingered in the air between them, she realized they were all wrong. She *did* know. Not in her head, but in her heart. Thoughts began to buzz through her head like bees in a confusing swarm. She couldn't think about this — not now.

He tossed another stone. "I hope he doesn't mind us being friends. I like talking to you."

"I wish we had become friends earlier. I somehow got the impression you weren't interested," she said with a coy smile. "Though I guess I was pretty unfriendly myself at first."

"Dagger lady. I almost pulled my gun in self-defense a few times."

Her mouth dropped open in feigned shock and denial. "You almost shot the dog! Sweet little Dukie. Never even hurt a flea — and he has access to plenty of them."

They both snickered. "You scared me in a different way," he said.

"What do you mean?"

He shook his head, his lips still pulled into a half smile. "Maybe I'll tell you sometime."

Smoke from the fire rose and dissipated into the sky. The momentary silence was comfortable. "Alex, why didn't your dad and Amilia ever marry?"

"I don't know. Maybe it was because they both loved my mom so much. 'Milia was engaged once, but the guy died before they tied the knot. I was so young, I don't remember him and she never talked about him much. But that missing ring was from him." He chuckled. "And then there was 'Milia's college degree. I think Pop was too macho to get past that little piece of paper, to tell the truth."

He stood slowly, stretching and gazing up at the deepening sky. "I suppose we should get back. I hope someone got 'Milia up."

His face was pleasant when he looked

down at her, extending his hand. No more Clint Eastwood glare. She placed her palm in his and he pulled her to her feet. His touch sent a current through her blood. He held on to her hand. " 'Milia's not the only wise woman around here," he said. "Between the two of you, some of that wisdom might rub off onto me."

She didn't correct him, though she wondered how he could perceive wisdom in a woman who couldn't even discern her own heart.

Twilight came early that time of year. Warm light glowed through the windows of Carmen's house as Alex, with his hand firmly on her back, guided her up the trail. She clung to the comforting peace of the moment, inhaling scents of fallen alder leaves and wood smoke, relishing the nearness of the intricate man beside her who wanted to be her friend.

Now was not the time to think about what she dreaded, this thing she knew she had to do.

27

Another Sunday afternoon of Seahawks and salami. This time Sidney made no effort to learn the characters in the meaningless, monotonous play being acted out on her TV screen, though Jack pointed out individual players, commenting on their accomplishments as if these were facts that were essential to know. Millard sat with one leg crossed over the other, his Velcro-tabbed shoe tapping rhythmically in midair until some event made him uncross his legs and lean forward to shout his wasted advice. Ty, absorbed in a computer game in his room, appeared from time to time to refill his bowl with chili while the girls strung bead bracelets at the dining room table.

Sidney wove a pencil between her fingers and stared at the sketch pad on her knees. Vine maple leaves trailed across the page, curving into a scroll pattern at either end. The little pumpkins had looked stupid among the leaves so she rubbed them out with Sissy's pink eraser. It was just practice; at the moment she had no furniture to paint. When she glanced up, her eyes fell again on the pot of golden chrysanthemums on the coffee table. They were beautiful. Bright spots of sunshine on a nasty fall day, and she wished they would go away. No, she wished they had never arrived.

Jack was being too kind. If only he would do something wrong or say something absolutely rude and insensitive, her task might be easier. He *had* presumptuously produced a duffle bag full of stinky laundry just after presenting her with the flowers, but that could hardly be cited as grounds for demoting him back to "just friends" status. After all, she had started the whole laundry thing.

Jack glanced over, touching her arm as she began to stand. "Hey, are you done with your doodling?"

"For now." She bent to remove empty chili bowls from the coffee table. "How much longer is this game going to be?"

"Not much. It's the fourth quarter. Why? Do you have plans?"

She shrugged. "Not really. Well . . . actually, I was thinking you and I might go for a little drive."

"You should do that," Millard said. "Get out, just the two of you. I can stay here with the kids if you like."

Good old Millard. Sidney hugged him and went to her bedroom to change from her soft slipper-socks into her Wal-Mart boots. She stood in her closet for some time, her eyes roving over a selection of sweaters, not really seeing. How was she going to do this? She had come up with some great breakup lines the night before, but now they eluded her. She should have turned on the light and written them down. Jack's words to her on the night of that first kiss continued to interrupt any cohesive thought that tried to form in her mind. "I can't handle that 'just friends' line again," he had said. But she had assured him, she had actually believed, that this time it was different. She had been so sure that he was the one.

The Seahawks won again. The words *Super Bowl* tumbled from Jack's lips often lately. He was like a boy anticipating Christmas; surely the day would come. He was buoyant, charged with energy as they rushed from the house to his car in a pelting rain.

Sidney shook the rain from her hair as he turned the key in the ignition. "Let's see if we can get a lane at the bowling alley," he said, pulling out of the driveway and pointing the nose of the car toward town.

"Actually, I was hoping we could just talk. This is the perfect opportunity. It's been pretty hard lately with the kids around so much."

"Talk? We can talk while we bowl." He chuckled, shaking his head. "I still can't get over that forty-yard dash. Shaun Alexander is my hero. Did you see that play? He charged over bodies like a marine in a kid's obstacle course."

She stared out her rain-pocked window. "I don't want to have to shout over the clamor of bowling balls and noisy kids. And I don't want to discuss football." She turned to look at him squarely. "I don't like football. It bores me."

His face flinched and his head drew back. "Whoa." The windshield wipers fanned back and forth, the only sound other than intermittent sprays of road water hitting the underside of the vehicle.

"I'm sorry. That probably hit you like a slap. I didn't mean to do that."

"It's okay. I know I get a little obsessive sometimes." She had dampened his mood. There was an awkward silence before he spoke again. "Okay, so you just want to talk. What do you want to talk about?" He drove past the bowling alley.

"Us."

He began rubbing his neck, stretching it from side to side. They were approaching Rosie's Rib House. He glanced over. "You wanna talk over a pile of —" He stopped himself. "No. I guess not." He had a hard time remembering that she was a vegetarian. "So where do you want to go?"

"I don't care. A parking lot would be fine."

He kept driving. She waited for him to ask the obvious question. *What about us?* But the question didn't come.

"Jack."

His look was apprehensive. "Yeah?"

"A woman needs someone to talk to. Not just about daily events or car problems or movies. I mean on a deeper level. It seems like we talk about things on the surface and never get down to our true feelings."

He scoffed. "Feelings are overrated." When he glanced back at her, his smirk faded. "Just kidding. You can talk to me about your feelings anytime you want. Is that all this is about? Talk away. I'm listening."

She sighed, shaking her head. She couldn't change him. He was perfectly happy bobbing along on the surface of life. Why should she pull him under to view a realm he was inexplicably afraid to explore? She remembered her long talk with Alex at the campfire, the comfortable honesty between them. Her resolve strengthened, though this was not about Alex. She and Alex might never become more than friends. "Jack, I know now what I didn't understand before. I know why I had to break it off even though you were such a wonderful, kind, positive guy."

He continued to stare straight ahead as he drove along the back side of town.

"We have no intimacy."

He rolled his eyes. "Dang, I hate words like that."

"Foreign language?"

He nodded. "Pretty much." He halted at a stop sign, turned on his blinker, and turned right. "But I've heard it before. That lady I mentioned to you once — the schoolteacher in Dunbar. As I recall, that was one of the words that came up in her good-bye speech."

"Oh. You never actually told me you two were dating."

His brows rose innocently. "Oh?"

"Case in point."

"I can't be what you want. I don't even get it, to tell the truth. I'm like an ape trying to land a plane. Can't read the controls, can't see the runway."

She smiled softly, feeling a weight lift from her. She reached out to touch his arm. "I made a big mistake when I lured you from the jungle, where you were happy."

He put his hand over hers, giving it a squeeze. The corners of his lips rose into a sad smile. "Me go back to jungle now. Jane go home."

28

"I don't need the confounded Internet," Millard stated emphatically. "I've survived all these years with good old-fashioned books and I'm doing just fine." He gestured toward the neat row of burgundy bound volumes on the lower shelf of his living room bookcase. "Anything I need to know I can find in the *Encyclopaedia Britannica*."

Tyson shook his head. "Those things are ancient. I looked up U.S. presidents and the last one in there was Richard Nixon. What if you want to know about something that happened last week? I promise, once you see how it works, you'll be hooked. You'll probably be online all day."

"I'm too old and it's too complicated. Now, quit changing the subject. I believe we were discussing your science project."

Tyson frowned, sighing dramatically. "I don't want to do this. I'm not even interested in science."

"Yes, you are." Millard gestured out the window. "Everything out there in those woods that fascinates you is science. What do you wonder about when you're out there on your belly observing the animals? Surely you must have questions. Don't you get curious when you look at the stars and galaxies? What holds our universe together? How is it that the human body needs the very things that nature provides?" The boy was slouched and practically oozing from a dining room chair, tapping his fingernails on Molly's mahogany table. Was anything Millard said getting through? "All you have to do is come up with a question. Your project is simply the process of finding your answer."

"I can't think of a question."

Millard huffed a sigh of frustration as he pushed out his chair. He walked to the window. Why did this kid have to make everything so hard? It was a drizzly November Tuesday. The trees in his yard were almost bare except for a sparse crowd of stubborn leaves still clinging to their branches. They might as well let go, Millard thought. They were destined to rot along with the others that carpeted his yard. He had given up on raking them, partly because it was a hopeless cause and partly because they hid the unsightly molehills that dotted his once immaculate lawn. "I don't know if I've got one tenacious mole or an army of them," he commented. "Wish I could see what's going on underground."

Ty joined him at the window. "Are there any new mounds?"

Millard pointed. "There and there. I'm going to have to break down and order one of those traps, I guess. Trouble is, I don't know where to put it. How am I supposed to know where the little rat is headed next?"

Ty glanced over at him smugly. "You get on the Internet and find out about a mole's network system. I'll bet it'll even tell you if moles are territorial, in which case you'd know whether he's working alone or not."

Millard rubbed his chin. "Maybe how to trap 'em, too."

"I could hook up my computer over here. All we'd need is an outlet and a phone jack." The kid's motives were not pure. He had complained since day one of not being able to play his computer games while imprisoned at Millard's house. "Did I mention that you can play *Wheel of Fortune* online — and you don't have to wait until seven o'clock?"

Millard pretended that didn't interest him in the least. "I'll make you a deal," he said after some thought. "I'll get the Internet. You get me that mole."

Tyson's brows rose. "Huh?"

"Do your science project on moles. Their habits, motivation, active seasons — everything we've ever wondered about them. And then you create a way to destroy him — or them. Maybe even build a trap. We could certainly put something together out in that garage. I've got a soldering iron, you know."

Tyson seemed to ponder as he strolled from window to window. When the phone rang, the boy answered, responding to the court's computerized voice recognition system automatically. The daily phone calls were just an accepted part of their day. He hung up and turned back to Millard. "Okay. I'll get that little sucker." He glanced around the room. "Where do you want to set up the computer?"

Millard was clearing the top of the little desk in the dining room where he managed his mail and paid bills when he heard a string of expletives escape from Tyson's throat. The boy jumped to his feet, staring out the window. Millard's eyes darted to the house across the street. A man was reaching up to Sissy and Rebecca's window, trying to push it open. He moved to the next window — Tyson's — and when it didn't budge, he slunk around the corner of the house. The boy charged toward the front door.

"Hey!" Millard yelled. "Come back here!" By the time he got to the door, Tyson was already across the street. He snatched the phone from its cradle and punched in 911.

"There's an intruder at — well, directly across the street from 727 Boulder Road."

"Is anyone in the home?"

"Yes — I don't know. My" — he floundered for the right noun — "my grandson ran over there. I can't see anyone now."

He couldn't wait for the operator's next question. He tossed the phone to his chair and ran out the door. His breath came short as he rounded the corner of the Walker house. There was no one in sight. Suddenly he heard loud shouts and a thud. The back porch railing wiggled in his hand as he climbed the steps. The back door was open.

"Get out of here!" The boy's high-pitched voice came from the direction of Sidney's room. "There's nothing left to steal, you bastard!"

"Back off, kid. I just came for a visit, that's all. This is between your mother and me. Just stay out of it."

Millard heard a loud crash. "Get out of my mom's room. Get out of my house!"

Millard glanced around the kitchen, grabbing a marble rolling pin, for lack of a better weapon, as he headed toward the hall. Another crash. The strange man backed down the hall toward Millard, Tyson menacingly pushing him forward with the legs of a spindle-backed chair.

The guy had a gruesome tattoo crawling around his neck. An evil snicker crept from his throat. "You playing lion tamer, boy? You always liked to pretend. Think you can tame your old man?" He chuckled again. "You're not the first one to tr—"

Millard brought the rolling pin over the stranger's head, jerking it tightly against his Adam's apple. "Maybe you're not worth the trouble, you pathetic ground-dwelling mole." He liked his little analogy, surprised by it as much as the fact that he had just apprehended the bad guy. Suddenly he felt a painful kick to his shin. An elbow thrust like a battering ram into his rib cage and he folded.

He saw a flurry of legs. Tyson hurled his weight forward and both bodies crashed to the dining room floor. Millard tried to stand erect. The pain in his ribs made him catch his breath. Tyson's fists flailed wildly against the intruder, his lips murmuring fevered words that no lady should ever hear. A lifetime of grievances, no doubt.

Tyson's father pushed him off. "Don't make me maim you, you son of a —"

"Son of a what? A loser?" Ty grabbed at him again. The man swung his arm hard, smacking the boy across the face and sending him sprawling against the wall. He grabbed one of Sidney's heavy oak dining chairs and held it over Tyson, poised to bring it down.

Millard dove. Man and chair came down hard against the table. He heard the sound of breaking wood. Millard started to push himself up from the floor. Another kick caught him, this time on the side of his head.

Tyson screamed a curse. "You touch him again and I'll kill you! I'll kill you! I mean it!" The boy sobbed between threats.

Millard wanted to get up, but his body wouldn't move. He heard more scuffling, more taunting, a shattering crash. The window. They had broken the window. He pushed himself into a kneeling position. There was blood on the carpet where his face had been. Sirens. Help was coming. One set of footsteps pounded through the kitchen toward the back door, and then there was silence. "Tyson? Tyson, are you all right?" He felt around for the nearest chair, using it for support as he tried to pull himself up. A sharp stab of pain made him sink back to the floor amid shattered pieces of Sidney's lovely hand-painted table.

The boy crawled to him. "Millard!" Ty's lips were bloody and swollen, his eyes still wild with terror. He reached out, touching Millard's arm. "What did he do to you?"

Millard shook his head, wrapping the boy tightly in his long, gangly arms and pulling him close. He was trembling. "The question is, what has that bastard done to you, son?" Tyson's body melted into his embrace.

29

Sidney's office was only a few minutes away from the Ham Bone branch of the Winger County Sheriff's Department. She found herself speeding, though Alex had assured her over the phone that Tyson was all right. She pulled into the parking lot, grabbed her purse, and headed for the entrance of the century-old building without bothering to lock her car.

A middle-aged woman greeted her at the front desk and led her to a room down the hall. "Would you like a cup of coffee?" she asked as she opened the door. Ty sat alone at a weary oak table in the middle of the small room. Sidney shook her head absently. "No, thank you."

"Tyson." She went to him, appalled by the damage on her son's face. He held an ice pack to one cheek. His lips were split and swollen, and a butterfly bandage had been placed on the brow of one already colorful eye. "Your father did this to you?"

Ty looked away from her.

"Oh, Tyson." She began to cry. The door opened and Alex walked in. He acknowledged them with a nod as he pulled out a chair for Sidney and sat opposite them. "Are you sure nothing's broken?" she said.

"The medics checked him out before releasing him to me. We should know something from the hospital about Mr. Bradbury soon. Thanks for waiting, Tyson. I couldn't question you until your mom was here."

Tyson ignored him, fixing his narrowed eyes on his mother. "Why didn't you tell me you were seeing him again?"

"I'm not seeing him! What made you think —"

"He said he's moving back to Ham Bone and you know all about it. He's been at our house before. He was going through your drawers. He's the one who stole your money and your stupid jewelry! I told you it wasn't me."

Sidney dropped her head into her hands, vaguely aware of Alex sitting across the table from her. "Ty, I'm sorry." She raised her eyes to his. "I had no idea. It never occurred to me that it was your father who stole from me." She shook her head. "I'm so sorry."

411

Tyson refused to acknowledge her. His eyes, still burning with anger, were fixed on a spot on the old plaster wall.

Alex scribbled a note on a pad of paper, raising his brows toward Sidney. "I don't believe you reported a theft."

"I'm missing a gold bracelet, a couple of diamond rings and other jewelry — and some cash. I'll make a list. Did you catch Dodge?"

Alex nodded, pulling something from his pants pocket and dropping it to the worn wood table. A stone-studded gold ring rolled toward the center, wobbled, and fell flat. "Look what I found."

Sidney breathed a sigh of relief. "Amilia's?"

"Yes."

"Did Dodge have it?"

Alex shook his head. "Tyson, I owe you an apology, too."

Ty's head moved slowly in the deputy's direction.

"I moved Amilia's TV console to make room for the chest your mom painted. This was hiding in the dust behind the drape. 'Milia thinks it must have been knocked off when she watered her plants. She just didn't notice it missing until the other things were stolen."

Again, Ty looked away, feigning disinterest.

Alex cleared his throat and turned to Sidney. "We have your ex-husband in custody. His old beater was parked a half mile down the road from your place. That's probably how he snuck into the house unnoticed before." Alex rubbed his shoulder. "It took two of us to wrestle him down. He was as high as a kite — probably PCP." She noticed for the first time a slight abrasion on Alex's temple, a bruise on the knuckles of his right hand. "There are two existing warrants out for his arrest — auto theft and possession of narcotics with intent to sell. You've got him for failure to pay child support, breaking and entering, theft." He glanced at Ty. "If he's convicted of all these crimes, he'll be put away for a long time. Is that what you want, Tyson?"

Ty's lips quivered. "I hope you send him straight to hell."

The bottled rage in her son's words chilled her. She reached for him but he pulled away. She had not believed him. His own mother. How alone he must have felt. It was no wonder he was bitter. She felt helpless. Sinking. How would he ever heal?

"I want to see Millard." Ty's face was void of expression, his eyes hard.

Alex stood, reaching for a phone on a small table against one wall. "I'll call the hospital." He punched in a number and waited. "Sheriff's Department. Checking on Millard Bradbury. He was brought into emergency about forty minutes ago." He waited. "Can he talk on the phone? Well, what do you know? Broken ribs," he repeated aloud, "possible concussion. Anything else?" He listened intently, his mouth slowly forming a smirk. "Okay, thanks." He snapped the phone closed. "Apparently your friend Millard has a daughter who doesn't like him playing the hero. Sounds like she's giving him a worse beating than he already got."

"When's he coming home?" Tyson asked.

"They want to keep him overnight."

Sidney stood staring out the window as Alex began to question Ty about the specific events of the afternoon for his report. She cringed hearing her son repeat his father's lethal remarks and the graphic details of the fight. The day had started out like any other. Now looking at Ty's face was like gazing at an open wound. One she didn't have the power to heal. Millard — dear, wonderful Millard who lived a sane, serene life before getting involved with her — lay in a hospital bed, broken and beaten by her ex-husband.

Sidney felt the weight of a ship's anchor lodged in her soul.

"Okay," Alex said, "we're just about done here. But we have one more issue to discuss, Tyson. You're still on house arrest. Technically, you broke the stipulations of the court by leaving Mr. Bradbury's custody, even just to run across the street to your own home. You know the rules. Also, according to all three statements, you were the one to initiate the physical attack. You took the law into your own hands instead of letting me and the other deputies do our jobs. Your probation officer will be notified of the incident and the court will have to decide —"

"Screw the court!" Tyson flew from his chair, knocking it backward; it crashed to the floor. "Screw you! Screw everybody!" His brown eyes almost bulged from his battered face. He charged for the door. "I'm not jumping through anybody's hoops anymore. I'm out of here! Shoot me in the back if you want. I don't give a crap!" He flung the door open.

In an instant Alex had Tyson pinned against the outside wall, Tyson's arms pulled tautly behind his back. Alex snapped metal cuffs onto his wrists and shoved him back into the room, holding up a hand to signal to another deputy who had come running that he had things under control. He closed the door behind him and pushed Ty roughly into a hard-backed wooden chair. He leaned into Ty's face. "You'd better start giving a crap!"

Sidney backed against the far wall, knowing she shouldn't interfere.

Alex paced, saying nothing for a few moments. Tyson watched him, his eyes ablaze. Finally Alex turned back to him. "You and I have something in common. A major problem. We're both trying to live life with wounds that won't heal up and we're so bitter that we're self-destructing."

This apparently was not what Ty expected to hear. His narrowed eyes showed signs of interest.

"Your father was supposed to love you. That's what fathers are for. He should have been there for you, taken you places, told you he was proud. But he didn't, did he? He should have kept his promises. He should have been a man of his word. Someone you could be proud of."

Ty seemed to follow every word.

"I'm sorry he lied to you. I'm sorry he turned out to be a loser. I wish I could change that. I know your mom does, too, in the worst way." He stared pensively at the floor. "I guess all our anger is never going to change another person's character."

Alex went quiet.

"So what happened to you?" Ty finally asked.

Alex shook his head. "It's pretty hard to talk about." He sat down, resting his elbows on his knees, letting his head drop, then glanced up as if he had a revelation. "Do you ever feel ashamed to talk about it — like it's your fault or something?"

Ty's eyes began to flood. He looked away.

"My big brother screwed me over." There was a long pause. "He seduced my wife. The thing went on for months right under my nose, and my brother was shining it on and lying to me the whole time." Sidney noticed that Alex made no eye contact while divulging his secret. "She divorced me and married him." He glanced up at Ty. "This is just between us, by the way."

Ty nodded.

"I've been a jerk to you, haven't I?"

Ty shrugged.

"I guess when you hate someone so much it comes out of you one way or another. It wasn't fair for me to take it out on you. I'm sorry."

"That's okay."

Alex stood, pulling Ty gently to his feet,

unlocking the metal cuffs, and sitting him down again. He placed them on the table and then sat facing the boy, leaning forward and studying his hands as he rubbed them together. "You ever lie in bed at night with your gut twisting so bad you want to get up and break something?"

Tyson scoffed. "Or drink a case or two of beer?"

Alex chuckled. "Yeah. Tried that. Believe me, it didn't help." He looked at the airborne dust particles illuminated in a stream of light pouring through the window. "Some people say I need to forgive my brother. It was the last thing my pop said to me. How's that for a guilt trip?" He directed his gaze to Ty's swollen face. "I don't know how to do that. It would be one thing if my brother were sorry, but he's not. He's moved on and I'm still walking around bleeding."

"Yeah. It's not fair."

Alex stood again and began pacing. "You don't go to church, do you, Ty?"

Ty shook his head; Sidney looked down at her feet.

"I take Amilia every Sunday, but I haven't enjoyed it in a long time. I kept hearing things I didn't want to hear. Like you have to forgive others if you want God to forgive you." He stopped at the window, his eyes searching the sky. " 'Milia says God won't ask us to do something we can't do — with his help." His eyes shot back to Tyson where he sat attentively, face upturned. "Do you believe in God?"

"Yeah. I'm not stupid."

Sidney's heart grew warmer by the second.

"I don't know how to fix us, Ty. But I'm suggesting we start by going to church together. Are you game?"

"Will I get credit toward my community service hours?"

Alex stepped back to the table. Ty's chair had been scooted away from it, and Alex pulled his up and sat where their knees almost touched. "Yep. That's what the program says. And maybe sometimes your mother and sisters will join us." He glanced at Sidney, and she nodded, smiling softly.

"Okay, I guess I'll go," Ty said.

"I know you're hurting," Alex said. "Your dad has been beating you up for years, even if it hasn't been physical before now. Those bruises go a lot deeper than the ones he gave you today. No one but you knows that pain. But you need to let it go somehow. What do you say we do whatever it takes to get free of the bitterness before it eats us alive?" Alex extended his hand.

Ty sat motionless, his eyes fixed on the deputy's. Then he lifted his hand, gripping Alex's as if finally being rescued from certain drowning. They held their steady gaze.

Sidney couldn't move. The scene would be etched in her mind forever.

Man and boy stood. "Why don't you let me talk to your mom for a minute? You can wait outside."

Ty hesitated, glancing at the handcuffs on the table before stepping out.

When the door closed behind him, Alex turned to Sidney. "Are you okay with all that?"

She stared into his humble eyes. He wore the same stiff uniform, but it seemed to be filled with a different man — one that was soft and touchable. The wall at her back was the only thing holding her up. She nodded, blinking away tears. "Alex." She inhaled deeply, hoping words would come. "You are a wonderful man."

"I didn't mean to say all that. It just happened." He gazed up toward the window. The afternoon light warmed his dark complexion, lit up the long fringe of lashes that shaded his brown eyes. He shrugged. "Funny. I suddenly saw myself in him. I didn't want him to shut down like I have.

He's so young."

"You don't sound shut down." She smiled. "I see definite signs of life."

The tough, confident deputy sheriff stood awkwardly in front of her, his hands smoothing the sides of his pants as if he didn't know what else to do with them. The vulnerability made him irresistible. "Yeah. I feel it," he said. "Like something is about to change."

Their eyes held a long gaze, one that made Sidney suspect his heart might be pounding as loudly as hers. The silence was charged with unspoken words. Finally, he slipped his hand around her back and guided her gently to the door.

30

Millard opened one eye. Rita was still there, gazing out the long window of his hospital room, her arms locked across her chest. He thought of feigning sleep again, but last time he had actually dozed off. For how long? He glanced at the clock: 6:30 p.m. "Shouldn't you be home, cooking dinner for your family?" he asked.

His daughter turned. "Not until we've had a little talk." She pulled a chair up to his bedside, frowning at the goose egg that he could feel without touching the side of his head.

He grimaced involuntarily as he tried to push himself up. The doctor had bound his rib cage tightly but the two cracked bones felt like broken spokes on a bicycle wheel jabbing his insides. A little talk? What had all that been preceding his nap? What more could she possibly have to say? Rita helped him up, propping pillows behind him. She sighed loudly, shaking her head. "Didn't I tell you those people were nothing but trouble, Dad? I'm not trying to rub it in, honestly. I just hope you can see now that they're not our kind. That man was crazy on drugs. You could have been killed!"

Millard looked beyond her, remembering the events of that morning. Dodge Walker had been more than crazed. He had thrust a heavy oak chair above his head like it was cardboard with a savage, inhuman glare — pure evil, and it was fastened on Tyson. The man's own son. No doubt, he could have killed the boy. He wondered what could possess a man to do that and then answered his own question. The devil himself. Rita rambled on, still in the process of *not* rubbing it in. He barely heard her. Tyson had seen the detachment on his father's face, heard the snarl of twisted pleasure as he lay helplessly beneath the man. The boy's tear-filled eyes had widened in disbelief as one mortally speared in the chest by someone who was supposed to love him. And that pained Millard more than the knot on his head or the bruises and broken bones.

"Dad? Are you okay?"

He swiped at the tear that had escaped from the corner of his eye. "I'm fine. They must have me on some kind of medication."

She shook her head. "Just Tylenol. Do you need something stronger?"

"Why? Are you packing a bottle of bourbon in that big bag of yours?"

She scoffed. "You don't drink."

"Well, I'm thinking about taking it up."

There was a tap on the door and it opened slightly. Sidney Walker poked her head in tentatively. "Excuse me."

"Sidney. Come on in." He gestured with his hand.

"We don't mean to interrupt," she said.

"You're not interrupting anything."

Ty followed his mother into the room. Rita squared her shoulders, scowling at them as if they had conspired together to inflict the damages on her father that had put him in the hospital.

"Hello, Rita." Sidney dropped her eyes uncomfortably at Rita's grim-lipped nod and stepped to the opposite side of the bed. She reached for his hand. "Oh, Millard. I'm so sorry about this." She stared at the bump on his head, the gash that he could feel running from his lower lip to his chin, shaking her head sadly. She tried to speak but the words seemed to catch in her throat.

Tyson planted himself midway between the door and Millard's bed, probably frozen in Rita's icy glare.

"Don't get all sentimental on me," Millard said. "I'm not dying. I'll be out of here by this time tomorrow. Sooner if I can find my pants."

"We'll see about that, Dad," Rita interjected. She glanced at Sidney. "He has broken bones and a grade-two concussion. I just hope there isn't more serious damage that hasn't shown up yet." She raised her chin, fingering the loose skin at her throat. "These injuries would be serious for anyone, let alone a seventy-three-year-old man. This involvement with your family has been nothing but —"

Millard reached for her hand, squeezing it hard. She defied his not-so-subtle signal to close her mouth, pulling her hand away. "No, Dad. It's time I speak my mind. He's too stubborn to admit it, but he's too old for all this. I realize your family has . . . issues, but it's time you work them out on your own. I'm sure there are social agencies —"

"That's enough!" A pain shot through his ribs. "My torso may be bound up but my mouth works just fine. I can speak for myself."

Rita recoiled.

"She's right, Millard." Sidney's head was dropped, her fingers kneading the turned-down edge of his sheet. "We've put you through a nightmare. You've given us so much." She dabbed at her eyes. "And this time it could have cost you everything." She lifted her head and ran her hand through the top of her shiny, sun-touched hair, which fell immediately back to drape on her shoulders. "Tyson said you saved his life. You're our hero."

Millard scoffed but he knew it was true. At least he had saved the boy from certain maiming. He hadn't meant to be a hero. It was merely reflex that made him dive into Dodge Walker before he could bring the weighty captain's chair down on Ty's body with what appeared to be superhuman drug-enhanced force. There hadn't been time to talk himself out of it.

Rita rolled her eyes and began stuffing her gloves and a small box of hospital tissues into her oversize bag. "I'll call you later, Dad." She nodded curtly at Sidney, ignoring Ty, and headed for the door with her coat over one arm.

"All right, then," he said.

"Rita." Sidney's voice trembled. "Can we go get a cup of tea?"

"Good idea." Millard gave his daughter a look that he hoped she would interpret as a command. "Tyson and I could stand some time to talk, too, man to man." He saw Rita's chest rise and fall in one of her infamous sighs as she and Sidney left the room.

As soon as the door closed, Ty was at the bedside, his face pinched with what appeared to be genuine concern. Millard patted the edge of the bed and the boy sat facing him, staring at the side of his head. "Man, I've never seen a bump that huge. What did he hit you with?"

"I believe it was his foot." Millard chuckled. "Everything happened so fast; I don't remember the exact order of events. Maybe I clubbed myself with that confounded rolling pin."

"No. You dropped it when he jabbed you in the ribs." His face wrinkled. "Are the bones sticking out?"

Millard pulled back the sheet, exposing his bandaged torso. "Nope. They say they're just cracked. This is to hold them in place while they heal up. I'll be as good as new in a few weeks." He knew that the boy's purple eye and the cuts on his face would soon be gone also. It was his lacerated heart that worried Millard.

Ty held his eyes on the white binding. "I'm sorry . . . about everything. Sorry I got you into this whole mess."

"I'm not."

Ty glanced up.

Millard tried to sink into a prone position without letting his face telegraph pain. Tyson pulled the extra pillow away. "You're the best thing that's happened to me in a long time, son."

Ty's brows drew together in disbelief. "What?"

"I had a boy once." Millard hadn't spoken of him to anyone in years. "Jefferson. Jefferson Ray Bradbury." He rolled his head toward the window. "I wasn't a very good . . . No, I was a lousy father." There. He'd said it aloud. It didn't make him feel any better. In fact, the silence was thick. This was not the thing to confess to a boy whose own father had turned out to be such a disappointment. Still, his mouth opened again. "He was born with Down syndrome. Do you know what that is?"

Tyson shook his head.

"He was mentally retarded."

"Oh."

"A happy boy, though."

"What happened to him?"

"He was born with a weak heart and it finally just gave up on him. He died when he was only fourteen. We didn't have any warning. One day he's out playing in the fall leaves, throwing them in the air like

$100 bills he had just won in the lottery. The next morning I find him cold in his bed." Millard stared up at the stark white ceiling. "Still smiling. He died with a little smile on his face as if he had seen the angel that carried him away."

Tyson cleared his throat but didn't speak.

"I held him then. Picked him up and held him like a gangly baby." He was embarrassed by the water welling up in his eyes and turned his head back to the window again, where he could see only the whitewashed corner of the hospital's south wing lit by streetlights. "I hadn't done that in a long, long time. But by then it was too late."

He felt a tentative touch as if a butterfly had landed on his arm. He still couldn't look the boy in his eyes. There was more to be said. Maybe it was the painkiller that had unfettered his carefully concealed and guarded emotions, or maybe it was just time. Maybe the hospital was the perfect place to lance this festering wound and let it drain.

"I'd always dreamed of having a son who was an athlete and a scholar. A fishing and hunting companion. A normal boy. I couldn't take Jeff fishing. His line somehow wadded into a rat's nest every time I turned around. When he miraculously hooked into a trout, he got so excited that he threw the rod into the water and splashed out into a strong current after the fish."

"Well, at least you took him fishing. That's more than my old man ever did."

Millard didn't mention that he had taken Jefferson out to the river only a couple of times, and that had been when the boy was nine. He had given up on his son. In all honesty, Millard had been embarrassed by his mentally handicapped son. Molly and the boy had come to watch his wrestling matches on occasion, but Millard cringed when she brought him down to the gym floor afterward. The coach's kid. Laughing too loud, his head tipped back with that moronic, gaping, often drooling mouth. Millard had silently wished that his son were invisible.

But Jefferson had loved his father with the devotion of a faithful dog.

"I was too hard on him. I wasted the few years we had being disappointed by what he wasn't, what he never could be." His ribs inflicted a punishing stab as he sighed. "I was the retarded one. He was perfect all along."

Tyson had gradually let the full weight of his hand rest on Millard's forearm. Millard reached across his body, letting his hand fall over the boy's, looking him in the eyes. "I just thought you should know that about me. I'm no hero, so don't set me up on some pedestal because I'll only fall off."

"Nobody's perfect," Ty said, his voice cracking. He cleared his throat. "What did you mean . . . about me being the best thing that ever happened to you?"

Millard chuckled. "You know what my life was about before you shattered the monotony? The daily crossword puzzle and keeping my old chair warm. Spent my days staring out the window, watching life like it was a movie with no plot. Poisoned dandelions for excitement. That cursed mole showing up was almost a blessing. Gave me something to think about beside my obituary." He grinned. "Then you came along."

"Yeah." Ty's brows lifted his face into a mischievous look. "And the plot thickened."

"Next thing I know I'm out working with concrete again, hopping freight trains in the middle of the night, teaching history and English. I thought I was all used up. But you've made me feel useful again." He tried to take a deep breath, but his ribs cut it short. "You've brought out feelings I didn't know I was capable of anymore. If I didn't care so much about you, I don't think I could have done what I did." He chuckled.

"If you told me a few months ago I'd be diving into a brawl with a lunatic —" He stopped himself. "Sorry. He's your dad. I shouldn't talk about him like that."

Ty huffed, his eyes narrowing. "He's not my dad. Never was. You can call him anything you want." The boy pulled his hand away and looked down, toying with his fingernails. "You're the closest thing to a dad I've ever had."

Millard caught his breath. He tried to speak, but couldn't. He squeezed Tyson's hand and the boy looked at him, saw the tears welling up in his eyes.

For a moment neither of them spoke. Millard was surprised to see Tyson's mouth clamp tightly as if he too was trying to suppress tears, but to no avail. They ran down his bruised face as his lips began to quiver.

"Your sisters call me Grandpa. I'd be proud if you would call me that, too."

Tyson nodded. He stretched the short sleeves of his black T-shirt to his face, swiping at his eyes. "Maybe we could go fishing sometime."

Millard's heart burst like a small, hard kernel of popcorn into a soft cloud. Imagine the possibilities. He willed his bones to knit together swiftly, to be strong. There was so much to live for. So much love to give.

31

Propped on a table in the far corner of Millard's living room was a hand-hewn coffin. It was a tiny casket made of pine, surrounded by flickering candles. The corpse held a small flower in one big, fleshy hand, and on its furry head just above a piglike snout was the paper pilgrim hat that Sissy had made at school.

Being Irish, and claiming to be the authority on wakes, Red, the barber, proposed the first toast. "To Digger the mole. May he never dig his way out of hell." Glasses and bottles clicked all around the room.

Rebecca frowned. "That's not very nice." She was the one who had woven the little geranium stem between the humanlike fingers, stating that the mole had just been doing what God created it to do — in which case Red was surely wrong about Digger's present whereabouts.

"And may he have left no relatives behind

in Ham Bone," Millard added.

"Okay, Ty and Millard," Sidney said, waving them into position. "I need a shot of the two of you with Digger."

They posed, one on each side of the deceased, tapping the necks of their root beer bottles together. Millard wore a red plaid hunter's cap, flaps down. Ty had borrowed a similar cap for the occasion. "Millard, you look an awful lot like Elmer Fudd," Sidney said.

"That's not the worst thing someone ever said about me." They grinned proudly, playfully jabbing at each other while she and Micki snapped photos. Millard let out a boisterous laugh, flinching slightly, his hand going automatically to his right rib. He was still wrapped tightly beneath his clothes, but to Sidney's relief his doctor said he was healing nicely.

"Okay, now hold up the trap and the notebook." Tyson sighed deeply as if annoyed by this request but immediately reached down for his science-project folder, holding it slightly forward and open to the front page, where the big handwritten "A+" was sure to show. Just below it, also in red, the teacher had printed "WOW!" Millard held up the steel plunger trap that the two of them had built in the garage using a modified design from a sketch Ty found on the Internet.

She clicked several shots and then picked up her half-full cup of licorice tea and leaned against the living room wall. Around the corner in the open dining room, Dennis and Andy filled their plates with food. Being potluck and three days after Thanksgiving, the main entrees were turkey casserole, turkey sandwiches, and Amilia's turkey enchiladas. Sidney had made a brussels sprouts and garlic salad and zucchini muffins. At least the muffins seemed to be moving well. Alex was the only one she had seen so far with brussels sprouts on his plate.

Alex. His name wafted through her like warm ocean air. He had grown excited when he saw Millard's collection of Washington State county maps on a bookshelf and had pushed platters of food and pumpkin pies aside in order to spread a map of the Cascade Mountains across the far end of the dining room table. Ty wandered over, gnawing on a carrot stick as he peered over Alex's shoulder. The room buzzed with conversation. She watched Alex trace a meandering line on the map with his finger. Ty responded with interest, pointing at something and asking a question.

Millard's daughter and her husband, Dan, sat stiffly on the sofa, observing the festivities as if they were visitors in a foreign culture. Rita had been disgusted by the whole idea of throwing a wake on behalf of a dead rodent. Ty assured her, however, that moles are not rodents; they are insectivores. It didn't help matters when Sissy blatantly called Millard "Grandpa Bradbury," which caused Rita and Dan to exchange alarmed glances, shaking their heads in failed subtlety as if this whole situation had spun way out of control. Sidney's attempt to befriend Rita over tea at the hospital had apparently done nothing to dispel her suspicions.

Sidney was pleased to see Amilia playing a game of Crazy Eights with Rebecca and Sissy at a card table in the corner. The older woman seemed to be having more good days now. Since Enrique's death, the family had tried to keep their matriarch busy, but Sidney found that sometimes all Amilia really needed was someone to sit and go through photo albums with her while she told stories of good times as well as bad. Amilia was a realist. Enrique had been far from perfect, but he had been her dearest friend. Sidney walked across the room. "Amilia, I'm headed to the kitchen. What can I get for you?"

"Have you got a deck of cards back there? I need you to sneak me a couple of eights."

Millard appeared, leaning over Rebecca's shoulder. "Got a good hand there?"

"Come play with us, Grandpa B," she said.

"Oh, I don't know about that. I haven't played that game in years."

"It's like falling off a bike," Amilia said. "It'll come right back to you. Pull up a chair."

He complied almost shyly, rubbing his gangly hands together as Rebecca shuffled the deck. "Well, those were some fine enchiladas you made, Amilia," he finally said. He held his fist to his stomach. "I'm afraid I'm going to regret them tonight, though."

Her brows drew together. "Were they too spicy for you?"

He nodded. "Yes, but I put them down anyway. Couldn't help myself."

She gathered up her cards as they were dealt. "I'll make you a batch without so many jalapeños next time."

Millard's interest was definitely piqued. "Well, that would be fine." He nodded. "Just fine." Millard loved to eat as much as Amilia loved to cook. "Maybe I can do something for you in return sometime."

She glanced at his bookcase. "I see you like poetry. You have some books there I'd like to read."

Millard's eyes ignited. "You like poetry?"

"Hello!" Sissy interjected. "Are we playing Crazy Eights or not?"

Sidney laughed as she walked away. Alex glanced up when she passed, his lips curving into his familiar closed-mouth smile before going back to his conversation with Ty and now Dennis, who also seemed intrigued by the map.

In the kitchen she began to reach for the refrigerator door but stopped, her arm dropping to her side. Among other artwork that Sissy and Rebecca had bestowed on their new "grandpa," a picture that Sissy had colored in Sunday school was stuck with magnets to the front of the door. Peter walking on the water, his boat at his back, and Jesus with outstretched arms beckoning him to come. Her eyes watered.

The kitchen door opened behind her. She dabbed at the tears in the corner of her eyes as Alex came and stood by her side.

"Enjoying the art gallery?"

She shook her head. "The whole time I was praying for a mentor to love my kids, Millard Bradbury was living right across the street." She sighed. "He was right here all the time. I thought I had to figure it all out — to orchestrate it somehow. My plan was just to get Ty through this house-arrest situation and move on."

He chuckled. "Old Millard's a good guy. Ty respects him. It's a shame that so many kids don't have adults in their lives that they can respect."

She twisted her neck and looked up at him. "He respects you."

He was quiet for a moment. "I hope so."

She turned to face him. "What were you guys talking about out there?"

He raised his dark brows. "Would you trust me with your son for two weeks this summer? We're thinking about hiking the Pacific Crest Trail through the Goat Rocks Wilderness area. Sounds like Dennis and Andy want to go, too."

This summer. Alex was planning to be a part of their lives for a while. She made a face. "I suppose as long as Ty is with you, you'll all survive. You'll be in his realm, you know."

Alex scoffed. "The wilderness was my realm before it was his. Besides, I'm the fishing expert. We're going to bring pack rods so we can fly-fish the alpine lakes. It's beautiful up there on the ridge. The views will take Ty's breath away."

"So you've been on this hike before?"

He nodded. "Pop took Ernesto and me when I was Ty's age. Ernesto must have been seventeen." His lips straightened. "We liked each other back then."

Her smile was sympathetic. Alex was apparently no closer to liking his brother, but he seemed determined to forgive Ernesto for the atrocity he committed against him. "One day at a time," she had heard him remind Ty. She too was struggling with wishing the worst for Dodge, who was being held temporarily in a jail cell in Seattle awaiting trial.

"I think it changed my life somehow," he said. "Standing on top of the world gave me a new perspective. I was so small and the world was so big. I guess I realized I was a part of it, but not the center."

She thought about that. "Is that why you want to take Ty up there? So he can get a new perspective?"

He nodded slightly, turning to gaze at her with intense eyes. He started to speak, but sighed instead.

"What?"

His hand brushed her cheek. "You've given me a new perspective."

Her face automatically rolled into his strong hand, and he caressed her temple with his thumb. Without thinking, she let her body melt against his, and his arms slid around her back. He smelled of spicy soap. She felt at home, though in his arms for the first time. She had imagined this moment often, wondered if it would ever come.

"Sidney," he whispered into her hair. "You know when I started falling in love with you? That day at Amilia's when I smashed my thumb." He chuckled softly. "I heard you laugh. I love your giddy, spontaneous laugh, the way you cry at sad songs. The honesty on your face. Anybody can read you like front-page news. I admire that."

She wanted to tell him that she admired him, too. That her heart melted like butter every time he opened up to her, sharing his private thoughts and feelings. She remembered Carmen's comment after the funeral as she gazed tenderly at her wounded brother: *He feels things deeply. He always has.* Jack was a good man, but he didn't know how to recognize, let alone discuss, the soft, fleshy part of his soul. He had been content to live as if he were only a shell. And he had expected Sidney to do the same. In her head she had believed that Jack was perfect for her — for her family. But her heart had known differently. That was why his kiss had stirred nothing.

But as she looked up into Alex's dark, passionate eyes and their lips finally touched, flurries of confetti and fireworks burst through her soul.

EPILOGUE

"Mom, they're home!" Rebecca called from the front yard.

Sidney tossed her dish towel to the counter and dashed to the front door as Alex's silver pickup pulled into the drive. Ty jumped out and soon Alex's head popped out on the other side of the truck. The girls, sopping wet from a water fight, converged on them, chattering excitedly.

Alex grinned over Rebecca's head. He apparently had not shaved at all during the two weeks he and Ty had been hiking the Pacific Crest Trail, and of course the girls had to run their fingers through his beard. He bent down to accommodate them. Sidney patiently waited her turn.

She hugged Tyson. "I missed you. Mmmm, you smell good. Like campfire smoke and pine needles."

"And trout. Mom, you wouldn't believe how many fish we caught! And fighters, too.

They're all native fish." He held out his hands. "I got this one lunker; I swear it was this big. We had to cut it up to get it in the frying pan!"

Alex nodded. "This kid can fly-fish like a pro. I've never seen anyone learn so fast. He's a natural."

"Did you bring some fish home?" Sissy asked.

Ty shook his head. "Nah. We were hiking, Sis. We couldn't exactly haul an ice chest up the mountain."

"I wish I got to go."

"Oh, no, you don't. You would have wussed out the first day. It was all uphill in the hot sun." Sidney had never seen her son so vibrantly healthy, so tan. He must have grown an inch or two. Best of all was the glint of happiness in his eyes, more brilliant than the late July sunshine.

Alex came around the car, slid his arms around her, and rubbed his beard against her cheek. "What do you think?" he asked softly.

"I don't know yet. Let me try it out." She kissed him. Oh, those two weeks had been long. The skin of his neck radiated warmth, smelled salty, manly. She pulled back momentarily with a contemplative expression. "I'm not sure. I'd better try that again." The next kiss was longer.

"Hey, give us a break," Ty said. Sidney noticed he was smirking. "Isn't there something you want to say, Alex?"

Alex punched his arm playfully. "Get out of here."

Ty snickered.

Sidney narrowed her eyes. "What? Don't you two even try to keep secrets from me. What happened up there?"

Man and boy exchanged glances, Alex's with a warning sign attached, Ty's mischievous.

Ty glanced over his shoulder. Millard had come out his front door. "Millard!" he called. "We saw bears!" He scrambled through things on the front seat of the truck, emerging with Alex's digital camera and ran across the street. Sissy and Rebecca went back to squirting each other with the hose.

Sidney turned back to Alex, running her hands over his solid brown forearms and up to the rounded biceps protruding from his T-shirt. "So what's this secret?"

He ran one hand through his hair. "It's not really a secret. Just something I ran by Ty one night around the campfire." He raised one dark brow. "He seemed to think it was a good idea."

She waited.

"Could you live in a house where you can hear the train clank past your backyard in the middle of the night?"

Her heart fluttered. "You mean your pop's place?"

He nodded. "It has three bedrooms. Rebecca and Sissy would have to share a room, but they do that now. Ty could have the attic bedroom. It's pretty big. There's an alcove where he could put a computer desk. I figure with your decorating skills you could make the place look nice. Especially that big dining room. I'll paint the walls any color you want. You could use the garage to paint your furniture until we can get your own shop set up in town and —"

"Alex, you're rambling." She knew what he was getting at but she needed to hear it out loud. She had to be sure that there was a good reason for the blood gushing through her veins like water surging through a hole in a dam. "Are you putting your dad's place up for rent?"

"My place now, you know." He blew out a stream of air. "Have I mentioned lately that I'm in love with you? I can't believe I was so afraid of letting it happen, but now I'm more afraid of letting you slip away."

She grinned, stepping closer. "Does that

mean you're going to cut me a sweet deal on the rent?" Her hand went to his face. She loved the shallow grooves that had begun to appear on his forehead, the slight laugh lines at the corners of his eyes. She rose on tiptoes and kissed him.

His arms closed around her. His kiss was so tender that it brought tears to her eyes. Eventually her heels sunk back to the brittle summer grass but her heart hovered somewhere above her.

"I'm talking about a long-term lease," Alex said, touching a tear from the corner of her eye. "A lifetime."

She smiled. "Where do I sign?"

READING GROUP GUIDE

1. At the Harvest Fair, Sidney prays for a man to help her with her lost son. What lesson does she learn from the course of events that follows?

2. What initially causes Millard Bradbury to take on the responsibility for a shaggy-haired, delinquent teenage boy?

3. Compare Millard at the beginning of the story to the man he is at the end. Discuss his journey.

4. Sidney believes that the one thing Tyson learned from school is that he is bad. Do you think this is a common problem for children with ADD or other learning challenges? Is medication the answer?

5. Like Sidney, many women are raising children without a husband who is physically and/or emotionally *there* for them. How important is the father's role in a child's life? What should that role look like?

6. Can you think of people in a community or entities that might help compensate for the needs of a fatherless child?

7. Compare Millard's relationship with his daughter to his relationship with Sidney.

8. Was Jack a good father figure for Tyson and the girls? Why or why not? What about Alex?

9. If Sidney had married Jack for the sake of her children, do you think they could ultimately have been a happy family? Why or why not?

10. What are some of the factors contributing to Ty's frustration and anger?

11. What traits do Deputy Sheriff Estrada and Tyson Walker have in common?

12. How does Millard's relationship with his own son influence his relationship with Tyson throughout the course of the novel?

13. How and why do Tyson's attitudes toward Alex Estrada change? Is there a single turning point, or does it seem to be a gradual change?

14. Is it possible to forgive such devastating betrayals as those experienced by Alex and Ty? How might lack of forgiveness affect their lives?

15. Would this story make a good movie? What was your favorite scene?

ABOUT THE AUTHOR

Karen Harter is the author of *Where Mercy Flows*. Her stories and articles have appeared in numerous publications. Karen and her husband Jeff live in northwest Washington State and have three grown sons.